"I knew ye'd make it this time,"

William whispered, pulling her into his arms in the darkness of the forest.

Before Mary could speak, she felt his lips on hers. He might think himself to be ancestor Slaytor MacEachern, but when his mouth claimed her for his own, he ... William.

For a few blissful seconds, she forgot everything except the sensation he was creating in her.

"I knew ye'd come," he whispered. "When I saw the sky was thick and black, I knew you'd pick tonight. If only I could see you."

Awareness came back to Mary. The man holding her in his arms was William—but he was not. And if the moon suddenly found a hole in the clouds, he'd see that she wasn't the woman he was expecting.

CAROLINE BURNES

Caroline Burnes has published thirty-five Harlequin Intrigue novels, many of them featuring horses, cowboys, or the black cat detective, Familiar. From the age of four, Caroline wanted to be a cowgirl and write mystery books. Though she is far from a cowgirl, she lives on a farm in south Alabama with six horses, six cats and six dogs. One of the cats, E. A. Poe, is a prototype for Familiar. Although she spent most of her riding career jumping, she recently took up team penning, a sport that demonstrates that cows are far smarter than humans.

CAROLINE
BURNES
SHADES OF FAMILIAR

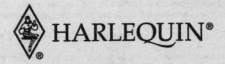

HARLEQUIN®

TORONTO • NEW YORK • LONDON
AMSTERDAM • PARIS • SYDNEY • HAMBURG
STOCKHOLM • ATHENS • TOKYO • MILAN • MADRID
PRAGUE • WARSAW • BUDAPEST • AUCKLAND

To Ann Herbert and Pat Sellers,
two newspaperwomen who helped me along the way—
and excellent friends forever

ISBN 0-373-80954-9

SHADES OF FAMILIAR

Copyright © 1994 by Carolyn Haines

www.eHarlequin.com

Printed in U.S.A.

CAST OF CHARACTERS

Familiar—This time the crime-solving cat must fight a phantom.

Mary Muir—Her hasty engagement may cost her everything—including her life.

William MacEachern—Can his love for Mary overcome the pull of the past?

Sophie Emerson—Once Mary's best friend, now she seems to have a hidden agenda.

Abby Connery—As the castle cook, she has access to the essentials of life...and death.

Kevin Connery—His ambitions rise higher than becoming head horse trainer.

Chancey Darnel—She makes no secret of her jealousy of William's bride-to-be.

Erick MacEachern—He'd been sole manager of Mayfair—until William came home.

Slaytor MacEachern—Had this fierce horse lord really returned from the grave?

Clarissa McLeod—She has an old score to settle with the MacEachern clan.

Darren McLeod—Is Mayfair his last chance to escape his mother's clutches?

Edinburgh

SCOTLAND

Mayfair Castle

Kelso

Arran

Borders

Jedburgh

Cheviot Hills

ENGLAND

Chapter One

So this is the borderland of Scotland. Rolling hills, hardwood forests. Almost as beautiful as my dark-haired Eleanor. The only trouble is that Eleanor is worried. And Peter, too. They've hardly spoken a word since we crossed the Irish Sea, but the sense of impending doom is thick enough to cut with a knife. Even though I have incredibly sharp ears, I could detect only so much from that one frantic phone call Eleanor received from a Mary Muir in Kelso, Scotland, and here we are, flying along these narrow, winding roads at breakneck speed.

Apparently something is terribly wrong with someone named William MacEachern. He must be important. The dame is fighting back tears, and Peter is driving straight through to Kelso without a wink of sleep or even a decent meal. If only they'd talk, whisper, anything! This pent-up emotion is killing me.

I've racked my fertile brain, and the best I can remember is some wild talk about a man named MacEachern who was a Scottish warlord. Compared to my ancestors, this Slaytor was a real pussycat. But humans tend to glorify the past. It seems this Slaytor was a master of horses and the broadsword, and he started the family from which my Eleanor, with a few sidetracks, descended. But I've never heard of William MacEachern.

Hey, there's a castle in the distance. I mean, an honest-to-goodness, storybook, Sleeping Beauty, wicked witch castle. Check out those ramparts, those turrets, those battlements. Not to mention the neat slots for bows and arrows. Ah, but there isn't a moat. Too bad. If we weren't in such a blistering hurry, I'd like to stop and poke around in that old creaky joint. No telling what I might uncover.

But wait, Peter is taking a turn into the old castle drive. He's driving right up to the open gates and into the courtyard. I hope these people don't have guard dogs. I mean, this place looks like the Hound of the Baskervilles could be hiding around a cold stone corner.

Check out that door. It must be six inches thick and bound with metal bands. The bell is positively frightening. I'm expecting to see the ghost of E. A. Poe, or possibly a relative of the Ushers. Uh-oh, the door is opening.

Oh, my, the little lass who's answered the bell is all eyes and elbows. A pretty pixie, a vision of delight. And she's drawing Eleanor and Peter into the house. So this is Mayfair Castle, home of Lord William MacEachern and the source of our sudden departure from Ireland.

What a lovely woman this Mary Muir is. So delicate and dreamy. Whatever has this William done to frighten her so? Or maybe it's this place. Mayfair Castle is a bit much. Ghosts could literally walk in here and it wouldn't seem out of place. Not a bit. Whatever is troubling her, the poor young woman looks distraught.

"Dr. and Mrs. Curry." Mary looked behind her as if someone might be spying on her, then shook her head. "Forgive me. I'm Mary Muir, William's fiancée. I'm so sorry to have called you here like this."

"What's wrong with William?" Eleanor stepped forward and took Mary's slender but strong hand. "What's wrong here, Mary?"

"I wish I knew," Mary said, biting her lip to hold back

sudden tears. "I know how much William thinks of you. If you can't help him, I don't know what I'm going to do." Suddenly realizing that they were standing in the foyer, she urged Peter to leave their bags.

"Come and sit down. Have a glass of port." Impulsively, Mary turned back to Eleanor. "We have to find out what's happening to William." She tried for a smile but failed; her bravado melted. "As incredible as it sounds, I'm beginning to believe Mayfair Castle is haunted." Before Eleanor or Peter could respond, Mary led them down the long, stone corridor where their footsteps echoed all around them.

By the time they were seated in a large formal parlor, Mary had composed herself. Back erect, she sat in a beautifully carved chair and met Eleanor's direct gaze.

"This is going to be hard to explain. But first, let me tell you that I love William unconditionally."

"I love him, too," Eleanor replied. "We don't see each other often now, but we were very close when he was younger. Even when his parents were alive, he was so alone."

"I know." Mary glanced at Peter and felt warmed by the encouraging smile he gave her. "You see, since we've come here to Mayfair to plan our wedding, William has been...has become...strange." She tried to swallow the emotion that almost choked her. "And it's getting worse. He's risking life and limb with wild midnight rides, and he's... Well, it's as if he assumes a different personality. A personality for his past."

"Like a split personality?" Eleanor couldn't believe it. Not William. Not the cousin who'd spent summers at her home, his blue eyes dancing with mischief and fun.

"Not exactly like that. More like he's been invaded by a...ghost." She hurried on. "A specific ghost. That of Slaytor MacEachern, Lord of the MacEachern clan." Mary felt the tingle of fear that came with speaking her worst fears aloud.

WHAT IS SHE SAYING—a ghost! Here at Mayfair! One that invades her fiancé and forces him to prowl the halls and ride horses at night! This is crazy. But judging from my Eleanor's face, she's taking this very seriously. This beautiful redhead believes her fiancé is possessed by a ghost. And not just any ghost, but the shade of his late, centuries-dead antecedent, one Slaytor MacEachern. I remember the story now. This Slaytor was the horse lord for the Clan MacDonald. A legend, of sorts.

This is, indeed, a fascinating situation. If any set of circumstances ever called for the unique talents and abilities of one very observant black cat, this is it. Ghosts! Castles! Ancestors haunting the living! Perfect for me. And I'll stay. Just as long as they don't try to make me eat any of those haggis things.

"SURELY YOU CAN HELP him?" Mary Muir pushed a tangle of soft red hair away from her face. "He spoke so highly of you, of the summers you spent together, and I didn't know who else to call." She cast a glance over her shoulder as she stood.

"He honestly believes he's possessed by a ghost?" Eleanor Curry looked at her husband. Her brown eyes were pinched with worry. When they'd gotten the emergency message to hurry to Kelso to assist William, they'd had no idea of the nature of the emergency. A haunting had never crossed her mind. Now William's bride-to-be was standing before them with a tale that was hard to swallow—and disturbing in a number of ways. For all of her enormous green eyes and gentle manner, Mary didn't seem to be the kind of woman who frightened easily. But was she the kind to imagine a haunting of her betrothed?

"William believes it, sure enough." Mary looked behind her again, obviously waiting for something to happen. "He'll be down for dinner in a moment."

"I see." Peter stood, also, giving his wife a sideways look.

"Have you seen that blasted cat?" He could tell by the way Eleanor was sitting rigidly in her chair that she was uncomfortable. A change of subject would be good for everyone. It would also give him a chance to evaluate the woman who seemed to be the source of so much turmoil.

"He's over beside the suits of armor," Mary said, indicating with a flutter of her fingers the black cat tail peeking out from behind a metallic leg. She turned back to Eleanor. "You have to help William. Someone has to help him. He's...at the breaking point."

"Mary, maybe it isn't a good idea for you to be here alone with William if he isn't well. Mayfair is an...impressive place. More than a little intimidating." Eleanor felt as if she were walking on very thin ice. She hadn't seen her cousin William in five years, and she had no idea what his relationship with this beautiful young woman might be. She only knew that Mary Muir was obviously beside herself with concern—real or imagined. "If you're worried, maybe it would be best if you went back to Edinburgh for a week or so. It would—"

"I'll not leave him." The fiery disposition that her red hair promised flared into life. "He's tried to get me to leave, that afraid he is of doing something crazy in the dead of night. But I won't go. I've loved William since I was a child, and I'll not abandon him now when he needs me most." She cleared her throat, softening her voice. "Besides, I have my best friend here with me. I've known Sophie Emerson since I joined the symphony five years ago. She's in the horn section, and she's staying with me until the wedding."

Behind her, a rich tapestry depicted a scene from ancient mythology. The golds and greens of the woven artwork made the perfect backdrop for the abundant red curls that tumbled around her shoulders.

Eleanor was about to resume her argument when she heard someone else speak. "Mary won't leave. I've tried to get her to go."

The voice on the stairs drew everyone's attention. Eleanor rose to stand beside Peter and just to the left of Mary as a tall, darkly handsome man came into the room. "Eleanor, my loveliest cousin, what a pleasure to see you here at Mayfair at last."

At the mention of the word "cousin," Familiar's bright green eyes blinked around the gray metallic leg of the armored knight. He stared intently at the man who continued speaking.

"After all of my visits with you and your family in the States, it's wonderful to finally have you here at Mayfair." William's smile was tired but filled with irony. "I see you've met my delightful bride-to-be, Mary. She insisted on calling you." He gave her a look that held no reprimand, only concern.

Eleanor walked swiftly to her cousin and hugged him. He was so tall she had to reach up to put her arms around him, and she was concerned by the thinness of his body as she embraced him. William had always been an athletic boy, tall and well made. He'd never suffered through the gangly stage that most kids endured. Now, though, he was terribly thin. And his face was pallid, as if he'd been ill.

"What has Mary been telling you?" he asked as he moved into the room, shaking hands with Peter and drawing Mary to him for a kiss on the cheek.

"I've told them about the ghost." For all of her fears, Mary was not one to back down from her own actions. "I know how fond you are of Eleanor. I knew you wouldn't mind."

"Fond. That's a rather weak word to describe how I feel about one of my last relations. Eleanor played at being my sister when I was growing up."

Eleanor heard the teasing note of the young William she remembered so clearly and she laughed. "All isn't lost if you still have that wicked sense of humor." She held out one hand to William and one to Mary. "Your bride-to-be is beautiful, William. Beautiful."

"Yes, she is." William looked past Eleanor at the petite redhead. "I have tried to convince her to leave...." An indiscernible emotion swiftly crossed his face.

"Enough of that nonsense. I'm staying right here with William, where I belong." Mary's clear-eyed gaze was leveled at her fiancé.

Footsteps sounded on the stones of the hallway, and they all looked up to see a slender, gray-haired woman standing at the open door. "If you've an appetite, dinner is ready to be served."

"Abby, these are my relatives, Eleanor and Peter Curry. They've come for a visit, as Mary has no doubt informed you."

"Yes, Mr. William. The table is set. Will Ms. Sophie be down?"

Mary looked up the stairs, reluctantly removing her hand from Eleanor's. "I'll see about her and be back in a moment. She's probably still deciding what dress to wear." Her chatter was slightly forced. "You know Sophie. She's such a dizzy thing. The most kindhearted person in the world, but dizzy."

William laughed. "Tell her I'm on my best behavior tonight. I promise not to terrify her in front of my cousin." William's face darkened. "If I can keep that promise," he said, almost under his breath.

Mary started toward him, then halted. "I'll get Sophie," she said softly, turning away, but not before the sheen of tears was visible in her eyes. Without a backward glance she ran out of the room. The eerie sound of her light footsteps echoed on the stones for several seconds after she was gone.

"She's lovely, William." Eleanor filled the conversational void that seemed to swallow all of them.

"Indeed she is," he answered. His hands clenched at his sides. "Lovely, smart, talented. All of the things I require in a wife."

Eleanor quickly looked up at Peter. Her husband's concerned features told her that he, too, had caught an undercurrent in William's words.

"What's going on here?" Eleanor asked. "Mary hasn't told us much. She was terribly upset when she called yesterday."

William signaled them to precede him into the formal dining hall. The table, which could easily seat two dozen, had been set for five.

"I'm not sure." He looked around the room, finally settling his gaze on a small black head that peeped over the table. "It would seem we need another place setting."

Peter and Eleanor caught sight of Familiar at the same time. "Familiar!" Eleanor said, hurrying to retrieve the cat.

"Leave him." William laughed. "It's been so long since I've had a pet. Now that I'm home at Mayfair, I'd love to get several cats and a couple of dogs." The change in his features was remarkable. It was as if a prisoner had been released. Happiness touched his eyes and the corners of his mouth.

"Kitty, kitty." William went to the cat and extended a hand for Familiar to sniff. "Well, at least he has expensive taste." He looked at the plate of smoked salmon and the telltale crumbs on the edge of the plate.

"Familiar!" Eleanor was horrified. "I swear, that black rascal can get in more trouble than two dozen mobsters. He had a little misadventure in Galway. Horse racing." She sighed, knowing it would be impossible to explain Familiar's past.

"He's fine." William eyed the black cat speculatively. "In fact, I'd love to have him as my guest for a week or so." He looked up at his cousin. "That is, if you'd be willing to leave him."

"Leave him?" Eleanor didn't understand.

"Can I ask a favor of you, Cousin Eleanor?"

"What can we do?" Peter asked.

"I want you to go to Edinburgh and look into the family history. Especially Slaytor MacEachern. What kind of man was he? Did he die here at Mayfair?" William took a breath, and his voice had the faintest tremble as he spoke again. "There has to be something in the family history, something hidden. Eleanor, though it is a distant connection, is a MacEachern *and* a researcher. Peter, you have a medical background. If you can, would you try to find out why Slaytor MacEachern might be haunting Mayfair after all these years? Is he after something here, or is it me he wants?"

Eleanor closely examined her cousin's face. William was as close to the edge as any human she'd ever seen. She gave a slow nod, catching Peter's eye to make sure that he agreed. "We'll do what we can."

"Wouldn't it be better if we stayed here?" Peter asked cautiously. "I don't believe Mayfair is haunted by a ghost, but…"

William shook his head. "I can't leave, and someone has to try to find some answers for me. If you go, you could save my life. Or at least, my sanity."

Mary stopped in the doorway, and William's last words made her lungs contract painfully. "You shouldn't talk like that, William." She stepped into the room. A taller woman stood behind her, and her discomfort was obvious on her face. "Talking about this ghost will only make you feel worse. And whatever you feel, you're not close to losing your mind. Now don't be spooking Sophie again," she added as she drew her slender friend into the dining room.

"I'm not certain what's happening to me, Mary, and I won't pretend otherwise." William saw the effect his doubt had on his fiancée. More than anything, he wanted to go to her, but he held back. If he could convince her to leave, it would be best. Maybe she'd go with Eleanor and Peter when they went to the capital. She had to go. Before…

Abby brought in a tureen of soup. Conversation fell into an awkward lull as everyone took a seat, and a maid served them. Mary turned to her friend and reached over to touch Sophie's milk-white hand. "Eleanor and Peter brought a cat with them. His name's Familiar."

At the sound of his name, Familiar popped his head over the table. His performance brought laughter around the table. "I've never had a pet, but Mary has been talking about getting a dog." Sophie's dark, straight hair was pulled off her temples with combs, and her dark eyes showed intelligence and an alert nature.

Familiar placed both paws on the white linen cloth and looked directly at Mary, as if challenging her.

"A nice, well-behaved dog," Mary said, directing her answer to the cat, to the amusement of everyone. "A cute dog."

"Meow!" Familiar yawned, showing his disdain for the entire topic of dogs.

"He's adorable," Mary said, reaching over to pull him into her lap. Familiar basked in the attention.

"That's what this house needs, some laughter," William said. His gray eyes were bright. "We've been here at Mayfair for little more than a month, and our mood has gotten more and more solemn. Maybe Peter and Eleanor can bring some sunshine into this old mausoleum. I'd hoped my future wife would be able to do that, but..."

The slight change in William's voice went unnoticed by everyone except Mary and Familiar. Both tensed slightly and turned to look at William.

"That's exactly the problem here. The women don't know how to make their men laugh." William's eyes had begun to glitter dangerously and he stared at Mary.

Mary's quick intake of breath was muffled into her napkin. Familiar eased from her arms, his green eyes focused on William. The hair along his back began to rise.

"You have no respect for your master, Mary Muir." William lifted his empty wineglass. "You even fail to see to my needs at the table."

"William…" Mary half rose, then resumed her seat at his angry scowl.

William stood, faltering. His pale forehead was covered with a sheen of sweat. He glanced at the guests one by one, and Sophie shrank back into her chair and gave Mary a terrified look.

"He's doing it again, Mary. You said he'd be better now that his cousin is here. We have to get out of here." She cast an apologetic look at Peter and Eleanor. "I'm sorry, but the man is losing his mind."

"William." Mary pushed back from the table and started around to him.

"Get back, vixen." He slammed his hand down on the table hard enough to make his heavy pewter place setting jump. "Do you call that dressed for dinner?" His look ran down her pale green dress. "And where are the jewels I had sent to your room? If you're to be the bride of a MacEachern, you must learn to dress the part in front of company. I'll not have you mewling about like some gilded English wench."

Mary cast an appealing glance at Peter. "He needs to go to his room."

"He needs a doctor." Eleanor stood with her husband and together they closed around William.

"I'll go to my room when I'm good and ready." William drew himself up to his full height, a good two inches taller than Peter. "I am Lord of Mayfair. I set the rules in my own household."

"You're sick, William." Mary reached out to touch his arm.

William's reaction was severe. He jerked away from her and spun out of the reach of the others. "You're all conspiring against me. Even my own kinswoman." He threw Eleanor a bitter glance. "I'll not fall into your clutches. You're up to no good, a pit of vipers nesting in my own hearth."

He strode out of the room, his boot heels clattering on the stones.

"He'll go for a ride," Mary said, turning back to the others. Her thin shoulders sagged, and she tried to smile but failed. "He'll ride for several hours, and then he'll come back in and sleep."

"He's hardly had a bite of food," Sophie said, her voice still trembling. "I don't know what the man lives on. Every time we try to have a meal, he turns into Slaytor the Terrible and rushes out to the stables. He could be gone for an hour or six hours."

"I don't know what to do." Tears sparkled in Mary's eyes, and she angrily wiped them away.

"You have to leave here, Mary." Sophie went to the smaller woman and grasped her hand. She spoke as if they were alone in the room. "He's getting worse and worse. Surely you love him, but he's not right. Not even your love can make him well, Mary. And you can't sacrifice your life."

"I won't leave him." Mary's profile was stonelike.

"We could go to Edinburgh and find a doctor. We could—"

"You're free to go, Sophie. I don't expect you to stay. But I will not leave him."

Eleanor stepped forward. "Has he seen a doctor, Mary?"

"He refuses. It has something to do with his inheritance. That's why we're here at Mayfair. We were so happy in Edinburgh. And then we came here to plan the wedding." Her voice sounded stiff and brittle. "He was fine until we came here. It's Mayfair." She looked around at the big dining hall where the corners hid in darkness. "It could well be haunted. Sometimes I almost believe that it is." She clutched her arms as if she were cold.

"William has asked Peter and me to go to Edinburgh to do some research. Perhaps it would be best if both of you came with us. We can look for a doctor, and when we come back, maybe we'll be able to help William." Eleanor to help you plan the wedding. I know how much you've given up, your music and career. I won't abandon you.''

"And Peter and Eleanor are going to Edinburgh.'' Mary cast a look at Peter. ''Is there any family history of medical problems? Could you check into it?''

''I could, and I will,'' Peter said.

''This is very difficult to accept.'' Eleanor paced the polished wood floor of the library. ''I look at William and I see the young boy I loved like a brother. He was the kindest, gentlest young man. There wasn't a mean bone in his body.''

''That's William,'' Mary asserted. ''I was eight when I saw him on a school holiday at the palace in Edinburgh. He was the handsomest boy I'd ever seen. He was sixteen and traveling with his school chums.'' She turned away from the group and stared at the fire, but she was seeing a time past. ''He was standing on the battlement looking over the city, and he was completely oblivious to all of the tourists poking around.''

''You were eight?'' Eleanor spoke softly. There was something so fragile about the young woman. A unique blend of strength and vulnerability. Much like the William she remembered.

''Eight. I went up to him and asked his name. Then his address.'' She smiled. ''I wrote him, and he wrote me back. We corresponded until he was sent away to London to school.''

''When he was eighteen.''

''Yes, and I was ten.'' Mary fell silent. Staring at the fire, she was able to momentarily forget the trauma that marred her life. She was back on that summer afternoon when she'd first seen William, dark hair windblown against the blue, blue sky.

''How did you meet again?'' Eleanor asked.

''We'd just finished a performance with the Edinburgh Symphony.'' Sophie spoke up before Mary could answer. ''It was the most romantic thing. He sent flowers backstage with a note that was signed 'Your old pen pal.' Mary knew immediately who he was and I thought she was going to die of excitement. She was that gone for him. All of those years, she'd still been thinking of him.''

"Yes." Mary was completely unembarrassed to admit it. "I dated other men, but I never forgot William. This all seemed like a fairy tale, a dream come true. And now..." The light of pleasant memories left her eyes.

"Now it's like a nightmare," Sophie said sadly. "I know Mary loves him, but there's no way she can marry him."

"The trouble is, now I've learned that I don't really know him." Mary closed the ledger. "All of those years, it was as if we'd known each other for an eternity. Now I find I don't know him at all. And what's worse, he doesn't know himself."

Chapter Two

Mary stood beside the car as one of the staff loaded the picnic basket Abby had insisted on making into the trunk of Peter's rental car.

"Be safe," she said, impulsively hugging Eleanor. "And thank you for helping me—us. At least I don't feel so all alone in this."

"I don't know what we can do," Eleanor said. She shivered against the dawn cold. "Don't let Familiar be a bother. There are times when he can be helpful." She gave the black feline a speculative look. He was sitting at the doorway pretending he had no interest in Eleanor's leave-taking.

"Aye, he's a canny creature." Mary moved to pick him up, rubbing him behind the ears as she held him. "The entire staff is in love with him."

Eleanor bent and kissed the cat's head. "Stay out of trouble, you," she warned in a whisper.

"We're off." Peter gave Familiar a pat as he handed Eleanor into the car.

"And we're on our own," Mary said softly as she watched the car pull out of the courtyard and disappear down the tree-lined drive. When she was sure the car was out of sight, she allowed her shoulders to sag. "I'd give anything to be leaving with them," she said, "but I couldn't live with myself." She looked up at the enormous stone structure behind her.

"It's this blasted place. It's been remodeled three times and still hasn't been brought into the twentieth century. If William would only leave it behind, then things might get back to normal. But when he's in one of his possessed moods, he thinks he's Lord MacEachern, and when he's sane, he won't hear of giving up." She started toward the door. The cat's rough tongue licked her cheek, and for the first time that morning, Mary smiled.

"Thanks, Familiar. I only wish you *were* a witch's cat. I could stand a little help, even from the black arts."

"Meow!" Familiar's tone was commanding.

"Okay," she said, clucking softly at the cat. "You're right. We can't give up yet. Now let's go check on William. He didn't get to bed until nearly three o'clock this morning. I'd give anything to know where he goes."

As soon as Mary entered the castle, Familiar jumped out of her arms. He scurried toward the kitchen, and Mary smiled. He was one cat that liked his breakfast, and more than likely his lunch, dinner and snacks. She followed him into the kitchen and prepared a tray with tea and toast for William.

Bright sunlight spilled through the large kitchen windows—a modernization insisted upon by William's grandmother. Mary loved the kitchen in the early morning, and she enjoyed making the light breakfast she shared with William. She was smiling as she worked around the spotless room, thinking of the cook who would be in shortly after nine o'clock when the real cooking began.

Abby and her husband, John, who served as butler, lived in a small cottage on the grounds with their son, Kevin. Even though William had been absent from Mayfair for a number of years, his view of the Connerys was that of family rather than "hired help." Abby had been at Mayfair all of her life, and she'd been a source of MacEachern family history for Mary.

Kevin, an exceptionally talented man not much younger

been one of books and music. Nowhere had there been room for horses. Now it was time to change that. When the black mood came on William, he rode. She couldn't ask anyone else in the household to follow him. She would have to learn how to ride so that she could do it herself. Since he didn't remember what he did, she would follow. Maybe she could learn something that would help.

"Miss Mary," Kevin greeted her with surprise. "What are you doing out here?"

"I was hoping you might have time to give me a riding lesson." Mary fastened the top snap of her jacket. She couldn't be certain if she was cold or simply afraid. The horses at Mayfair were so large. There wasn't a pony or a small mare among them. They were all bred to carry the members of the MacEachern clan, long-legged men and women who seemed born to the saddle.

"Does William know you're about this?" Kevin looked puzzled. "He'd have my hide if anything happened to you."

"It's a surprise." She gave him a confident smile. "If I'm going to be part of the life here at Mayfair, I'm going to have to learn to ride. William loves it so much. I want to share this with him."

"I see." Kevin looked into the barn. "There's Suzy. She's getting on in years, a little arthritic, but smooth. She's not much of a challenge, but a good—"

"She sounds perfect!" Mary beamed. "I don't need a challenge for my very first lesson."

In fifteen minutes Kevin had shown her how to groom and saddle, and she was walking Suzy around a small open field, with Kevin watching sharply from the ground.

"Heels down, Miss Mary. If you stand on your toes, you're out of balance." He urged her to let Suzy trot.

Mary felt as if everything inside her were being jarred.

"Post!" Kevin said to encourage her. "You've good balance. You just need some muscle tone. There, now go up and down, keep it up."

Mary rode until she felt as if her legs had been pulled from her hip sockets. When she pulled Suzy back to a walk, Kevin was beaming. "You're not much of an outdoors lass, but you've balance and a cool head. You'll be an excellent rider if you work at it."

"I think I might die," Mary answered, afraid her legs wouldn't hold her if she tried to dismount from the gentle Suzy.

"So, William's bride-to-be is learning to ride." Sarcasm honeyed every word in the throaty feminine voice.

Mary swung around to find the owner of the sultry voice. She caught her breath at the sight of a tall, slender woman dressed immaculately in breeches, polished black boots, white shirt, stock tie and black wool jacket. A black riding crop dangled from her hand.

"I'm Chancey Darnel." The woman stepped forward as if she were the hostess and not the guest. "I'm an old friend of William's, and I came over to see if he might care for a ride. We used to tear up the fields and woods around Kelso when we were younger."

The implication that they'd torn up a lot more than fields was distinctly clear beneath her words.

"This is Mary Muir," Kevin stated to fill the awkward gap. "She's to marry William next month."

"So I've heard." Chancey smiled. "So I've heard."

"We haven't seen you around Mayfair in a long time," Kevin said deliberately. He walked over and held Suzy's bridle so that Mary knew she should dismount.

"Excuse me," Mary said, finally recovering. "I'm so jarred from my lesson that my brain is addled. Let me figure out how to get down from here, and we'll go inside for some tea. I believe Abby was making scones when I came out. I'll bet they're just out of the oven, and I do believe all of this exercise has given me an appetite."

"That's good," Chancey said, running a critical eye over Mary's figure. "You look a little anemic. It's critical to William that he produce an heir, as you no doubt know. You need to put a little meat on those bones. The winters here at Mayfair can be brutal.''

Mary slid to the ground, stifling a wince as her feet hit terra firma. Chancey Darnel was either the rudest woman she'd ever met, or she was deliberately being abrasive. She caught a look at Kevin's face and saw the thunderclouds there. Chancey's abrasiveness was deliberate.

''William wants a child, and so do I,'' she said sweetly as she turned to Chancey. ''He's often spoken of how simple it would be to reproduce if he were a stallion or bull. He'd simply pick out the biggest, strongest mare or cow and…well, let nature take its course.'' To her satisfaction she saw Kevin's wide grin. Chancey's lips were a thin line.

''You and William must have some blunt conversations.''

''Indeed we do. When you're in love, you can say anything to each other.'' She extended her hand, delighted to see Chancey's anger. ''So pleased to meet you, Miss Darnel. Won't you come in to Mayfair and have some tea?''

''I'd love to. Is William about?''

''He's with Erick, going over some of the books. I know he'd love to ride with you, but he rode this morning, and he's blocked out the rest of the day for estate meetings. Maybe another time.''

''Of course.'' Chancey followed Mary into the castle. They passed through a long dark hall with ancient weapons lining the walls before Mary led her into a small room on the west side of the castle. A fire was burning brightly, creating an atmosphere of cozy warmth.

Mary took a chair in front of the fire, signaling the tall blond woman into another. ''Abby will bring some tea. Like you, she's concerned that I'm too thin. Any chance she gets to put something hot and filling before me, she does.''

Chancey smiled, her gaze roving the room. ''There's something different here,'' she said.

''I rearranged the furniture.'' Mary smiled. ''William's

parents never used this room. I find it to be perfect for the afternoon. And in the summer, when the gardens are in bloom, I'll work here.''

"Then you and William are intending to make your home at Mayfair?''

"Absolutely. Where do you live, Chancey?''

"About five miles from here.'' She looked up at the sound of a gentle knock at the door.

"Come in,'' Mary called as Abby entered bearing a tea tray, casting a glance over her shoulder.

"It seems half the country has decided to come visiting today,'' Abby said, giving Chancey an unfathomable look. "Miss Darnel, it's been such a long time. You must have heard William was back in residence.'' She stepped aside. "And our neighbors, Mrs. Clarissa McLeod and her son Darren have also come for tea.''

A woman of average height with beautiful gray hair piled on top of her head stepped through the doorway. Behind her, a slender man in coat and tie smiled as he entered the room.

"And me,'' Sophie said as she hurried inside. "I watched Mary take her riding lesson from the upstairs window. I thought I would die of hunger before she came inside.'' There was a slight hint of disapproval in her tone.

Mary stood and went to greet her new guests. "It's wonderful to have my neighbors visiting,'' she said, wishing heartily that they'd all go home. Clarissa McLeod looked as if she could boss a frigate around, and Darren was a mere shadow. Chancey Darnel apparently had her sights set on William, and it would seem that everyone at Mayfair had long been aware of it. Sophie was the only truly welcome face in the room, and Mary went to her side.

"Everyone, please find a seat. Abby has—'' she lifted the edge of a lace coverlet and the delicious aroma of freshly baked scones filled the room "—a wonderful surprise. I'll help with some more cups, and we can all sit and chat.''

"Where's William?'' Clarissa demanded as she settled

girl that Slaytor had snatched on one of his raids across the border. She was a slip of a girl, hardly more than a child, and it was said that Slaytor fell in love with her before he could get her home to Mayfair. But Lisette would have nothing to do with him. She pined for her home and her relatives. No matter what he offered her, Slaytor couldn't win her heart or her interest.'' Clarissa paused. There was only the sound of teacups settling back into saucers.

"When Slaytor saw that he couldn't win her with kind actions, he decided that brutality would eventually wear her down. So he locked her into the small room on the third floor of Mayfair.''

"Mother.'' Darren's voice held a warning. "William hates this story, and we are guests in his house. I think—''

"Hush, Darren,'' Chancey said. "Let your mother finish the story. I've heard it a million times, but she always tells it best.'' She gave Mary a glance. "Besides, our little bride might want to hear the family history before she says 'I do.' ''

Clarissa continued. "The sound of Lisette's weeping went on for five months, day and night. She ate only what she was forced to eat, and with each passing day, Slaytor's patience grew thinner and thinner. On the eve of Hallowmas, he ordered the women of the castle to prepare her for the bridal bed. Without benefit of clergy or the blessing of the Lord Almighty, he took her to his bed.'' Clarissa leaned forward, her voice dropping. "And she became pregnant.

"That, my dear, is how he finally made her agree to marry. Lisette could not stand the idea that her child would bear the name bastard. To give her baby a name, she married the man who had kidnapped and tortured her.''

"And she bore him eight more children.'' William stepped into the room. His face was rigid with anger. "I had hoped the story of Lisette's abduction had long ago passed away from the local folklore. I can see that you're working hard to keep it alive, Clarissa. Perhaps I should contact the Scottish cultural department. I hear they're eager to record the oral stories of these parts. It takes someone with a passion for gossip and exaggeration to repeat that type of story with conviction."

"William." Clarissa rose to her feet, followed swiftly by Chancey and Darren.

"William." Chancey stepped in front of Clarissa and hurried forward to throw her arms around him in a warm embrace. "I've thought of you often. When I heard you were finally coming home, I couldn't believe it. Then I heard that you'd made arrangements to marry." There was a note of pain in her voice. "I wanted to come and give you my congratulations in person." Her voice lowered a bit, "Or condolences, as the case may be."

Mary's teacup clattered as she put it on a table and rose to her feet. She'd had enough of Chancey Darnel and the entire ill-bred crowd. Only William's gaze stopped her from further action.

"Thank you, Chancey. Your congratulations are accepted." He stepped out of her embrace. "Mary and I had hoped to have an engagement party." He motioned Mary to his side. "Perhaps we shall, yet. I want all of the people of the area to get to know my Mary. She's a rare one. A very special lady."

"Mary's an incredible musician," Sophie inserted. "I know she hates to perform solo, but she's wonderful. Why don't you play something for us, Mary? You never want to show off, but it would make me feel so much better after that…story."

"An excellent idea," William said. "I'll get your instrument."

"I…" Mary realized that protest was useless. As much as she hated performing alone for a small group, she would have to this time. William's look said that he was counting on her.

He went to get her cello, and Mary took a seat in a straight-backed chair.

"Music may be fine for Edinburgh, but Mayfair requires

a strong back and a healthy body." Chancey looked at William as he returned, as if to remind him that she had both.

"I want a wife, Chancey, not an agricultural worker." His voice was gentle, but the words stung. His tone changed as he addressed Mary. "Here, my love, play the sonata that I like."

Mary took the instrument from the case and held it between her knees. To steady herself, she drew in several deep breaths. Then she placed her fingers on the strings and slowly began to move through the first melancholy notes of the piece William had requested.

The music seemed to fill the small room, and as Mary played, she watched the reaction on William's face. He loved this piece, but it always seemed to sadden him. As she concluded the first portion, she stopped.

"I believe that's sufficient," she said, smiling. "Mrs. McLeod was eager to see you, William. I don't believe she came for a concert."

"That was lovely, my dear," Clarissa said with great enthusiasm. "You don't look as if you'll ever really master a horse, but you can play."

"Beautiful," Darren echoed, rising and walking over to Mary. "I love music. I hope you'll consider playing for us on a regular basis. Edinburgh isn't that far, but it would be wonderful to have our own musician."

"Of course I'll play," Mary said, pleased at the look in William's eyes. Clarissa McLeod might be a battle-ax who controlled everything her son thought, and Chancey Darnel was a spiteful troublemaker, but Mary wasn't going to let the neighbors spoil her life at Mayfair.

"Mayfair will be filled with the sound of music, laughter and children," William said. He was smiling, but his eyes also dared anyone to correct him. "Mary has agreed to marry me, and we intend to make our home here. Like the MacEacherns before us."

"And what of Erick?" Darren's question was softly put. "Will he stay?"

"Of course." William looked slightly bewildered. "Why wouldn't he? He's done a remarkable job here. I wouldn't want to try and manage without him."

Darren gave William a crooked grin. "Good, then. It will be nice to have my old school chum back here. Maybe we can resume some of our adventuring in the woods here and about."

William smiled. "We had some adventures." He went over to Mary and gently kissed her head. "Of course, now my Mary will have to join us on our tromps. I want her to learn to love this country as much as I do."

"And I shall," Mary said gallantly. "I already do."

"She took a riding lesson," Sophie said. "I was watching from the window and she did quite well."

William's smile lit his face. "That's my Mary," he said proudly.

"Why don't we go for a ride together tomorrow?" Chancey spoke to William.

"I'm sorry, Chancey. I have some business to take care of tomorrow. Maybe Mary would like to be my substitute. You could show her some of the town and surrounding area. Just leave Mayfair to me. I want to show it to her myself."

Chancey's eyes hardened. "Of course. I'd be delighted to."

"I don't know…" Mary had a sudden sense of dread. "I've only had one lesson. I'm not really good enough. I'll slow Chancey down and spoil her ride."

"Of course you won't." Chancey was smiling now, but it wasn't friendly. "There's nothing I'd rather do than show William's bride-to-be around the area on horseback. It's all settled, then. I'll be here at one." Chancey caught and held Mary's gaze. "I'd better get home."

"As should we." Clarissa rose, and Darren stepped to assist her with her wrap but she shrugged him away. She turned to Mary and scooped up her hand, drawing her away from the others. ''Just remember, if you hear crying coming from the turret on the third floor, spare a little pity for the beautiful Lisette. The MacEachern men can be a headstrong and brutal lot.''

Chapter Three

Mary buried her face in the cat's warm black fur and tried to forget the story of Lisette and Slaytor that Clarissa McLeod had told her. "It was only a tale," she whispered to Familiar, but she couldn't shake the idea that it was a bit of bloody history that was very much a part of William's heritage. Strange, but she'd never connected him with such a family. She thought back to the days—and nights—in Edinburgh when they'd dined and danced their way through the summer. Even further back were the letters she'd received from a young man gifted in the art of writing and humor. He'd of course mentioned Mayfair, but never in any way that made the reality of the castle and the family holdings seem more than the average home where Mary had grown up. It wasn't that William had hidden anything from her, it was just that he was his own person—not a prisoner of his past or his possessions. If only they could step back in time, back to the days of lunches and the nights of dancing and long, sweet kisses that had driven her nearly mad with desire.

"Mary?"

William's voice echoed along the third floor, and Mary started guiltily. Curiosity, morbid curiosity, had driven her up to the turret room that Clarissa had described. And what had she discovered? Only that the door to the chamber was locked, and that she was a fool for listening to the tales of

Clarissa McLeod. Worst of all, William would easily ascertain her motives in searching out the room—and he would be further upset.

"Come on, Familiar." She set the cat down and hurried toward the stairs. Perhaps she could meet him on the second floor.

"Mary?"

His voice was concerned.

"I'm coming, William." She hurried down as fast as she could, breathless when she finally met him on the second-floor landing.

"What were you about?" He smiled as he brushed a curl from her cheek. "You look capable of magic, a beautiful fairy."

"Exploring," she answered, smiling herself. "Learning all about Mayfair is going to be great fun. There are so many rooms. And I'll bet there are secret passageways and—"

"I don't know of a single one, but I'll have them built to please you." He took her hand, turning her to face him. "You played beautifully today. I'm so proud that you're going to be my wife. I should have taken you around to visit the neighbors sooner. It's rather embarrassing that they had to come here, to Mayfair, to see my bride."

"They're an interesting…group." She stumbled. She didn't like any of them, but if they were his neighbors, she would do her best. "What about your friend, Darren? Did you really grow up together?"

"We did. Up until I was sent away to England. Darren and I spent almost every day, after we'd done with our separate chores, tromping around the woods. He liked to fish, and I liked to daydream." William was smiling as he remembered the happy days of his boyhood, but a scowl quickly followed. "I begged Father not to send me away, but it was the MacEachern tradition to go to school abroad. And God knows, my father loved tradition." He shrugged away the bitterness as he turned to her and lifted her hand to his lips. "I swear to you, Mary, that when our children are born, I won't send them away from Mayfair or from us."

Caught by the passion of his vow, Mary smiled. This was the William she knew and loved. "No, we'll keep the whole brood here until we die of old age." She leaned forward and kissed his chin. Even so, she had to stand on tiptoe. Her breath rushed out as his fingers closed around her small waist. With almost no effort, he lifted her against him.

His kiss was neither hesitant nor timid. His lips demanded a response. And Mary gave it to him. It had been such a long time since he'd allowed himself to show his passion for her. He'd been afraid—not for himself, but of somehow hurting her. That restraint, coupled with the turmoil of the past month, intensified the pleasure of each touch, each sensation.

Mary felt her knees weaken. She'd dreamed of making love to William, of learning every inch of his body and knowing exactly what pleased him. His marriage proposal, the fairy-tale visit to Mayfair, all had been part of her dream, and that included the physical relationship that his embraces had made her desire. Mary's love had grown from satisfaction in a few romantic kisses to a searing physical need. As his arms held her and his lips claimed hers, she told herself to ignore all of the doubts that had grown between them. The man holding her was William, her William, and whatever happened between them, he would protect her.

For the weeks of her visit, William had forced himself not to dwell on his desire for Mary. She was in Mayfair, learning the routines of his family's ancient home. When he caught sight of her walking down one of the long corridors, her face lighted by the arched windows, his need for her almost made him insane with desire. But it was the very thought of madness that had prevented him from taking her into his arms and carrying her off to his bedroom.

After his first episode, he'd been afraid to pull Mary any deeper into his problems. She loved him, that he didn't doubt. But if he was mad, if he was losing his mind, he could not drag her down with him. They were not yet married. She was still a free woman, and if something tragic happened, she could pick up the threads of her life and move on, unencumbered by a madman for a husband.

He'd asked her to marry and had brought her to Mayfair to make certain that she could—would want to—fit into his future. The life of Lady MacEachern, surrounded by the duties that the title brought with it, might be too isolated for her, too different from her life as a symphony cellist and city girl. Once he'd seen her at Mayfair, though, his doubts had disappeared. Mary was perfect for life in the country, and more importantly, she was perfect for him. He could not imagine a future without her.

His need for her had finally outstripped his desire to protect her. He slid his arm beneath her legs and lifted. She was as light as a feather in his arms. Sometimes, when she was out in one of the fields and walking in the sun, she seemed like a sprite. With her red hair afire in the sunlight and her tiny figure running across the green yard, she was the most beautiful creature he'd ever seen. Now, she was completely woman. Her breasts pressed against him and her fingers clutched at his back.

"Take me to your room, William," she whispered in his ear. "For pity's sake, take me now."

"I will," he answered, pushing his own concerns aside. For an hour or two, he wouldn't allow the uncertainty of the future to mar his love for Mary. He would have her, and he would take care of her.

There was the sound of rapid footsteps coming up the stairs, and the sudden intake of breath as Sophie caught sight of the lovers. Mary was in William's arms, her body pressing upward to claim his lips.

"Excuse me." A red flush touched Sophie's cheeks and neck. She turned and started to rush back down the steps.

"Sophie," William called after her. She'd looked so

shocked. He started down the steps, Mary still in his arms. "Wait a minute."

"Terribly sorry," she called back over her shoulder. "I'm always blundering into other people's private business. I...I..." She reached the foot of the stairs and stopped.

"Sophie." Mary had refocused on her surroundings. William placed her deftly on her feet, and she started to run after her friend. "Let me talk with her a minute," she called back to William with a grimace of regret. She didn't wait for an answer, but turned and ran after her friend. "My lord, Sophie, it was a kiss. Quit acting like you've seen something shocking."

Mary couldn't help the impatience in her voice. Sometimes Sophie acted like such a goose. It was the late-twentieth century, and Edinburgh was certainly not a backward city. Sophie had seen and heard plenty in the movies, in magazines, from her friends. A kiss shouldn't drive her into flight like a terrified rabbit.

"Sophie!" Mary let impatience twine with regret in her voice. "Sophie Emerson, you'd better stop and talk to me or...or...or I'm going to tell Abby not to make another single batch of scones." They'd run almost to the kitchen, and Mary heard the sound of footsteps halting.

"Whatever has happened to you to make you act so foolish?" Mary regretted the harshness of her tone, but she was aggravated. Sophie, unintentionally, had interrupted the first private, passionate moment she'd had with William in over a month. They'd made that physical connection and were on the verge of moving their relationship to a different plane—a plane that Mary felt would help William through his time of trouble. Sophie's presence had shattered the moment between them.

It was the harshness that finally stopped Sophie. She was at the kitchen door, hand on the knob, when she turned around to face Mary. "It's nothing important."

Her voice trembled so badly she could hardly speak. Mary

felt a lightning bolt of regret at her harsh tone. "What is it, Sophie? I'm sorry I was short, but it's just that William and I haven't had a lot of time lately...."

"I know how much you want to be with him, Mary." Sophie stepped forward. Her eyes were enormous in the slightly darkened room.

"What's happened that you were so eager to find me?" Mary looked around the room for more light. It suddenly dawned on her that the day was gone. It was already nearly eight o'clock, dinnertime, and the sunlight had long abandoned this part of the world.

Sophie hesitated, her large eyes glancing left and right in a frightened manner. "Mary, there was someone in the hall, standing just outside your door when I went up to your room."

"Just now?" Mary was trying to remember the last time she'd gone into her bedroom. Had it been just after the neighbors had all left? Yes.

"It was about an hour ago." Sophie's gaze would not connect with Mary's.

"Who was it?" Mary couldn't understand the dire significance of what her friend had seen. So, someone was standing outside her door. It could have been any of the household help.

"It was William." She swallowed. "I think."

"Well, he found me, as you no doubt know." Irritation at Sophie renewed itself. This was Sophie's big news?

Sophie reached out and touched her friend's arm. "But maybe it wasn't William." Her voice had dropped to a whisper. "I didn't see his face clearly. But he was tall, broad-shouldered."

"That does sound like William." Mary tried to interject a light note. "Or any of his kin."

"Oh, Mary!" Sophie clenched her fists at her sides. "He was wearing this costume, like he was some warlord or something. He frightened me. I did see him, and William was acting out some strange fantasy. He was terrifying.''

Mary felt her body tense. For a split second, as she digested Sophie's news, she didn't breathe. She felt as if her heart had stopped beating. Her friend was telling her that William was dressing up and playacting like a Scottish warlord. That alone might be peculiar, but combined with what had been happening to William, it was frightening.

"Sophie, are you sure?" Mary felt her body swing back into life, and with it came a sick sense of panic. "Maybe it was bad lighting, and you're mistaken about what you saw.''

"No." Sophie swallowed. "There was this fur thing across one shoulder, and he was wearing very tight leather breeches and a sword. It was a short sword, but wide, and he had a round shield, like the ones on the wall.''

Mary knew them. She'd studied the history of the Mac-Eachern family in the heirloom weapons they'd collected. Where some families collected china and crystal, the MacEacherns seemed to specialize in weapons and armor.

"Mary, when he saw me…" Sophie hesitated. "The look he gave me frightened me to death. It was like I was a tender morsel of meat, and he meant to roast me on a spit. It was downright cannibalistic.''

At any other time Mary would have laughed at her friend's description. Sophie had a way of exaggerating the most mundane things and making them sound terrifying. This time, though, Mary could not find the humor. What was William doing running around the castle in a costume? Especially when everyone was already worried about him.

"Did he say anything?"

Sophie shook her head. "He laughed. He turned around so that the light was behind his face, and he just laughed, like a devil.''

"And then what?"

"I don't know. I ran into my room and locked the door.

I've been in there ever since, trying to get up the nerve to find you.''

Mary put her arm around her friend's shoulders. Even though Sophie was a good three inches taller, Mary was the stronger of the two. "Think hard, Sophie. Could it have been someone other than William?''

"Who?" Sophie shook her head. "It looked as if he had longer hair than William. The same dark color but longer. And…" She looked up, her eyes round. "I think he had a beard. Not a long one, but a beard. There was this darker shadow around his chin.''

"William doesn't have a beard," Mary countered. Somehow, that fact didn't make her feel any better at all.

"But it had to be William.''

"It had to be?" Mary didn't want to push Sophie too hard, but the accusations she was making could have serious consequences. There could be no room for error; either it was William or it was not. "Why did it have to be William?''

"He was tall, taller than anyone here, like William." Sophie saw the fallacy of her own logic. "But it could have been someone else.'' She closed her eyes and put her fingers to her forehead. "I was so frightened, I didn't look all that close. That's the truth. It looked like William, so I assumed it was him.'' A new thought made her snap her eyes open. "But if it wasn't William, who was it?''

"That's a good question," Mary said. She'd already begun to debate that point in her mind. Who would be stalking the upper halls of Mayfair, standing outside her bedroom, if not William? And why was the intruder wearing a fur and leather breeches? None of it made sense.

Surreptitiously casting a glance at the troubled Sophie, Mary tried to ascertain how upset her friend was. Had Sophie seen anything? Really? She had a vivid imagination, and during their friendship, Sophie had "heard" and "seen" intruders in her apartment often enough so that it was something of a joke in the police precinct that sent the officers to check out her complaints. Sophie was frightened at Mayfair. She disliked the castle, and she hated what was happening with William. Had her subconscious conjured up a William look-alike?

"You're thinking I frightened myself into this, aren't you?" There was no anger in Sophie's voice, just misery. "I didn't, Mary. I was coming out of my room to go and talk with you. That's when I saw him. There are things here at Mayfair, Mary. Bad things. Buried secrets."

"Where did the man go?" Mary asked. If there was a stranger in the house, he might be found. It was worth looking for him, at least. And if it was no stranger, and not William? Was Mayfair haunted? That thought made her suddenly cold. She stepped closer to her friend.

"I don't know where he went." Sophie sighed with self-deprecation. "I didn't bother to look, because I was frightened. I suppose he could have gone into your room and murdered you, and I would have been cowering under the bedclothes."

Mary put her arm around her friend and squeezed. "I don't think so. I would have screamed, and even though you might have been frightened, you would have come to my rescue." The idea of someone in her room was terrifying. Especially if the intruder was a ghost.

Sophie gave her a long look. "Probably not, but at least you don't think I'm a total coward."

"You have a very vivid imagination, Miss Sophie Emerson. It's one of your charms." She gave Sophie a peck on the cheek. "And I do believe you. I'm just wondering who you saw and what they were doing."

Sophie cast a worried glance at Mary. "If it was William, do you suppose he was...pretending again? To be Lord MacEachern."

The statement went right to the heart of Mary's worries. She wanted to deny it, but she and Sophie had been close friends for the past five years. She would not lie to her. "I don't know, Soph. If that was what was happening, then William is not getting better.'' She chose her words carefully. "I'll speak to him about it and see if he will at least talk with a doctor.''

"What kind of doctor?''

"Maybe a psychiatrist.'' It tore at Mary's heart to say it. Saying the word aloud gave power to the fact that William might be very sick, sicker than anyone wanted to believe. So far she'd convinced herself, and Sophie, that William's illness was stress related. Something that rest and love could cure. If he was living in the past... She took her friend's hand. "I have to speak with William. Alone.'' She shushed away Sophie's startled expression. "He won't harm me, Soph. No matter what else, he'd never harm me. You go and tell Abby that we'll be ready to eat in fifteen minutes. Okay?'' She gently pushed Sophie toward the kitchen door. "Go on. You'll feel better in the kitchen.''

And she would. The room was bright and warm and always filled with the delicious smells that were a part of Abby Connery's days. Mary maintained her smile until Sophie was safely in the kitchen. Then she turned to find William. Worry knotted her forehead.

She hurried down the long hallway, passing the library and the sitting room, moving on past the parlor and the dining room. At the sound of voices, she stopped and listened. Two men were talking, but neither of them was William. They were in William's office, the room that matched her afternoon room, except it was on the east side of the house.

Feeling guilty for eavesdropping, she stepped to the slightly opened door and listened.

"He's a fine stallion, Erick. I'd hate to see him sold, but he needs work. Either I need the time to train him, or he should be sent on to someone who will. If he's not worked, he'll go rank on us, and then he'll be worthless to anyone.''

"You're right.'' Erick's voice was contemplative. "We'll find a lad to take over some of your other chores, Kevin.

You're too good a trainer to waste on feeding and cleaning. We'll get you another boy to work in the mornings and afternoons. How would that be?''

"Fine. That would be fine," Kevin said. There was satisfaction in his voice. "Thanks, Erick. Now about that horse for Miss Mary."

Before the conversation could go any further, Mary tapped lightly on the door. "Excuse me," she said, entering. "Have you seen William?"

"He was supposed to stop by and see me at seven, but he didn't show," Erick said. He looked at the horse trainer.

"He hasn't been to the barn. At least, I haven't seen him," Kevin said. "Is something amiss?"

Mary forced a smile. "Not at all. I just know how you men are when you start talking about the affairs of Mayfair. I was hoping to find him holed up here with you. And neither of you have seen him all evening?"

"Not since five-thirty or so when he decided to check on you and your company." Erick smiled. "He actually felt guilty about leaving you alone with Clarissa and Chancey. How strange that both women should arrive at the same time. And how unlucky for you." He chuckled. "They're both very strong women."

Mary couldn't hide her grin. She liked Erick, and respected him for all the work he'd put into Mayfair. He was a handsome man, an obvious member of the MacEachern line. But he was not nearly as tall or good-looking as his cousin William.

"Chancey could make you a good friend," Erick went on, "but be wary of her, Mary. She's had her cap set for William for many a year." His face closed. "It's a blow to her that when he returns to Mayfair at last, he's brought his bride-to-be with him."

"Was there…" She tried to think of the right way to say it without appearing jealous. "Was there ever anything between William and Chancey?" She looked at both men. She was the outsider here, and if she was going to fit in, she had to learn the past. "I don't mean to pry, but I need to know how shaky the ground I'm walking on might be."

Erick shook his head. "Not on William's side. He and Chancey often rode together when he was a young boy. On holidays, when he came back from school, she was often at Mayfair. There were parties and such, and she was always invited. It was clear she cared for William, but he was never unkind to her."

"You say she could make a good friend?" Mary waited.

"Aye, she could. She knows this area, and she knows the people. If she took it into her head to introduce you around, she could make your acceptance go smoothly. She's well respected."

"And if it doesn't go smoothly?" For the first time Mary was aware that community approval was a big item on the agenda she faced. Marrying William was not enough. She had to prove that she could be Lady MacEachern. This was something she hadn't bargained for.

"Mayfair is crucial to the community. It's the center of the agricultural industry around Kelso. It's always been the heart. If the community doesn't take to you, and I can't imagine that they won't, it won't be the end of the world. But it would be so much nicer for William, and for your children, if it all went well."

Kevin stepped forward. "Don't worry, Miss Mary. The people here will love you. They'll see right off that you're perfect to be William's wife."

The conversation had rattled Mary down to her shoes. Never in her wildest dreams had she imagined she'd have to pass some community test of approval. And neither Erick nor Kevin was aware of the problems that William had been facing.

"I'd better find William," she said.

"I've been talking with Erick about a horse for you,"

Kevin said. "We should have you something suitable in a day or two."

"Suzy is perfect for me," Mary assured him. "We get on fine."

"But in a few weeks, you'll want to go out with William and you'll need something with a bit more spunk."

"Please, don't bother yourselves about me."

"It isn't a bother," Erick assured her. "We'll find a lovely animal for you. Something reliable yet with some pluck."

"Thank you." Mary hurried out of the room, hoping that her dismay wasn't too obvious. She checked her watch and discovered that it was time for dinner. Passing the dining room once more, she saw that it was empty, though the table was glowing with candles and the china and crystal were in place.

"William!" She called his name as she ran up the stairs to the second level. She passed her own bedroom door, hurrying as she raced to the end of the corridor where the master bedroom was located. Only five weeks before he'd laughingly teased her about what he wanted to do to her inside that room.

The memory was like a knife wound as she knocked on the door. When there was no answer, she knocked harder. "William!" Still no answer.

The doorknob turned in her hand and she stepped through the doorway. It was a beautiful room, with banks of windows on the south and east sides. It was a perfect place to wake up in when the dawn was just breaking.

She saw the room was empty, as was the dressing room and the bath. "William?" Where could he have gone? She stepped forward, almost tripping on something on the floor. She bent to pick it up, her fingers burying deep in the thick pile of the fur. As she held it up in the lamplight, she recognized it as the type of clothing a warlord would wear— the garment Sophie had described—a fur to be cast over one shoulder to protect the arm that held the sword.

Chapter Four

Mary tightened the girth on Suzy and checked the bridle once more to make sure the cavasan wasn't too tight. "If it were left up to the two of us, neither would go on this ride," she whispered to the old mare as she straightened her forelock. With a nervous glance, she looked for the hundredth time to the open door of the barn. Chancey was late.

"Would you like for me to come along?" Kevin asked. His gaze roved over snaps and buckles, making sure that everything was in order.

"Do I look that nervous?" It was a stupid question. Her hands were trembling visibly.

"Aye, you do." Kevin grinned. "Just don't let Chancey bully you into more than you feel you can manage. Stick to the trot and the walk. Tell her you aren't secure at a canter, yet. In another week, you will be."

"I hope." She gave Kevin a smile. He was trying hard.

"Erick will make certain that he finds a very nice mare for you."

"I like Suzy." Mary could hear the stubbornness in her own voice, and she didn't care. She didn't want a young horse. She liked Suzy, who was slow, reliable, and had plenty of experience.

There was the sound of a commotion outside the barn, and Mary felt a twinge of nerves as she recognized Chancey's voice, along with William's and Erick's. She and William had not really talked since she'd asked him about the article of clothing she'd found on the floor of his room—and he'd denied knowing anything about it. And when they went back to check on it, it was gone. Vanished! As if it had never been there.

Was Mayfair haunted? A ghost could walk in and out of a room, leaving things at will. What other explanation was there?

"She's a real beauty." Chancey's voice traveled clearly into the barn, shattering Mary's thoughts. "Mary is going to love her."

"William thought of the new saddle and bridle," Erick said. "I got her for a real bargain. She was in a pasture, and no one was riding her. She'll be perfect for Mary. Not as big as some of our finest horses, but big enough for your petite bride-to-be."

"She's classy," William added. He raised his voice and called for Mary to join them.

Mary hesitated, knowing that she was going to ruin the entire surprise by her reaction. She felt Kevin's hand on hers as he gently took over Suzy's reins. "Go on out there and show your delight," he advised. "I know you're afraid, but don't show it. For William's sake, don't show your fear in front of Chancey. It'll be all over Kelso in a matter of hours."

"I am afraid."

"Bah! Stiffen your spine, girl." Kevin's voice was adamant. Even though he was only a year or two older than Mary, he spoke with authority. "You're going to be Lady MacEachern. Slaytor MacEachern was the horse lord for the Clan MacDonald. This is not the time for you to show a jellied backbone, if you'll forgive me for saying so. If you can't fill the shoes, you'd best consider other alternatives."

Mary took no offense at Kevin's words. His tone was kind, and she knew he was trying to help. "You're right." She released Suzy's reins and squared her shoulders. When she walked out into the stable yard, she was smiling.

"Your first wedding present," William said as he led the blood bay mare over to her. "Her name's Shalimar. She's an Anglo-Arab."

"William, she's beautiful." Mary wasn't lying. The horse was exquisite. Her intelligent brown eyes watched Mary, and her nostrils flared as she took in the smells of her new home.

"She's well trained. Erick made certain of that."

"Indeed she is," Erick said, stepping forward. "She's been out in pasture, but she'll settle right back to work. She just needs to be ridden."

Mary stroked the mare's sleek neck. "Maybe it would be better if Kevin rode her for a few weeks. I wouldn't want to mess up her training—"

"Nonsense," William interjected. "She's your horse, Mary. You said you wanted to ride and now you can. Anytime and anywhere you want."

"And I think we have a ride planned," Chancey said, glancing pointedly at her wristwatch. "We should leave now so we have plenty of time to see the area. I've made some scheduled stops for us. People you'll want Mary to meet and know." She looked at William, and for a moment her longing was apparent.

"You're a jewel, Chancey." William leaned over and kissed her cheek. "You've always been my friend."

"Shall we?" Chancey ignored his last remark and looked at Mary.

"Of course." Mounting as Kevin had taught her, Mary managed to get in the saddle without breaking her neck. Only William's beaming face made her decide to stay mounted. Shalimar was standing perfectly, but her ears were twitching back and forth, a sign that she was alert and intelligent, Kevin had told her.

"I'm trusting my lovely Mary to you, Chancey. Take good care of her." William stepped to Mary's knee. "Soon we'll be riding the borderlands together, Mary, just like we planned. And in a few years, our children will be with us."

The image he evoked was so filled with love that Mary eased her heels into Shalimar's side and nudged her forward. She wasn't a coward; she wouldn't disappoint the man she loved.

"Have fun," Erick called.

"We will," Mary answered. As she followed Chancey and her big black mare out of the courtyard, she said a silent prayer that she'd be back alive.

Chancey kept the horses at a walk for the first half hour. She was an impressive tour guide, as William had promised. As they rode the beautiful lanes that wound around the estates—none as big or as prosperous as Mayfair—Chancey told Mary some of the history of Kelso and the most famous personality, Mary, Queen of Scots.

"Since she's your namesake, I thought you'd know more of her history," Chancey said, one eyebrow arching in a condescending manner. "History is very important to us here in the borderlands. Especially to William."

"Our *future* is important to me and to William," Mary corrected easily. "But I have an interest in the past. I know a great deal about Queen Mary, though I was named after my mother's favorite aunt and not a queen. But I'm not well schooled in the history of the borderlands."

"Yes, you are a product of Edinburgh. A city girl," Chancey conceded with a touch of disdain. "Mary is a beloved figure here. She suffered a terrible, tragic life."

"She was a victim of the times and her lineage." Mary spoke the words before she realized their significance. Could not the same thing be said of William? If Chancey knew the details of what was happening at Mayfair, she would no doubt draw that conclusion.

"Are you pregnant?"

Chancey's question caught Mary completely off guard. Mary turned to her, a nasty reply at the ready.

"I'm not asking because I care. I was going to propose a canter, but not if you were pregnant. Not many people get hurt in a fall, but it isn't recommended for someone who's with child. If you're carrying William's precious heir, I wouldn't risk a canter."

"I'm perfectly fine to canter," Mary said. She had to force the words out. Her temper was raging, and it took all of her control not to show it.

"I'm certain William will want to start his family as soon as possible." Chancey's eyes were bright as she swept her gaze over Mary's body. "Time is running out for him, you know."

"What are you saying?" Mary sensed that Chancey's remarks held some deeper meaning.

"Let's canter." Without a backward glance Chancey urged her horse into an easy gallop. Shalimar followed with no encouragement from Mary.

The rocking motion of the horse was terrifying to Mary, but she clutched the reins and tried to relax as Kevin had taught her. It was with a sigh of relief that she saw Chancey pull her horse back to a walk. Shalimar followed suit without any instructions.

"We're running late." Chancey nodded toward a large house clearly visible but still some distance away. "If we cut through the fields, we can eliminate about twenty minutes." She checked her watch again. "Mrs. Daugherty gets in a temper when her guests are late. I'd hate for you to make a poor impression on her at the very beginning. She's rather prominent in this area."

Mary didn't understand the dilemma. "If it's closer, then let's cut across the fields."

"Are you sure?"

"Yes." Shalimar tugged at the reins and moved sideways. She was ready to be moving again.

"There are a couple of low fences."

"There's a gate, right?" Mary caught a glimpse of delight in Chancey's face.

"No. We have to jump them. But they're very small."

"Chancey, I…"

"Of course, we can go the long way. Mrs. Daugherty probably won't hold it against you. You know she never got on with William, anyway. She thought he was an ungrateful brat for trekking all over Europe instead of coming home to run Mayfair. She's already set to oppose him as much as possible."

"William wanted to come home. He didn't get along with his father." Mary rose to defend him with hot words before she'd even thought through what she should and shouldn't say. She couldn't allow Chancey to goad her. "He studied ways to improve production at Mayfair the entire time he was away," she added in a more moderate tone.

"You can explain it to me, but I'm hardly the one who cares about such things. The best thing you can do for William is show your respect to the elders of the town, but that's up to you. Now, is it the road or the fields?"

"The fields." Mary knew she was being pushed, but she couldn't make a different decision. If Mrs. Daugherty was such a dragon that she wouldn't understand how horses could interfere with a schedule…but then Mrs. Daugherty and the rest of the people would just view her as weak and unable to manage as Lady MacEachern.

Chancey put her heels to her horse's side and started across the green meadow. "Lean forward and hang on to the mane," she called over her shoulder as she allowed her horse to gather speed.

Terrified, Mary tried to lift her posterior out of the saddle as Chancey was doing, but the motion of the horse defeated her. Every few strides her bottom bounced so hard on Shalimar's back that the mare bolted forward, making a bad situation worse. "Easy, girl," she whispered, trying to soothe the horse.

The first fence came at her so suddenly that she was over it before she knew what had happened. The landing was a bit rough, but she managed. In the distance, Mrs. Daugherty's house looked no closer, and there were several fields still to go.

Chancey was thirty yards ahead and moving faster and faster. Mary tugged on the reins, trying to slow Shalimar, but the mare shook her head fiercely, nearly pulling Mary from the saddle. To save herself, Mary abandoned the reins and clutched at the horse's mane. Freed of Mary's guiding hand, Shalimar lengthened her stride to an all-out run.

Clods of soft, rich dirt were flying from the hooves of Chancey's horse, and Mary felt one strike her shoulder as Shalimar drew closer and closer to the first horse.

With all of her energy focused on staying on top of Shalimar, Mary didn't see the fence—or the sheep on the other side. Chancey cleared the stone wall, and the flock parted. Shalimar rose easily in the air, the wall no obstacle for her—until a lamb, confused by Chancey, darted back under Shalimar's hooves.

"No!" Mary's cry slipped from her throat. She could hear the bleat of terror from the lamb and the answering cry of alarm from its mother. She could feel Shalimar twisting as she tried to correct herself in midair to miss the small creature. Turning sideways, Shalimar landed hard and stumbled, missing the lamb by only inches. Mary managed to stay on until Shalimar surged forward to regain her balance. Already leaning to the left, Mary could cling no longer. She felt herself going over the horse's neck. She hit the dirt hard, sending a sharp pain racing from her head to her eyes. Blackness crashed down over her, as frightening as the intense pain. For a split second she heard the thunder of hooves beside her head, and then she felt herself floating.

WARMTH WAS THE FIRST sensation that Mary noticed when she awoke, warmth and a loud steady noise that was somehow comforting. She struggled against waking. It was so peaceful in the darkness of her sleep. When she came too close to consciousness, there was a terrible pain in her head and back. But the loud motor beckoned her toward the light, and she slowly opened her eyes.

Two very bright green eyes stared back at her.

"Familiar," she whispered, reaching up to stroke the cat that stood at her side. Pain rocketed through her. Familiar seemed to sense her discomfort and moved closer, to curl and snuggle just at her waist.

"She's awake!" Sophie Emerson rushed to the side of the bed and gently touched her friend's face. "Mary, thank God, you've come to. You've frightened me nearly to death. What in the world were you thinking, jumping stone walls when you've only ridden once?"

"Shalimar? And the lamb?"

"What?" Sophie leaned closer. "What?" She looked toward the tall, grim man who'd entered the bedroom at the first sound of Mary's voice.

"She's asking about her horse and the lamb that was nearly trampled." William went to the bedside. His gaze was tender as he brushed Mary's curls from her forehead. "Shalimar is perfectly fine. And so is the lamb. It seems you were the only one who took a fall."

Mary smiled and reached her hand slowly to William's face. "It all happened so suddenly...."

"So Chancey told us," he said. There was a hardness in his voice. "I thought she had more sense than to put you at fences. But she said you insisted. Mary, I love the fact that you've taken to riding like a duck to water, but you can't go jumping fences when you hardly know how to sit."

"I—"

He took her hand and pressed her fingers to his lips. "I was frightened out of my wits when Chancey rode back and said you were injured. And then when you didn't wake up, I was afraid you were seriously hurt."

"But the doctor says it was only a nasty bruise on your head and back," Sophie interjected. She sat on the other side of the bed. "And I'm going to stay right by your side until you're feeling better."

William eased Mary's hand back to the crisp sheets, but his fingers still caressed hers. "Dr. Sloan was here, and he said the best thing for you was to take it easy. Those are his orders. Rest and take it easy. He'll be back after dinner to check on you again. And this rascal—" he gave Familiar a scratch "—hasn't left your bedside."

Mary tentatively moved her right foot, then her left, making sure that each part worked before she tried to ease up into a sitting position. The pain reminded her that she was bruised—in a million places.

"I hate to leave you, even for a few hours, but I'm going over to Woodlands. Clarissa McLeod called, something about a dam on Mayfair property that affects the flow of water to three of her fields. She's hysterical, says it absolutely can't wait until tomorrow. The workmen are there, and she's going to have them tear it down." William rolled his eyes. "Just rest, my love, and I'll be back for dinner." He kissed her forehead. "We'll have something sent up to your room, and I'll keep you company," he said.

Sophie jumped to her feet, her jerky movements betraying her state of anxiety. "You don't have to do that, William. I'll stay with Mary!" She flushed a bright red. "I mean, you have so much to do, and I have so little. It would be best for me to take care of Mary. I mean, tend to her needs...." She faltered to a stop.

"Your offer is generous, Sophie, but I'd love the opportunity to take care of Mary." He kissed Mary's cheek and left the room.

For a long moment Sophie stood poised beside the bed. She was staring at her friend, but she was listening to William's footsteps fade away. When the last trace of his steps was gone, she ran to the closet and began pulling out Mary's suitcases. The large one was almost more than she could manage.

"Sophie, what are you doing?" Mary ached in places she'd never ached before. When she tried to move, Familiar shifted so that he could sit up and watch her.

"We have to get out of here. We haven't much time, Mary. We have to get our things and be gone before William gets back. He'll try to stop us, of course, but—" She threw the suitcase to the floor. "Damn it all! Forget the clothes. We can send for them. Just try to sit up." She rushed to Mary's bedside. "Can you sit?"

"What are you going on about?" Mary couldn't keep the sharp tone from her voice. Every time she moved, lightning forks of pain zapped her.

"They're trying to kill you." Sophie's face was white. Her voice was little more than a harsh whisper. "I haven't figured out why yet, but it's true."

"Don't be foolish." Mary felt irritation with her friend. "Who's trying to kill me?"

"I overheard Erick and Kevin talking. Kevin said it was a crying shame that William had sent you off with Chancey when you'd only ridden once. He said that he knew Chancey's passion for riding wild and free—that she was reckless. And then Erick said that he'd told William that the horse hadn't been ridden in a year. He'd urged William to let Kevin ride Shalimar for a few weeks to make sure she remembered all of her training. And Shalimar has racing blood in her, so she's supposed to be fast and high-spirited. Is that the kind of horse he should buy for a beginner?"

Mary saw the real worry on her friend's face, and it tempered her irritation. Sophie was often foolish, but always a true friend. William's odd behavior had unnerved Sophie to the point that she was totally paranoid. "All of the horses here at Mayfair have racing blood of some type, or some other fancy bloodline. William wouldn't buy a horse that wasn't well bred, Sophie. It isn't some plot to kill me, it's simply that horses are such an important part of the Mac-Eachern heritage that William wants me to have one that's special.'' She saw that her words did nothing to reassure her friend.

''Then why didn't he allow Kevin to train her a little?''

Mary forced her body up in the bed without wincing. ''She was a gift. William was very proud of her, and he wanted me to have something to ride as good as Chancey's horse. Don't you see? He didn't want me to be at a disadvantage as we went around to the neighbors. He didn't want me to be riding an old, decrepit horse because it might look, to some of the neighbors, as if he didn't love me enough to do better by me.''

Sophie lifted the large suitcase and stood it up. She nudged it with her toe. ''You only see the good in him. Mary, he's disturbed.''

''He thought Chancey would behave more…sensibly. But it was me who insisted on cutting across the fields. I thought if she could do it, so could I. If that lamb hadn't frightened Shalimar, we would have been perfectly fine.'' She spoke those words with conviction, though she didn't completely believe them.

Sophie returned to sit on the side of the bed. Even her slight weight sent a tremor of aches through Mary, but she ignored them. She was beginning to realize that many of her pains were simply sore muscles. The sooner she got up and moved around, the better off she was going to be.

''There's something else.'' Sophie's soft voice held none of the hysteria that it had before.

''What?'' Mary smiled at her friend.

''I was so worried about you that I was crying, and Abby took me into the kitchen for some tea.'' She hesitated, looking down at her hands. ''Mary, Abby has seen someone wandering the castle late at night.''

Familiar shifted positions on the bed. His intense green gaze resting alternately on each speaker.

"A prowler?" A chill made Mary pull the covers higher.

"She believes it was a ghost." Now that the words were spoken, Sophie's eyes begged Mary to consider what she was saying.

"Sophie, that is completely ridiculous." Mary felt her anger beginning to stir. "I'm going to have a talk with Abby, too. She knows better than to pick on you with those stories. She knows how easily frightened you are. It seems everyone in Kelso is ghost crazy."

"She was concerned." Sophie touched the blanket covering Mary's foot. "She *is* concerned for you."

"For me?"

"She said that, for the most part, the legends of Slaytor MacEachern have been laid to rest. They're still a source of local gossip and entertainment, but a sighting hasn't occurred for...well, for as long as anyone can remember."

"A sighting?" Mary couldn't believe it.

"Yes. And I did see someone outside your door, whether you want to believe it or not. And the night that Eleanor and Peter arrived, Abby saw something, too. It was after William had gone riding and we'd all gone to bed. Abby was at her cottage, and Kevin and her husband were sound asleep, but she got up and went into the kitchen. Kevin had forgotten to bring in some wood, and she wanted the comfort of a fire in the hearth, so she went outside to get a few sticks."

"She must have really wanted a fire," Mary said sarcastically.

"She couldn't sleep. She said something was troubling her and she wanted a chore. Getting the firewood was just an excuse. Anyway, she was outside when she heard a noise. She said it was late. About three o'clock in the morning. The noise came from one of the battlements. When she looked up, she saw him."

"Him?"

"Slaytor MacEachern. He was standing on the battlement, a man larger than any ordinary man. He had his sword and shield. She said he nearly frightened her to death. But he just looked down at her and laughed, and she described it exactly the way that he laughed at me in the hallway.''

"And why hasn't Abby come forward with this story before now?''

"She didn't want to make trouble, and she didn't want to stir any rumors. She wants you and William to be happy here, Mary. But she is worried about you.''

"Why me? Why not William?'' Mary forced her voice to remain calm. Sophie had only her best interests at heart, and it would do no good to get angry at her. She was easily influenced by tales and stories.

"Well, Slaytor is his kinsman. And it was Slaytor's wife who suffered, according to the stories. And…''

"And what?''

"Well, he was standing outside the room where he kept his wife locked up like a prisoner.''

"A regular Bluebeard,'' Mary said.

"You can laugh at me if you want, but I'm only trying to keep you safe.'' Tears hovered in Sophie's eyes.

"I know that.'' Mary felt a stab of guilt. Sophie was her best friend. "I don't mean to be sarcastic. It's just that I find it difficult to believe all of this ghost of Slaytor MacEachern hysteria. There are no ghosts.'' She reached down and captured Sophie's hand. "I promise you, Sophie, there are no ghosts. This castle is old, and spooky. I'll give you that. You're nervous and upset, and your eyes and ears are playing tricks on you. Look at Abby. It was late. She was tired. She was worried about something else altogether. Her mind gave her a little diversion.''

Sophie sighed and stood. "I knew you wouldn't listen. That's why I wanted to pack you up and get you out of here.''

"And you knew that I wouldn't leave.'' Mary smiled at her friend. She leaned down to pet Familiar as he rested by her leg. "Look, if there were any ghosts about Mayfair, Familiar would sense it. Cats have an ability to tune in to supernatural things. Especially black cats.'' Mary lightly stroked Familiar's back. Obligingly he flipped over and gave her access to his stomach. ''This cat couldn't be more relaxed. Now could he?''

THE TRICK to being a successful cat is to look relaxed, especially when some lovely elfin creature is willing to stroke and caress you. But that's a secret from the cat's survival manual I intend to pen as soon as I get back to the States and Eleanor's electric typewriter. Now that she's caught up in her computer, the IBM Selectric is all mine.

It's difficult to concentrate on my potential literary successes, though, while Sophie is sighting ghosts and Mary is nearly breaking her neck. Something isn't right here at Mayfair. No, something is definitely wrong. But I can't seem to get a handle on it.

When William and Mary are together, I could swear he loves her with every corpuscle of his big, tall body. Yet, that first evening at the dinner table… He was in a rage at her, for no reason. He didn't have to stab a dagger into the table to let me know he was capable of violence. Little Sophie is a goose, but I certainly understand why she seems to be afraid. I'm more than a little concerned for Mary's safety myself. It just doesn't make sense, though. Why would anyone want to harm Mary? She isn't even part of the MacEachern clan. At least, not yet.

Methinks I'll take a little tour of the stables. During my visit in Ireland, I picked up a bit of chatter involving horses. If push comes to shove, I'm sure I can get in touch with Patrick and Katherine. It's a comforting feeling to know I have my own horse experts just across the water. Yeah, I'm picking up on this north country lingo pretty good. I can't wait to get back to Washington and impress Clotilde with my new vocabulary.

But first things first. I'm going to the stables. Kevin and Erick seem to hang out there, and if there's something rotten in Kelso, I may get a whiff of it from those two.

Chapter Five

William stood at the head of the table. The enormous dining hall only made their small party of three seem even less significant. Sophie wouldn't meet his gaze, and Mary was so insistent on being cheerful that he knew something had gone wrong in his absence. Although he'd tried to make her stay in bed, she'd insisted on coming down for dinner. Once Dr. Sloan had reassured him that she was only bruised, he'd relented. In his experience with falls from horses, it was better to move around some if possible.

"Have you seen Familiar?" Mary asked as she buttered a slice of the homemade bread that Abby baked daily.

"He was out at the stables." William poured more wine for all of them. "Kevin said he was sitting on Shalimar's stall as if he was communicating with the mare. He said it was very amusing to watch. I'd give anything to know what goes on in the head of that handsome black feline."

"Now that's a thought." Mary lifted her wineglass. "A toast. To the improvement of my riding skills and to my new horse, Shalimar."

Sophie forced a smile and sipped her wine.

"I think it might be a good idea if you took a few days off from riding and then started on the lunge line with Kevin helping you," William said.

"Good idea," Mary agreed. "I think Shalimar and I will

get on fine if we take it slow—and if we stay away from frightened lambs."

William slapped his forehead. "I almost forget to tell you. Mrs. Daugherty was so upset over what happened that she sent that lamb up here as a gift for you."

Mary looked up from her plate. "What am I going to do with a lamb?"

"I suppose we could eat it."

"William!" Sophie and Mary cried out in unison before they saw the smile widen on his face.

"Ah, ladies, it's good to see some enthusiasm and life around this table. Of course, the lamb will be well cared for. It was an amazing gesture, coming from Mrs. Daugherty."

"I hear she isn't one of your biggest fans." Mary didn't want to get into the details of what had happened with Chancey regarding Mrs. Daugherty's penchant for punctuality. She'd spent half an hour thinking through the fact that Chancey had told William that she, Mary, had insisted on taking the fences. Was it possible that the tall blonde had interpreted the events in that fashion? Was it Chancey's guilt that made her lie? Or had she really twisted the facts that violently? All in all, Mary had concluded that it didn't matter. In the future, she determined to use her good sense and not allow herself to be bullied. If blame was to be laid at anyone's door, Mary had to take her share for being too easily pushed around.

"Mary, I hate to be the bearer of dismal news...." William's smile took some of the sting out of his words. "Clarissa McLeod has invited herself over here for dinner Saturday night. She and Darren, and she's suggested that I might want to invite Chancey and a few of the other neighbors. She has a surprise. What do you think?"

Mary didn't know if she'd be able to move by Saturday night, but she couldn't put off meeting the members of the community forever. "That sounds lovely."

"It's just that I feel Clarissa manipulated me rather easily." He reached across the gleaming table and touched her hand. "You see, I've gotten used to dealing with a woman who doesn't resort to manipulation. I'd forgotten that people like Clarissa are masters of the verbal ambush."

Mary laughed. "I'll have to pay attention to her tactics. If you ever start to become difficult, I can take lessons from Mrs. McLeod."

"Heaven forbid." William rolled his eyes.

"This is a lovely meal," Sophie said. She was watching William closely. "I mean, it's usually in the evenings when he begins to…feel ill." She looked from William to Mary and then back down to her plate. "I shouldn't have brought this up. I'm always saying the wrong thing."

"No, you have every right to talk about my bad moods since you've had to suffer through them." William reached on either side of him and took both women's hands. "This scare with Mary may have jolted me out of my own selfish world. I believe I've been so concerned with Mayfair and my responsibilities that I've become overwrought to the point of…well, of some peculiar behavior. Today, though, I realized how easily Mary could be taken from me. I think both of you will see a change, for the better."

Sophie sipped her wine, spilling a few drops of the blood-red liquid on the white tablecloth. "I'm so sorry," she said, blotting it with her napkin.

Mary's laughter rang brightly in the room. "Oh, Sophie. Don't worry so much." She gripped William's hand. "Sophie is such a fussbudget, and I'm so happy. You make me so happy." After the doubts and anxieties, she did feel extraordinarily happy. *This* was the William she'd fallen in love with.

"You're the most important thing in my life, Mary. I've been so stubborn about leaving Mayfair, and I know how frightened you and Sophie both have been. Because of me. I believe all of that's behind me now. Behind us." He lifted her fingers and kissed each one.

Sophie had recovered and lifted her wineglass. "To your future," she said. "To all the happiness you both deserve."

Laughing, they drank to the toast.

Mary finished her glass of wine and put it back on the table. "I hate to be the party drag, but I've had enough sitting in a hard chair for one evening. If you two will excuse me—" Mary pushed back her chair "—I'm going to soak in a hot, hot tub and hobble back to bed."

William stood and went to help her. "An excellent idea. I'll bring up some brandy and dessert when you've had a chance to settle into bed." His gaze touched her like a caress.

Mary felt her heart catch. There was a definite promise in William's eyes—a promise of tender embraces. Her body was sore, but she felt an immediate response to William. "Yes, I'll be waiting," she said.

"Abby has made something special," Sophie said. "I was watching her in the kitchen. It's going to be delicious."

"I'll keep that in mind," Mary said. "While I'm soaking these battered old bones, I'll be thinking of…dessert." The look she gave William made it clear she was thinking about him.

"Can I help you?" William offered.

"No, I need the exercise. I'm afraid if I don't move, I'll rust." Mary laughed as she slowly made her way out of the dining room.

In the hall, she paused. Abby had brought her a cup of herbal tea earlier that had done wonders. With the prospect of William's visit hanging deliciously before her, Mary decided that a second cup could not hurt. She started toward the kitchen, hoping that Abby still had plenty of the herbs left.

As she walked along, Mary found that it became increasingly easier to move. That was encouraging, and she pushed into the kitchen with a smile on her face.

Seated at the table, Kevin looked up, startled. A heavy silver spoon slipped from his fingers and crashed into a delicate glass bowl. At the sound of broken glass Abby whirled from the sink, her hands filled with a mortar and pestle where she was crushing up a yellowish powder. She placed it beside her on the counter.

"I didn't mean to startle you," Mary said, entering the room and closing the door behind her. "I was wondering if you had any of that wonderful herb tea left?" She looked from Abby to Kevin, whose face was now stained a dull red. He hurriedly began to clean up the pieces of the broken glass.

"I'm afraid I've made a terrible mess," he said. "And it's one of the crystal pieces, too."

"Kevin." Abby said with a sigh. "You've a delicate touch with a horse, but you're an oaf with the dishes." She went to help him and swept the glass and custard into a paper towel. "I'm terribly sorry, Mary. That bowl was part of a set that belonged to William's great-great-grandmother. If there was any way to replace it, I would. But there isn't." She nervously went to get a cloth to clean the remainder of the mess.

"Well, the way I look at it, it's at least fifty percent my fault for blasting in here like that. I startled Kevin or he wouldn't have dropped the spoon. And dishes are bound to be broken. There's really no need for apologies. It was an accident."

Kevin eased back into his chair, and slowly the flush left his cheeks.

"The tea," Abby said. "Yes, I have some left. I'll bring it right up to you as soon as I brew it."

"Don't be silly. I can wait and take it up myself. I'm not a total invalid." Mary started to take a seat at the table with Kevin, but Abby hurried toward her.

"I'll bring it up to you, Mary. Please. That way you can have it nice and hot."

Mary hesitated. She suddenly realized that she might be interrupting a personal conversation. "Of course. That would be fine.'' She looked over at Kevin. ''It won't be tomorrow, but I can promise I'll be back in the saddle soon.''

''I'm sure that's so,'' Kevin said. Whenever he talked about the horses, he relaxed visibly. ''The next time Chancey decides to take you for a ride, you'll be ready for her tricks.''

''Indeed I will,'' Mary promised. ''Indeed I will.'' She was chuckling as she left the kitchen. The only thing she could think about was a hot bath—and William. He'd been perfectly fine at dinner. He'd been charming and gentle and wonderful. Just like before. And he was coming to bring her dessert. She felt her heart lift higher than it had in weeks. Maybe things were going to get better at Mayfair. Maybe there would be an early November wedding yet in the ancient old hall of the castle.

As she turned to close the door to the kitchen, a black shadow flew by her feet and raced inside the door. Her smile quirked up on one corner. The black cat never missed an opportunity to ingratiate himself with Abby. He was no doubt already getting the best cut of meat and the most delicate morsels of fish. Familiar had a way of getting people to come around to his way of thinking. He was some kind of cat.

WILLIAM DIPPED the spoon into the dish and lifted lush raspberries and cream to Mary's mouth. The tart, rich taste was sinful, and she allowed her body to slide another inch beneath the bubbles and hot water. Raspberries, her favorite thing in all the world. And William had had them prepared just for her.

William had surprised her in the bath—with two desserts and two glasses of brandy. The herb tea Abby had delivered, the hot water and the brandy were having a decided effect on her, not to mention the fact that every time she looked at William she felt a surge of desire. She was caught in a world where all of her senses were aroused, and she was loving every minute of it.

Perched on the side of the large tub, William held the spoon. "One more bite," he urged.

"Have some yourself," Mary said, laughing as she allowed him to feed her.

"In a moment, after you've finished yours." He held the brandy snifter for her to drink. "I'm having homemade custard. My favorite." He smiled. "Abby has indulged us both tonight."

"I feel wonderfully decadent." She met his gaze. "And a little afraid."

"Afraid of me?" His blue eyes were concerned.

"No." Mary shook her head, sending a few more of her curls into the bathwater. The red hair clung to the white skin of her shoulders, and William automatically reached out to touch them.

"I'm afraid of the future, and the step we're taking."

"Before I brought you to Mayfair, you weren't afraid. You would have married me in Edinburgh without any hesitation or fear."

William spoke the truth, and Mary couldn't deny it. To doubt their union would never have crossed her mind during the courtship in Edinburgh. There had been no time or room for doubt in the magical six months. But the month at Mayfair had taught her a lesson about the complexity of the man she intended to wed.

"I suppose I was acting like I'd stumbled into a fairy tale in Edinburgh. Everything was perfect, so perfect that it was like some fairy godmother had written the script for me. I just accepted it because it was so wonderful. Mayfair has brought home to me the reality of what marriage to you will be like." She wasn't complaining, but she was no longer so naive. Mayfair and the life of Lady MacEachern would be difficult at times.

"And you've changed your mind?" William swallowed.

"No." She laughed and reached for his hand, trailing bubbles along the leg of his trousers. "I haven't changed my mind, at all. I intend to marry you, William. And if what you said tonight at the table is the truth, then I see no reason why we can't continue with our plan to marry the first of November.''

''Mary!'' He put the tray and glasses on the floor and slid to his knees beside the bath. ''I love you so much. And I'm so sorry for what's happened here. I have no idea what came over me. I've been so selfish, and I wasn't even aware of what I was doing or why.''

''I'm just glad it's over.'' She leaned forward, her breasts rising from the warm water and bubbles.

William's arms dipped into the hot bath, and he lifted her up into his arms.

''I'm dripping water all over your clothes,'' she said as she began to kiss his neck and cheek.

''I did feel something warm running down me,'' he teased. He kissed her forehead. ''Are you sure, Mary?''

''I'm sure.'' She picked up a heavy towel off the counter as he carried her past. She might not be positive about the future, but she was certain that she had to have this time with William.

''What about your bruises?'' he asked as he settled her in front of the fire burning in the hearth.

''What bruises?'' Her hair fell around her shoulders, clinging in places to her wet skin. The firelight played across her body, emphasizing the creamy skin and lush curves.

''You are so lovely,'' William said as he took the towel and slowly began to dry her. He blotted her shoulders, her back, her arms and breasts and waist and legs. And each place he dried, his lips warmed her.

''William.'' Mary's voice was uneven. She placed her hands on his shoulders, and he slowly lifted his face. ''I love you.''

''And I you.'' He rose to his feet, and once again swept her up into his arms. ''You're like a magic creature, Mary. So delicate and beautiful. I'm afraid I might hurt you.''

"Hurt me?" She laughed softly. "Ah, William, you could break my heart, but you couldn't physically hurt me. That much I know about you." Even when Sophie had been terrified of him, Mary had felt no physical threat. He was frightening—but only because she did not understand what had happened to him.

"Even these past weeks, you haven't been afraid?"

"Not of physical abuse. But there were times I believed I didn't know you at all."

"Those times are over."

"Then you promise I won't lose you? Not to the past or Mayfair or your duties?"

"You won't, Mary. Not ever." He placed her gently on the bed and stood to remove his own clothes.

WELL, WELL, WELL, the lovebirds have finally wound up in the same cage. And what a scene it must have been. This bathroom is a wreck. Water everywhere. Lace underthings strewn about. Brandy on the floor. And a crystal cup of untouched egg custard, one of my personal favorites.

Abby is a wonderful cook, and she's more than generous with the fish and meat, the cream and cheese, the gravies and butter. But she hasn't considered the fact that a well-traveled feline such as myself requires a taste of sweet at the end of the meal to satisfy the palate.

I doubt that Mary and William will mind if I help myself to this little delicacy. After all, it's going to ruin here on the floor. I remember my mother giving me the old lecture about the starving kitties in China. How many times did I hear her tell me to clean my bowl? I'm also protecting Abby's tender feelings. She made this custard especially for William. How would she feel if she saw it returned to the kitchen untouched? So, here goes.

Hey, this stuff is great! Dense, rich, creamy. Perfection. Well, that's an empty bowl. In the morning, I wonder if William will think he did this. Now, since my place in Mary's room is occupied, I think I'll wander around that spooky old turret room for a little while. I spent the entire afternoon in the stables, and I learned zip. But then, I am a stranger. It may take a few days for me to catch the drift of what's normal and what's not.

If the ghost of Slaytor is walking tonight, he should be up in the turret room at one time or another. Gee, I'm going to ghost watch. When I get back to Washington, Clotilde will never believe this.

MARY AWOKE, her body tense and aching. Beside her, William was fast asleep, his profile relaxed and happy in the still burning flames of the fire. Looking at the height of the flames, Mary realized that she'd been asleep only a few moments. What had awakened her?

She listened, hearing only the pop of the fire. Snuggling back beneath the covers beside William, she noted that she was still sore and bruised from her encounter with Shalimar, but she was getting better all the time. She smiled as she thought of the hot bath and the lovemaking with William. Perhaps she should recommend the combination as a cure for falls and other such injuries.

The noise came from the foot of the bed. She sat bolt upright, every nerve tingling with alarm. It was a hiss, like that of a large snake.

''William.'' She shook his shoulder and softly called his name. ''William.''

''What?''

''There's something in the room. A snake.''

''A snake?'' He was half asleep.

''Wake up.'' She touched his shoulder again. ''Please.''

The terror in her voice brought him completely awake. ''I don't hear anything,'' he said, reassuring her.

''Listen.''

He did, but there was nothing except the soft crackle of a

log in the fire. "Mary—" The deep growl and the hiss that followed stopped him short.

"What is it?"

"I don't know." He eased back the covers. "But there's something in this room." Reaching over Mary, he snapped on the bedside lamp. Soft light flooded the room, but there was nothing to see.

William sat up and put his feet on the floor. Sharp claws tore into his bare legs.

"Holy—!" He pulled his legs up on the bed. Blood from three deep claw marks oozed down his right calf.

"What is it?" Mary asked, terrified.

"I think it's a cat."

"No, that couldn't be a cat." Mary felt her heart pounding. "No cat would deliberately attack like that." She thought suddenly of their black feline guest. "Do you think Familiar has cornered some strange cat in here?"

"There are some wild ones in the woods. People put them out, thinking they'll take care of themselves. But they can't. They turn feral, and they begin to starve. Sometimes they go mad with hunger." William's gaze roved over the firelit room for his clothes.

There was no sound at all from under the bed.

"Do you think Familiar's okay?"

"It seems to be only one cat," William said. He darted his hand to the floor and snagged his pants. Quickly he began to put them on.

"How do you think it got in?" Mary held the covers up to her neck.

William shook his head slowly. "I don't know, but a more important question is, what are we going to do? We can't stay here in bed like this."

"Can we catch it?" Mary was thinking ahead. "Maybe if we catch it, we can feed it and tame it back down." She felt her fear lessen. "It must be scared to death, William. And desperate."

"Aye, desperate." He had seen cats and dogs gone wild. He knew their prospects for survival were dim. Often they were so badly malnourished and consumed with parasites that not even the best medical attention could save them. But he had no intention of telling Mary. They would catch the cat and let the local veterinarian decide. "We have to capture it before Familiar decides that it's invading his territory."

"Who would put an animal out to starve?" Mary asked.

"I can't say for certain, but if I find out, I'm going to make sure they never do it again."

Mary heard the threat in his voice, and she didn't pursue it. If anything, she knew she'd help William. "Maybe we could get the sheet and wrap the cat in it when it starts to attack. Maybe we can catch it without hurting it."

"That's probably the smartest idea I've heard." William reached across the bed and touched her. "You know how much I love you. Instead of being upset or angry, you're concerned for a stray cat. You're not worried about getting clawed or bitten, you're worried about the animal."

"Somehow we'll survive. I'm not so certain about the cat, though." Mary had seen enough stray animals in Edinburgh to know the suffering they endured. "Shall we try?"

"It's our best shot."

Working together, they pulled the top sheet from the bed. "I'll jump down over there." William pointed to a place beside the fire. "When the cat comes after me, I'll drop my end of the sheet and you follow with yours, then I'll bundle it up."

"Right." Mary stood on the bed, both hands filled with fabric. William took his end and jumped as far from the bed as he could.

Before he'd even had a chance to regain his balance, they heard the sound of a furious growl, and a large black shape charged at him.

"Familiar!" Mary cried as she leapt to the floor and secured her end of the sheet.

Beneath the snowy mound of white, a small shape struggled. Growls and hisses filled the room, and sharp claws tore ineffectually at the tight weave of the sheet.

Moving carefully, William bundled up the cat and held him, struggling, to his chest.

Mary couldn't help the tears. "It's Familiar. I saw him."

"I know," William said.

"What happened?" she asked. "Is he…mad?"

"There's been no rabies here or in Britain for years. The laws for bringing an animal into this country are very strict." He shifted the cat, trying to find a gentler hold on the thrashing animal. "I don't know how Eleanor and Peter got him in here, though."

"Surely he's had his shots. Peter's a veterinarian."

"Aye, he is." William held the cat as gently as he could, but he had a terrible feeling. He looked down at his leg, at the blood still seeping from the wounds.

"What should we do?" Mary asked. If she were in Edinburgh, she'd know how to get some help for the cat. She hadn't a clue in Kelso. Was there help available?

"Get dressed. We're going to Dr. Faulkner's clinic right away."

"At this hour of the night?" Relief made her almost giddy. There was help at hand.

"At this moment," William said, "Familiar's life may depend on it."

Chapter Six

Dawn was breaking when the gray-haired veterinarian came into the lobby where Mary and William waited.

"He's calm now," Dr. Albert Faulkner said. "I've never seen an animal so distraught, so violent. It's a puzzling case, and we won't know anything until the tests come back."

"Is he…?" Mary had to fight back the swell of emotion that almost overwhelmed her. "Is he going to live?"

Dr. Faulkner ran a hand through his hair and resettled his glasses on his nose. "Since I don't know what happened to him, I can't make any promises. But he is stabilized now. He's a strong, healthy cat."

William reached over to grasp Mary's hand. "Dr. Faulkner is the best. He'll do everything possible for Familiar."

Dr. Faulkner picked up Familiar's chart and scanned it as he spoke. "I can remember when your father wouldn't allow you to have a cat, William. Where did Familiar come from?"

William hesitated. "He belongs to my cousin. I'm caring for him for a few weeks."

"I see." Dr. Faulkner took a seat beside Mary. "Then you don't know his medical history."

"No," William said. "But my cousin's husband is a veterinarian, so I'm sure he's had all of his vaccinations, and the best of care."

"I see." Dr. Faulkner's tone was speculative, but he didn't press the issue.

"Can I check on him?" Mary asked. "Just a peek."

"He's asleep, and he's resting heavily," Dr. Faulkner cautioned her. "It might be a good idea for you to see him. And I want to talk to William."

Mary made her way to the examining room where Familiar had been placed in a large kennel. He was on his side, as still as death.

Mary unlatched the door and reached in to stroke his black hide. Familiar's normally sleek fur felt rough and dry, but his body was cool. When they'd captured him in the sheet, he'd been burning hot. William had been afraid he was going to convulse from the fever.

"How is the black boy?" she asked softly, stroking his head.

One green eye opened and gave her an unfocused look.

"Familiar?" Mary bent down so that she was very close. As her fingers stroked his fur, she heard a ragged purr. "Oh, Familiar," she said, wanting to pull the cat into her arms but afraid to disturb him. There were no broken bones—that much she knew for certain. But had there been internal injuries from the fever?

"Meow." Familiar lifted his head and looked around the room.

"Everything's going to be fine," Mary said as she stroked his head. "Just fine."

EASY FOR YOU to say, Miss Pixie. My head is throbbing like a jackhammer is ripping into it. And where am I? The last thing I remember is strolling up to the turret room to see if I could catch a glimpse of old Slaytor MacEachern. I was comfortably curled beside the door, listening. And then— wham!

I've never had anything like that happen. It was almost as if I'd lost control of my own body—and my mind. I had this incredible impulse to bite and claw, to lash out at anyone who came near me. It's a good thing my beautiful Clotilde didn't see me in such a state. She would have been terrified. And the strangest thing is, I knew I was acting wild, but it didn't seem like it was really me.

I remembered the feel of cold marble beneath my paws, and the smell of the mountains in Tennessee. It was so incredibly sharp, like a very concentrated smell. My body began to burn, and I had to pant. The fire was crackling in Mary's room—very loud. I could smell the oak burn and hear the fibers snap. My sense of smell and hearing were so intensified. And I knew I had to hide.

It was so primal, so ancient, the survival of the cat, the hunter. The king. I couldn't help myself. Moving from shadow to shadow I made it under Mary's bed, and I knew they were both there.

Hunkered down under the bed, I remember thinking that it was my time. The rest is a blur.

The next thing I knew, I was wrapped in a bed sheet and being held down. A totally humiliating experience, let me assure you.

But the real question is, what happened to me? How did I go from Familiar the Lovable to Familiar the Hunter?

I'll figure it out, that's for certain, but right now, I think I'll give up thinking for a little while and allow myself to yield to the luxury of Mary's hand stroking my temples. She has such a wonderful touch. And she's so upset. She's even crying. The child has a heart as tender as a flower. I'd better make a little effort to purr so that she knows I'm okay.

"JUST REST, Familiar," Mary whispered. She wiped the tears from her cheeks. She was so relieved to see the cat awake—and giving it his best attempt to purr. There was no trace of the wild, furious animal from the night before.

When Familiar's eyes closed again, Mary latched the kennel door and went back to the waiting room. William and Albert Faulkner were discussing possibilities.

"I'd say chemical," the vet was saying. "Check the house and see if you can find out what he might have gotten into."

"There's nothing." William's voice was insistent. "Erick and I discussed the use of pesticides months ago. Like every large farm, we have to use something, but we're extremely careful."

"What about rat bait at the barn?" Albert Faulkner asked.

"I've thought of that. It isn't possible." William was sitting on the edge of his chair, his expression adamant. "Whatever Familiar got into, it wasn't a poison."

"He's awake," Mary said, deliberately interrupting the conversation. She could tell that William was worried and frustrated. "He's even purring."

"An excellent sign," Dr. Faulkner said with his first smile of the morning. "Now, you two look worse than the cat. You'd better go home and get some sleep."

"And you, too, Dr. Faulkner." Mary liked the vet. He'd been so careful with Familiar, and extremely thorough.

"Aye, I'll catch a few hours. I'm due over at Chancey's barn to check on a horse for her."

"Give her my regards," Mary said quickly. "And tell her I'll be ready for another ride soon."

Albert Faulkner shook his head, but he was grinning. "You're a spunky lass. Gossip runs through this area faster than the wind. I heard you took a spill just yesterday. And ready to go again. It must be the love of horses that you share with William and the MacEachern clan."

"She is a rare treasure," William agreed as he put his arm around Mary's shoulders. "We'll call about Familiar later in the day."

"He seems to be making a rapid recovery, but I'll watch him for a bit more. Go on with the two of you. And, William, check the barn for poison."

"You're right," William agreed. "I will check very thoroughly."

He opened the door for Mary, and they walked out into the new day.

"Dr. Faulkner thinks Familiar was poisoned," William said as he assisted Mary into the car.

She waited until he'd gotten behind the wheel before she answered. "So I heard. Is it possible?"

"Anything is possible. But we don't use rat bait. Or at least, we shouldn't be using it. Erick and I both agree that it's dangerous. But I'll ask the grooms and everyone else." William's shoulders ached from the stress of the night.

"I'm sure Dr. Faulkner will find out what happened to Familiar." Mary placed her hand on William's neck and gently massaged the tense muscles. "The important thing is that he's going to be okay. But I think we should call Eleanor and Peter."

"I agree." William sighed. "It would break Eleanor's heart if anything happened to that cat."

"He's going to be fine." Mary continued the massage until she felt William's neck begin to loosen up. "We're all going to be fine, William. All of us."

IT WAS LATE afternoon and, over Sophie's protests, Mary had dressed for a riding lesson.

"Shalimar is perfectly fine." She took a breath. "If I'm ever going to learn to handle the mare, I need to do it now. If I wait too long, I'm afraid that I'll become scared of her."

"But she hasn't been ridden!"

Mary's smile was secretive. "Ah, but she has. Kevin rode her this morning. We're going to double team her."

Sophie's concerns lessened and she sighed. "Mary, you are the most stubborn person I've ever known."

"It's my nature," Mary agreed. She laughed at her friend's expression. "It's true. I am stubborn. My father used to tell me I was half mule."

At that, Sophie finally smiled. "I can sympathize with him."

"Things are better, Sophie. Last night William was wonderful. He was kind, tender…so loving." She felt the blush begin to creep up her skin but she didn't look away from her friend. "Things are going to be okay. I can feel it in my bones."

"Are you sure?" Sophie touched Mary's shoulder. "I know you love William. But love isn't everything."

"I know." Mary soothed her friend's worries. "Right now, I'm more concerned about our black cat than William. I'm expecting Dr. Faulkner to call, and William has gone down to check on some of the cattle. Erick said there was some problem with a fence."

"I'll come and get you if the vet calls," Sophie assured her. "If you insist on riding when you can hardly hobble down the stairs, just be careful and have a good ride."

"Cheerio." Mary's laughter floated behind her as she walked—as normally as her sore muscles allowed—toward the barn.

Shalimar was none the worse for wear from the accident the day before. Nostrils flaring, she sniffed eagerly at Mary and gave her an easy butt with her head.

"She likes you," Kevin interpreted.

"I like her." Mary rubbed the mare's forehead and gave her the carrot she'd taken from the kitchen.

"Ah, so you're trying to bribe her?" Kevin's dark eyes sparkled.

"I'll try anything not to find myself eating dirt again." Mary felt a real rush of excitement as she mounted Shalimar. As frightened as she'd been, and as much as the fall had hurt, she'd enjoyed riding. With some practice, she knew she could become a good rider. And then she and William could ride together, galloping over the beautiful borderlands.

Under Kevin's firm but gentle instruction, Mary found that

she progressed rapidly. She was just learning to sit the gallop when she saw Sophie headed her way.

"Is it Dr. Faulkner?" she asked as she reined in Shalimar.

"It's Peter. Just checking in, but he didn't have any news. I told him what had happened, and he's going to call Dr. Faulkner so they can consult on Familiar's test results."

"Good." Mary had been trying to find Peter and Eleanor all morning, but they hadn't answered the telephone in their Edinburgh hotel. She didn't know Peter at all, but his reputation at research was excellent. Between the two vets, Familiar was in the best hands.

Sophie leaned on the fence while Mary finished her lesson, and the two of them went inside together.

"You really can ride." Sophie didn't bother to hide her surprise. "You're such a petite person, I didn't think you'd ever learn to haul a big horse around."

"I'm learning, and it isn't as hard as I thought." Mary was exhilarated. "By next week, I'll be ready for Chancey again."

"Absolutely not!" Sophie shook her head. "Don't even think about such a thing. I found three gray hairs this morning while I was brushing my hair. You're making me old before my time. At the idea of another ride with that Scottish hellcat, I'll be white-headed."

"Sure those gray hairs aren't from seeing ghosts?" Mary's laughter seemed to fill the courtyard.

"I'm sure." Sophie laughed, too. "It's you. Not even a ghost can be blamed for this."

"Miss Mary?"

At Abby's approach, Mary let her laughter subside. "Yes?"

"Dr. Faulkner called while you were riding. I didn't want to interrupt your lesson, but he said that he's been unable to determine what was wrong with Familiar. Nonetheless, the cat has made a complete recovery, and you may pick him up today. And he said Dr. Curry spoke with him." Abby smiled.

"Don't worry, dear. Dr. Faulkner will figure it out. He's saved many an animal around these parts."

"Let's go get Familiar now," Sophie said.

"Right." Mary wanted a chance to talk to the vet in person—and she wanted Familiar home, safe and sound.

She left a note for William, and she and Sophie drove the six miles to the vet's office. Familiar was ready for them, his voice still sounding rough but his meow welcoming.

Dr. Faulkner had gone on a call to Chancey's barn, and the nurse at his clinic said the tests were inconclusive, so far. Not all of the results were in.

"He's fine," Sophie said, picking up the cat. "Let's get him home and let Abby feed him."

"He's a very picky eater," the nurse said. "Doesn't care for his dry food."

"A picky eater? Not Familiar," Mary answered. "That cat eats twenty-four hours a day."

"Yeah, salmon or cream or prawns or sirloin. He's spoiled rotten," Sophie added, but she stroked the cat's head.

"Dr. Faulkner would like to see him in three days for a follow-up." The nurse gave Familiar a goodbye pat.

"Meow."

"Thanks." Mary paid the bill and hurried to the car.

Familiar curled sleepily on Sophie's lap, and Mary drove slowly through the beautiful countryside.

"Have you given any thoughts to your menu for Saturday?" Sophie asked.

The dinner party had completely skipped Mary's mind. The fall from Shalimar and the incident with Familiar had wiped all thoughts of the approaching fete out of her brain.

"Not a single idea, and you can be sure that everyone will be looking at the menu, the decor, and my clothing to find fault." She hated to sound so antagonistic, but Chancey had rubbed her nerves raw about fitting into the community. She knew how important it was to William that she be accepted as a suitable Lady MacEachern. Her marriage to William was more than a union of two people. It was part of a much larger tradition and community.

"Are you going to play for them?"

"I hadn't thought about that, either." Mary considered. She was an excellent cellist, and even though she hated the limelight of performing in a small group, it might help pass the evening.

"I'll make a deal," Sophie said, her eyes bright. "You plan the musical menu and I'll take care of the food. With Mrs. Connery's help, of course."

"Would you?" Mary felt her burden lighten considerably.

"Sure. I like doing that sort of thing." She gave her friend a sidelong look. "I'm jealous that you'll be hosting parties and planning menus and entertaining on such a scale. I'll be back at the flat in Edinburgh trying to make the can opener work."

"Hardly." At the sound of Mary's laughter, Familiar lifted his head and purred.

"It's true." Sophie was smiling, but her tone was serious. "When I was a little girl, I dreamed of having a large estate where I could entertain. I loved the idea of china and crystal, polished tables and chandeliers. You're going to have all of that, Mary, and it doesn't mean a thing to you."

"I never knew that was your secret dream." Mary brushed back one of her unruly curls. "I dreamed of living in foreign countries, of danger and excitement and finding lost treasure. I wanted to be an adventurer. Planning parties with matching candelabra and silver was the last thing I wanted to do."

"Well, you'd better learn to enjoy it. As Lady Mac-Eachern, I'll bet you'll be the center of the social whirl here."

"You're probably right." Mary didn't sound enthusiastic. "But you can come and take care of all of that for me." Her voice bubbled again. "See, that's perfect. You love it, and you can do as much of it as you like."

Sophie shook her head. "You'll get the knack of it. You'll see."

"I'll do it for William," Mary said, making a martyred face. "But the sacrifices I'm going to make…" She burst out laughing, and Sophie joined her.

When they pulled into the yard, William was waiting for them. He took Familiar in his arms and led them into the house. Once in the library, with Familiar perched contentedly in Mary's lap in front of the fire, William poured the women a sherry as he listened to the report on Familiar.

"He does seem perfectly fine," William commented.

"He does," Mary agreed, stroking his back.

As she spoke, Familiar jumped from her lap and, with complete catlike dignity, walked out of the room.

"Maybe he was tired of being talked about," Mary said.

"Maybe." William refilled his glass of Scotch. "I'm just glad the black devil's fit and home. And I have a surprise for you two ladies."

"What?" they asked in unison.

"We're going to Killby's Tavern for dinner. There's an old friend of mine playing some tunes on the harp, and I thought it would do us good to spend an evening out."

"That sounds wonderful." Mary was enchanted with the idea. Since they'd been at Mayfair, and since William's behavior had been so erratic, she'd given up all thoughts of going out. Now, though, an evening of music and fun sounded perfect.

"You two go." Sophie stood and put her empty glass on the table. "I have a slight headache, and I don't think I could take the smoke or the music."

"Sophie!" Mary's voice was wheedling. "It'll be fun."

"No doubt, Mary, but it will be more fun for both of you if I'm not along complaining and whining about my head." She tapped her forehead lightly. "How could anything so empty ache?"

"Are you sure, Sophie?" William asked.

"I'm sure." She smiled at Mary, then William. "Besides, I like the idea of the two of you out together. It's like a date, of sorts. Romantic."

Before Mary could protest any more, Sophie hurried from the room.

"I don't think her head is hurting at all," Mary said.

"I don't think it is, either. But I think she's very wise for one so young." He slipped his arms around Mary and pulled her against him. "I'd love to take this lovely woman for a date, and I think it will be far more romantic if it's just the two of us."

"Do you think you know me well enough to take me out with you?" Mary asked, her voice soft, teasing.

"Aye, and I have intentions of knowing you even better before the night is over."

Mary stood on tiptoe and offered her lips for a kiss.

"Now run along and get dressed, before I have to change my plans and stay home," William said. He gave her bottom a friendly pat.

Warmed by his kiss, Mary hesitated. The idea of staying home sounded better and better. "Maybe we shouldn't leave Familiar."

William touched her cheek. "He's fine, Mary. Just to be on the safe side, though, I'd like to leave him in your bedroom while we're gone."

"He'll probably sleep," Mary agreed. She felt a momentary reluctance to leave the cat.

"Abby's in the kitchen now, poaching some salmon for him." William ran his fingers down Mary's cheekbone. "I'm sure Eleanor and Peter aren't going to want him back. He'll be too spoiled."

"I think he was spoiled when he arrived," Mary retorted. "I've never known a cat who made himself at home quite so easily."

"Then we're agreed. Familiar is perfectly fine, and we're going out."

"We're agreed." She turned on her toe, gracefully leapt away from William, pirouetted and bowed. "I'll be ready in half an hour, Lord MacEachern."

"See that you are," he said, making his voice gruff and stern. "I'll not be waiting for a mere woman."

Mary rushed up the stone steps, taking them two at a time in her exhilaration. William was completely back to normal! She felt as if she'd been freed of a terrible burden, and the future spread out before her was as wonderful and magical as she'd imagined it when William had first proposed.

Her footsteps echoed on the stones, reminding her that Mayfair was still old, big, and very drafty, but she was undaunted. She would learn to ride, and she would learn to entertain—as befitted Lady MacEachern. She would help William in his struggles to run the gigantic estate, and together they would raise their family.

Panting, Mary stopped halfway down the hall and settled into a more dignified walk. As nervous as Sophie was, if she heard running footsteps outside her door, she'd jump to the conclusion that the castle was on fire.

Thinking about her jumpy friend, Mary was smiling when she caught a sudden movement in the shadows at the end of the hall.

"Familiar?"

She paused for a few seconds, wondering if her eyes had played a trick on her. The movement had been sudden, like a cat slinking from shadow to shadow.

"Kitty, kitty."

She waited, but there was no response. If it was Familiar, he'd chosen to explore in another area.

Mary walked on to her room. Slightly nervous, she kept glancing down the hallway, but there was nothing. Not a whisper of sound or movement. It had obviously been a shift of light.

As she opened the door, her fingers felt the delicate chain that had been draped over the heavy knob. In the dimness of the hallway she disentangled the chain and drew it to her. At the sight of the beautiful ring dangling on the end, she gave an exclamation of surprise.

She stood staring at the ring, then burst into her room and turned on the bedside light.

The emerald was exquisite. Cut in a pear design, it was at least two carats, and the deep green of the stone was pure and brilliant. The gold setting bore a tiny crest of the MacEachern clan, and it was dangling from the most beautiful of fine gold chains.

"William." Mary felt a rush of pleasure at the thought that he'd entrusted her with a family heirloom. And what a beautiful way to surprise her, hanging the ring on her door for her to find. It was just like him to give such a magnificent gift in such an unconventional way.

She slipped the ring on her finger, admiring the brilliant stone against her pale hand. It was a ring designed for Lady MacEachern. She would wear it as William's bride, and as his wife.

The sound of footsteps outside her door made her leap to her feet in anticipation. William was waiting for her to discover his gift.

Running to the door, she threw it open.

"Thank you!" she cried before she realized the hallway was empty.

Expecting to find William standing there, Mary brought herself up short. She'd definitely heard footsteps outside her door.

Looking down the long length of the arched stone hall, she felt sure no one could have disappeared so suddenly. It had been maybe three seconds from the sound of the steps until she'd opened the door. No one could disappear in three seconds!

She stepped into the hall, wondering if William was playing a prank by hiding in some tiny alcove. In the poor lighting, it would be easy to miss him.

''William?'' She called his name and realized how frightened she sounded. ''William?''

''Lisette.''

The name echoed back at her, and she felt her stomach clench with such a fierceness that she thought she might be sick.

''Lisette.''

The name was a whisper spoken by someone in pain.

''I'll wait for you, Lisette. Forever. There is no escape.''

A noise at the far end of the hall made Mary cry out as she whirled around. From the dark shadows a small black shape hurled itself down the hallway. Remembering the ferociousness of Familiar's attack the night before, Mary involuntarily stepped back. But the cat streaked past her without stopping and ran to the end of the hallway.

Tail twitching, he stopped at the stairs and looked up, up toward the third floor turret room where Lady Lisette MacEachern had been held prisoner.

Chapter Seven

Mary's first impulse was to run into her room and slam the door, but that was quickly replaced by a desire to rush forward, to see who was speaking so plaintively into the darkened hall. The voice was familiar. Still, she could not positively identify it. It seemed to float out from the very stones of the castle walls. She felt goose bumps invade her skin, even as she fought against the notion of the supernatural.

That thought spurred her into action, and she hurried to where Familiar stood. If there was someone playing pranks in the halls of Mayfair, it was time he revealed himself.

At the stairs where Familiar waited, his steady gaze intently watching up the stairs, she hesitated. The man, or creature, who'd spoken in the hallway had probably gone up the stairs. Mary's inclination was to go down, down to safety and to the library where she prayed she'd find William. He had to be in the library. That would prove that he had nothing to do with the events that were happening on the second floor. She wanted to find who was tormenting her; she wanted to prove that William was innocent. Even if it meant confronting a ghost.

"Meow." Familiar, back arched, started up to the third floor.

"Familiar," she whispered. "Come with me."

The cat ignored her, going on up the stairs. Mary hesitated for a second more before she darted headlong down the stairs.

She found herself creeping as she neared the library. William would be sitting in his favorite leather chair, poring over a book as he waited for her to change clothes. She visualized him doing just that as she made it to the library door.

The huge oak door was closed. With the gentlest of pressures, she opened it and peeped inside. The room was empty. Doubt struck her with such force that she felt an acute pain in her chest.

Was it possible William had been on the second floor landing calling softly into the night? Was he playing some joke on her? Her doubts grew to staggering proportions in a few brief seconds. Worst of all, she wondered if William was sick, sicker than she'd ever imagined.

"Mary."

William's voice made her scream as she jumped away from him and into the library.

"I thought you were going up to get dressed. What's going on?"

He stood behind her in the hallway, a leather-bound volume in one hand and a glass of port in the other.

"William." His name escaped her lips, a plea.

"What is it?" Concern washed over his face. "You're pale as a ghost. What happened?" He went to her and guided her toward the sofa in front of the fire.

"Where have you been?" Mary could hear how choppy her words were. He stood while she sat.

"I went to get a glass of port. I thought you'd gone up to change your clothes." He stared at her. "Whatever happened? Is it Familiar?"

"No." Mary could feel her heart rate slowing. "No, it's not Familiar. There was someone in the hallway."

"Who?" William was instantly alert.

"I don't know."

"Did you see someone? What did he look like?"

Mary hesitated. How did William know it was a he? "I didn't get a clear look."

"What did you see?" William's voice held a tiny note of exasperation.

"Nothing, really. It was what I heard."

"Mary, what are you talking about?"

She saw the frustration in his eyes and she knew suddenly that he was changing. The shift was so subtle, so fine, that no one would notice it other than herself.

"Someone was in the hallway. He whispered 'Lisette.' And then he said he would wait for her forever. That there was no escape."

Mary watched the dawning of awareness on William's face, but it was overlaid with something else, a terrible struggle. She knew he was slipping away from her, deep into that black abyss where he was bedeviled and tormented.

"Ye speak as if ye knew Lisette." The gray eyes assessed her as the features hardened. "How would it be that ye know my Lisette?" The question was a warning and a challenge.

Mary reached out her hand and stroked William's forehead. He was burning hot, a dry heat that seared her very soul with despair.

"William, it's me, Mary. Look at me, love." She made her voice strong, willing William to hold on to her voice and touch.

"Mary?" William's face turned into a frown of concentration. "Mary." A more modern inflection made the name sound more familiar, and a fraction of recognition washed over his features only to be replaced with confusion.

"Yes, it's me. Mary, your bride." She placed her palm flat on his cheek, ignoring his fever and encouraging him to look into her eyes. "Stay with me, William. Don't leave me."

He lifted his hand, as if to stroke her face. But suddenly his face broke into an anguished mask; the effort to control was too great. He slammed his fist into the pillow beside her head, and Mary flinched, ducking her face into the soft cushion of the sofa.

When she looked up, there was no trace of the William she knew. The man who stood in front of her was surveying her with insolence and contempt.

"You'd seduce me with your soft words and kind glances, would ye, lady?" He gave her a knowing look. "The bed of Slaytor MacEachern has been sought by more than a few. But he'll wed only one. Do ye know her?" He gave Mary a sly glance.

"I—I know William..." She faltered.

"William?" The man who stood in front of her was puzzled. "William was killed at Loch Bane. Ten years gone. How did you know my brother?"

Mary knew then that William had lost all touch with reality. He was adrift, spinning back into the past, into a history she did not know, but was suddenly determined to discover.

"I was his friend," she said softly. "I love him to this day."

"Aye, he did inspire love, and loyalty. Twenty men died beside him, and not a one of them tried to run. It was a glorious slaughter, and they took more than four dozen of the MacAdams with them. Aye."

Mary shivered. William had never stayed in the room with her when he suffered an attack. In every other instance, he would become volatile, and then he would run away. But he seemed in no hurry to leave. He downed the port, cast a glance at the glass as if he'd never seen it, and carefully placed it on the table.

"Would you like something else to drink?" Mary asked. "I could get you something."

"Aye, not that sweet wine. It tastes like syrup gone bitter. I want something with some body, some heart." He picked up the glass and flung it into the fire, laughing as he did so. "Makes a pretty noise, doesn't it?" he asked, turning back to Mary.

"Lovely," she answered. It had been Waterford crystal from Ireland. William had said his great-grandmother had collected it. "I'll get you something more appropriate," she said, rising on unsteady legs. She started toward the door before she realized he'd moved to stand behind her. She ignored his presence as she reached for the door, but his hand caught her wrist.

"Where are ye from, lassie?" he asked softly, so close that his breath whispered against her hair.

Mary hesitated. Her heart was pounding, and she wasn't sure what to say. "France." She finally decided on that country as the safest. At one time, if she remembered any of her history correctly, France had been an ally of Scotland.

"Is that why you're dressed so…strangely?" He nodded down her length.

For the first time Mary was aware of her jeans and her sweater. And the ring! She clenched her hand into a fist to hide it. She'd slipped it on her finger in the hallway when she'd gone to investigate the voice.

"Yes, it's French custom," she said. "Denims. Very modern."

"Aye, the French have some modern ideas." William nodded wisely. "Fetch my drink." He released her hand as suddenly as he'd taken it.

Hurrying out the door, Mary shut it behind her and leaned against it while she took a breath. She had to hurry, before William went into one of his fleeing fits where he rushed out of the castle, to be gone for hours on horseback. Before she went a step farther, though, she took the ring off her hand and put it in her pocket. Better safe than sorry, and the sight of the ring might evoke too many memories for William to safely handle.

The liquor was kept in the bar in the second parlor, and she ran there as fast as she could. There was a collection of pewter goblets along the mantle, and she grabbed the biggest of those, filled it with a bottle of stout from the bar and hurried back to the library.

William's eyes lit up at the sight of the goblet. "A pretty piece," he remarked as he took it from her. "Lovely work. Far better than I recall at Mayfair, though there are some fine craftsmen here. Where was it wrought?"

"France," Mary said swiftly. It seemed the safest answer for almost everything he asked.

"Fine work." William smelled the stout and then drank several big swallows. "Yes," he said. "Now there's a drink."

"Another?" Mary asked.

William suddenly looked toward the door as if he'd heard something. "Lisette." He put the goblet down on the table as he blindly walked toward the door. "She's waiting for me."

"William." Mary went to him and touched his arm, but he didn't notice her. It was as if she no longer existed for him.

"Lisette. I'm coming." He shook off Mary's hand and strode toward the door.

"William!" Mary ran to him and put her arms around him. "Wait. Stay here with me. It's Mary. Your Mary."

"Away, woman." William shook free of her. "I told ye there was only one woman for Slaytor MacEachern, and she waits in the thicket for me to take her. It's a kidnapping, you see." He grinned. "And a more willing victim could not be found."

"William!"

Mary started after him, following him down the hall, out through the empty kitchen and into the cold dark night of the courtyard. She knew then that he was going to the stables.

His sharp whistle cut the night, and there was the answering whinny of a horse. Blaze! Horse and master had an uncanny relationship.

An uneven stone caught Mary's foot and she stumbled,

but she managed to regain her balance. When she looked up, William had disappeared into the barn. He seemed not to notice her presence, so she went in after him.

A terrible plan had begun to take shape in her mind. She knew how to saddle. Kevin had not allowed her to ride the first time until she had learned. If she hurried, she might be able to follow William. Shalimar was fast enough to keep up with Blaze. And Kevin had said the Anglo-Arab had more stamina than any horse in the stables.

But it was night, and Mary didn't know the roads the way William did. Could she honestly even attempt to ride after William, the finest horseman in an area dedicated to the horse?

Yes! At least she had to try. If she could only discover where William went, then she might be able to help him solve the why of what was happening to him.

Her bridle and saddle were hanging beside Shalimar's stall. Mary threw a pad on Shalimar's back and prayed. Even though her fingers fumbled with the girth and the buckles of the bridle, she had the mare ready to go by the time she heard Blaze's hooves on the cobblestones of the courtyard.

Shalimar shied to the right as she began to mount, and for one brief moment of terror, Mary thought she was going to be dragged under the horse's hooves. But the mare settled, and Mary sprang up and into the saddle as Kevin had taught her. She took up her reins until she could feel Shalimar's tender mouth respond to her touch, and then she urged the mare forward.

Blaze's hoofbeats sounded on the paved drive, and Mary gave Shalimar more rein and urged her into a trot. If William took the time to listen, he would hear the second horse behind him, but Mary honestly did not believe it would matter to him. He was riding toward his fate, toward an event or person who was long dead and gone. He had no time to listen to things of the present.

Low clouds swamped the moon and the stars, and Mary

zipped the jacket she'd grabbed from a peg in the stables up to her chin. She found a pair of gloves in the pockets and blessed whoever had had the foresight to leave them there. Shaking her red curls loose from a barrette, she used her own hair to cover her ears from the bitter wind and wrapped the muffler that had come with the jacket as high as she could. Had William stopped for a jacket? She didn't know, but she didn't think so. He was burning with fever, but when he came out of his "fit," would he freeze to death? That thought gave her another boost of incentive to keep up.

Shalimar had extended into a mile-gobbling trot, and up ahead she could hear the rhythm of Blaze's gait, also a long trot. That bit of knowledge gave her pause. If William were going only a short distance, chances were that he would gallop. The fact that he was trotting probably meant that he intended to ride for a long period of time. As she lifted her body up and down in the saddle, feeling each sore muscle and each tender spot from the lessons and her fall, she could only pray that he didn't intend to ride all night. She knew she'd never make it.

Beneath her, Shalimar moved as smoothly as a carousel horse. Sensing that the mare could follow Blaze far better than she could follow William, Mary loosened the rein and gave Shalimar the freedom to choose the path. There were times when the clouds parted long enough to let a glimmer of light through, and then Mary could see William riding on ahead of her. They were on a trail that led through the fields and toward the woods. It entered Mary's mind that they were headed due south, toward England.

Shalimar stumbled just as the moon broke through the clouds for a brief moment. Mary saw they were no longer on a trail. They'd begun to cut cross country, and the pace slowed.

Unfamiliar with the area, Mary had lost all sense of where they were—or where they might be going. Even if she turned back now, she wasn't certain she could find her way to Mayfair. Around her the night turned thick with a low, rolling fog that began to cover the land.

"William." She spoke his name softly into the night, knowing that even if he did hear her, he would not know she was talking to him.

William apparently picked up another trail, because the going became easier and Shalimar broke into a trot on her own. Mary gave herself to the rhythm of Shalimar's stride. Unable to see, unwilling to turn back, Mary committed herself to the sensation of riding. The only way she knew there was another horse and rider in the night was the sound of iron shoe on rock as Blaze and William continued to lead.

When Shalimar suddenly stopped, Mary almost flew over the horse's head. In the nick of time, she braced herself against the mare's neck. In front of her, the sound of hoof against stone had also ceased.

The darkness was so complete that Mary could see nothing. She waited, ears straining, to hear the slightest sound up ahead. A pebble slid down a rocky slope to her right, but there was no other sound.

Dismounting, she looped Shalimar's reins over a small shrub she discovered in the darkness. Step-by-step, she moved forward, hoping for a break in the clouds and the fog. While she was riding, the night had not seemed so bitter, but now she felt the nip of the wind against her face. Her nose was frozen solid, and she pulled the muffler up to conceal as much of her face as possible.

She moved forward an inch at a time, pausing often to listen for a sound from William. She heard Blaze, snuffling and shifting on the rocky land. William was nearby; what was he doing?

Walking with her hands extended in front of her, she felt him before she even knew what he was. Her fingers closed on the wool of his sweater, and she gave a small gasp of success at finding him.

"I knew ye'd make it this time, Lisette," he whispered, pulling her roughly into his arms.

Before Mary could speak, she felt his lips on hers. He tasted of William, and his kiss, so ardent and intense, still retained the tenderness of William. His hands pulled her against him while his mouth claimed her for his own. Before she knew what she was doing, Mary kissed him back. For a few blissful seconds, she forgot everything except the sensations he created in her with a single kiss.

"I knew ye'd come. I've waited here, night after night. When I saw the sky was thick and black, I knew you'd pick tonight. If only I could see you," William whispered when he lifted his lips from hers. "Where is your woman and your things?"

Awareness came back in sharp degrees for Mary. William was waiting for an answer to a question she didn't fully understand. The man holding her in his arms was William, but it was not. And he had assumed she was someone else. If the moon did suddenly find a hole in the clouds, he'd see that she wasn't the woman he thought she was. He was waiting for her answer.

"I came alone, with nothing," she said at last, her voice weighted with uneasiness.

"Lisette! There are men willing to run you through, or worse." William's voice was hoarse with disapproval. "Ye came alone?"

"I had no choice, Wil—If I was to come at all, I had to come alone." She spoke with more authority.

"I would not have ye risk yourself like that again," he admonished, but his chiding was overlaid with the roughness of his desire for her.

She could not let him kiss her again, for she couldn't be certain she could control her response. She loved him, completely. But more than anything, she had to find a way to help him. Searching for a safe subject, she hit upon the weather.

"It's a bitter night." She could feel herself slipping back into the less modern phrasing. She could never sound like William, with his brogue thickened to the point that sometimes she found it difficult to understand him. But the few times she'd spoken to him, the old expressions and phrases came back to her easily. Fear lurched through her stomach. Good God, what was happening to her? To them?

"Does something ail you?" William asked suddenly.

"No. I'm tired from the ride."

"A bonny lass like yourself, tired from an adventure in the night." William squeezed her. "Am I not worth a bit of an effort, Lisette?"

"You are, indeed," Mary answered. William would never know the irony of this moment.

"'Tis only a short ride back to Mayfair." William's voice rang with pride. "I've a room prepared, and it shall be as you asked. We'll say you are my prisoner." He pulled her against him and kissed the top of her head. "A prisoner by day, my own true love while the moon reigns."

Mary leaned against him, wondering about the man Slaytor MacEachern and his kidnapped bride. Whatever part of history William was playing out, it didn't seem as if Lisette were an unwilling victim. She'd met him halfway, at least, for her own kidnapping.

"Do you think this plan will work, Lisette? If your father firmly believes you've been taken against your will, then he will forgive you if you marry me?"

Mary couldn't think of an answer. She allowed William to assist her back to where Blaze remained, perfectly willing to stand and wait for his beloved master.

"I judge by your silence that you are not sure." William sighed. "Would that there was another way, my love. But he'll never give his permission for us to wed. Not willingly. Not even Mayfair could make him change his mind about me."

"Let us forget the future." Mary could hear the quiver in

her own voice. What was she saying? Had she gone completely mad trying to delve into some historical hallucination that William was having? Psychosis could be extremely dangerous, to the person and to everyone around him. By encouraging William, she might do permanent damage. Yet it was the only way Mary could obtain enough information to try to help him.

"You're right." He pulled her to him with such force that she felt her feet leave the ground. But his strong arms held her safely, and he put her down as soon as he'd kissed her.

"To Mayfair," Mary said, breathless and shaken. She had to get him home.

"To Mayfair." He kissed her again with a passion that went straight through her. He broke the kiss with a hungry laugh and swung her up onto Shalimar's back in an almost single motion.

"We'll ride like the wind, my love. And when we get home, there'll be a raging fire for you and some food."

Shalimar danced under Mary. She acted as if William's mere presence made her nervous. "Don't ride too fast," Mary said, trying hard not to sound afraid.

"Aye, I don't want to wear you out on a horseback ride," William answered with a chuckle. "I have other plans for you. Now home!"

The clatter of hooves let Mary know that he was mounted and on his way to Mayfair. Trusting to Shalimar's superior vision, Mary forced her protesting body into rhythm with the horse. She had to get him home to Mayfair. She'd find help. There had to be someone who knew what was happening to William, someone who could diagnose his illness and give him a cure.

Mary no longer doubted the fact that something terrible was happening. And it was much more frightening than she'd even dreamed. She'd thought William was getting better, but he was much worse. The only good thing was that now she could tell him exactly what he did and how he acted. Once she could talk to him—when he returned to being her William—then he would surely agree to find the right medical help.

A thought far worse than any she'd had made her gasp. What if he didn't change back? What if he was truly possessed? What if, this time, he didn't come around?

Chapter Eight

You'd think someone in this establishment would consider putting on a few night-lights for wandering guests in search of the kitchen. These stairs are treacherous, especially when there's the off chance that a ghost is going to pop out of nowhere.

Mary and William took off into the night. I have to give my little pixie credit. She's got a will of iron and a constitution to match. Whoever said not to judge a book by its cover was thinking of her. She looks fragile, but she is one tough cookie. Not many women would follow their man out into the wild Scottish night on horseback.

I've got to figure out what's going on around this place. I've spent some time thinking about my seizure and subsequent trip to the vet. I've never experienced anything like that before in my life. There would seem to be two possibilities. A supernatural source or—hateful thought—something I ate. But what?

Having exposed myself to all of Sir Arthur Conan Doyle's masterpieces, I know Sherlock would start at the obvious and work out in a tight circle. A bit of a cynic, he would put the ghostly aspects of this business aside to examine the portions where human intervention seems more likely. So, to the past evening's menu. I was perfectly fine through dinner. Abby gave me a few slices of the pheasant she'd prepared. Deli-

*cious with those mushrooms and shallots. I had a taste of
that pungent cheese that's made locally, and Kevin slipped
me a few dollops of that heavenly custard. I was feeling perfectly fine.*

*It was a bit excessive to eat the second custard my two
little lovebirds left in the bathroom, but no harm done. No,
if food is the source of the problem, it had to do with what
I ate, not how much. And I suspect that whoever has been
running around this castle in the dead of night can tell me
what I want to know.*

*Mary was just going into her room when I heard a male
voice calling for Lisette. My immediate reaction was that
someone was setting her up. But when I went up to the third
floor and she went to the first, I found nothing and she left
with William. Someone had to be there. And if that person
was flesh and blood, where did he go? I've searched every
nook and cranny of this old moldering pile of stones, and
there is no one on the third floor.*

*If I weren't a more sophisticated cat, I'd begin to believe
that Mayfair might really be haunted. If William is possessed
by some ancient and barbaric ancestor, then it stands to reason that I was possessed by some ancient and savage family
cat. Is possession contagious?*

SHALIMAR UNERRINGLY found her way home and, in a rare
burst of moonlight, Mary was never so glad to see the walls
of Mayfair. She heard Blaze in front of her; William was
already in the stables. As she slid from the saddle to the
ground, she heard someone fall with a groan.

"William!" She rushed to the light switches and flooded
the barn with illumination.

His face gray, William was lying on his back only a few
inches from Blaze. His chest rose and fell in fast, shallow
breaths.

"William." Mary dropped her reins and rushed to him,
finding a weak and rapid pulse in his carotid artery. Even

though he was sweating profusely, his skin was cool to the touch.

With no time to lose, Mary dashed to the Connerys' stone cottage. There were grooms somewhere in the barn, but she wasn't certain where they slept, and she knew where Kevin, John and Abby could be found.

Wrapped in a warm robe, Abby answered her urgent knock. In less than a minute, Kevin and John were dressed and at the barn. Picking William up between them, they carried him into the house. The stairs were too difficult to negotiate, so they placed him on the sofa in the library. John set to work to build a fire.

"Looks deathly," Kevin said in an awed voice.

"Aye," John Connery answered. "We should get a doctor immediately."

"Hush!" Abby warned them as she pushed them away. "You sound like he's all but dead." She looked at Mary and gave a reassuring smile. "He looks bad, but he's a stout man with a strong physique." She turned to her husband. "Now without terrifying Mary more than necessary, call Dr. Sloan. Tell him to come at once."

John nodded, but kept his opinions to himself.

"I'll take care of the horses," Kevin said. There was an unspoken question in his statement.

Mary looked from Kevin to Abby. She didn't understand what passed between them, but they were undoubtedly concerned about William and what he had been doing. She had to think of something to protect him, some way to explain what he'd been up to without revealing the depth of her concerns.

"William has been…troubled," she began. Gossip spread so quickly around the small community that she schooled herself from saying more. The Connery family had been with Mayfair for years, but Mary recognized the land mines ahead of her. If William was insane, if he was suffering from some terrible mental illness, then everything and everyone at Mayfair would be in jeopardy. Before she got them all worked up and excited, it would be better to find out what was wrong with William.

"He's been riding a lot at night. A dangerous habit," Kevin said evenly.

"Dr. Sloan should be here in the next fifteen minutes," Abby said briskly. "Now, Mary, help me get his shoes off and some warm blankets piled on him. Kevin, tend to your chores in the barn. And put a kettle on for some tea on your way out. William is sick, but Mary looks as if she could use a spot of something warm to drink."

In the bustle of Abby's orders, Mary found a respite. William's color was better, and the terrible sweating had diminished. She reached under the blankets Abby was piling on him and took his hand. There was a tiny degree of warmth in it.

Once he was better, she would make him confront the issue of his strange behavior. She'd waited, more patiently than most, to allow him time to work through the shifts in personality in his own way. She was no fool, though. He had to seek professional help. No matter that Mayfair and his inheritance might be at stake. Bother the estate and all that went with it. His health, and their future, was all that really mattered. Somehow she'd make him see that.

"I think he's coming around," Mary said. William's lips parted and closed, soft words were mumbled under his breath. Hands and legs moved beneath the blankets. A new worry nagged at Mary. Would he wake up in this reality, or the past?

She saw his eyelids begin to shift. They opened, revealing unfocused gray eyes. He looked at Mary and then around the room. "I'm near frozen to death," he said, his teeth chattering to prove it.

"You'll be warm soon," Mary said. She clung to his hand. "William, you scared half a lifetime out of me." She spoke softly, but she couldn't help the tension in her voice. "And everyone else here at Mayfair."

"What happened?" William's glance took in Abby, who'd left the room and was now returning with a tray laden with tea and biscuits.

"Ah, a little food might be the best thing for you," Abby said as she put the tray down beside the sofa. "I was thinking you'd come around as soon as we got you warm."

"I feel like I've been taken to the north country and left during a blizzard." William's smile was rueful.

"You've been riding that horse through the fog and chill. And your bride-to-be followed along like a foolish pup," Abby said, but her tone belied her stinging words. "What is it you seek in the night?" Her question was softly put and loaded with worry.

"I don't know." William's answer was equally soft, and puzzled.

The sound of John letting Dr. Sloan in ended the conversation.

"I think I'm well enough to go to my room," William said, swinging his feet off the sofa. "I'm sorry you were called, Dr. Sloan. I'm feeling perfectly fine."

"Have a cup of tea with the doctor," Abby suggested. "You'll feel better, and so will he." She pressed a cup into his hand before he could resist. Just as efficiently, she served Dr. Sloan and Mary, and then quickly left the room.

Mary cleared her throat. "William, you must talk with the doctor."

"I'm fine, now," William argued.

"For the moment." She went to sit beside him. "We have to talk with Dr. Sloan. Trust me, now. This can't go on. The next time…"

The resistance left William's eyes. "I was hoping there wouldn't be a next time. I thought it was done. Over. But it isn't, is it, Mary?"

"No, my love." She kissed his cheek, then gave him a smile as he started to speak to the doctor.

Together they told Dr. Sloan about the episodes William had been experiencing.

"It's far from my expertise," Dr. Sloan said, his deep concern clear in the furrows of his forehead. "I was your doctor when you were a lad, and a healthier, happier boy could not be found anywhere in Scotland. But stress and worry can manifest themselves in peculiar ways. And that's not to rule out some chemical or mental malfunction." His clear eyes caught William's gaze and held it steady. "It could be stress, or it could be something far worse, William. You have to find out. It isn't just your future, or that of your lovely bride-to-be. The community depends on Mayfair and your stewardship of it. You know that. Should you fall ill, there could be grave consequences."

"I know." William leaned forward so that his elbows were on his knees.

"I think I'll make us another pot of tea," Mary said tactfully. She wanted to give the men time to talk. William would eventually tell her everything, but he needed a chance to express his worries and concerns to his doctor.

She closed the library door and felt once again the chill of the night in the drafty hallway. It was as if a hand from the grave had slipped down her spine.

When she felt something brush against her leg, she almost screamed before she recognized Familiar.

"So, you and William are up to taking turns to make sure I go crazy with worry," she said, stooping to pick up the cat. He was fully recovered from his illness. "When do I get a chance to show my other side and drive the two of you crazy?"

Familiar took a graceful leap out of her arms. She was too tired to chuckle at his antics as he rolled on the floor. "I've a pot of tea to make, my fine, black friend. You'll have to wait until later for a belly rub."

As she started to the kitchen, Familiar grabbed her leg with his claws. He didn't break the skin, but held firm.

"Familiar." She shook her leg gently to disengage him, but he only clung harder.

"Give it up, my furry friend." When she bent down to untangle him, he jumped to his feet and meowed. Looking back at her, he led the way down the hall to the back door.

"I have to go to the kitchen," Mary said, following him, anyway. He was acting so strange, and the idea that he, too, might show another personality change, made her loath to ignore him. "Well, just for a moment I'll indulge you."

The cat immediately increased his pace. He didn't even pause at the back door but pushed it open and slipped into the night.

The idea of stepping back into the cold made Mary shiver, yet she didn't stop. She had to get Familiar back inside. It was a foul night out, not fit for man or cat. Searching the courtyard, she caught sight of him headed toward the stables. He stopped in a pool of light and looked back at her, as if waiting for her to follow.

"Okay," she said, hurrying after him. "But you'd better have a good reason for this."

At the barn, Familiar waited again. Mary caught up with him and was about to speak when she heard voices in earnest conversation. Something about the tone made her stop, and when she heard William's name, she listened.

"I'm going to tell William." It was Kevin who spoke, and he was agitated.

"Wait, Kevin. This isn't the time. William is not well." John Connery's voice was worn with weariness. "I've been trying to tell you for the past two months, this is something that will require time, patience, regard for everyone involved."

"If it's true, then we both have a right to know. We can't go on pretending."

"You're upset, and I understand." John's voice was strained.

"For two months I've waited, first for William to come home so I could discuss this with him, and now for the proper time. I can see there won't ever be a good time to bring up this subject. In the meantime, everything continues right along—he's the heir to Mayfair, and I'm the trainer at his stables." Kevin's anger grew. "That may well be the case, but if what you've told me is true, then some portion of Mayfair is mine."

In the darkness outside the door, Mary felt the blood drain from her face. What was Kevin saying?

"Abby and I have loved you like our own son," John said. "I didn't want her to tell you about Joanna, but she felt that you had a right to your chance of a heritage. I was afraid that if things didn't work out, it would make you bitter, angry. You're too fine a man to live the rest of your life feeling cheated, Kevin. Promise that whatever happens, you won't let this spoil your life."

"What are my legal rights? I've waited long enough to find out."

Kevin's question sent a chill down Mary's spine. It wasn't what he was asking, but the way he was asking it. Mayfair was incredibly important to William, and he would brook no threat against it, not even from a kinsman.

"You'll have to find a solicitor to tell you that. There are tests to prove blood kinships, I'm sure. We'll have to find your mother."

"And where is my dear sweet mum?"

Mary had never heard such bitterness.

"The last we heard, she'd emigrated to Australia, Kevin. Now you can't go blaming her. She was a child herself, and infatuated with William's father."

"So Lord MacEachern continued with the family tradition of seducing the servants, taking advantage of a young maid." Kevin spat the sentence out. "'Tis a fine inheritance."

"It wasn't that way," John said, his voice anguished.
"Such bitterness, Kevin, will be the ruin of you. Joanna was
a young girl. Young and foolish, but not mean or cruel. She
was as bright as a ray of sunshine, but she was obsessed with
William's father. She made up her mind to have him, and I
do believe she did. When she became pregnant, he offered
to help her. But she left during the dead of night. Six months
later, we found you on the stoop of the cottage with a note
from Joanna."

"Thrown away like an old shoe."

At that, John laughed. "Hardly. Joanna knew that Abby
and I wanted a child more than anything in the world. We
couldn't have any. She found you the best home that could
ever have been."

Kevin's sigh was audible. "That she did," he said. "I've
never gone a day without feeling the love of you both."

"Keep that in mind, Kevin, and bide your time awhile.
William is in a bad position. He's under pressure to marry,
as you well know. Should he fail in that regard, it will be a
real donnybrook in the courts to see who owns Mayfair. As
it is, he's been gone for many years, and has much catching
up to do. But he seems to be a fair man. Give him a chance
to hear your story and see if he isn't willing to settle fairly
with you."

"And what of Erick?"

"If William marries, as the trust decrees, Erick will have
little to say what becomes of Mayfair."

"And that's justice!" Kevin's tone was angry once again.
"Who's worked these last years to keep William's heritage
together for him?"

"That's nothing to do with William or Erick. That's the
way it's always been at Mayfair. And the way it will continue, I'm sure. First born is heir, as long as he meets the
obligations. If William fails, then Erick will have his
chance."

"And me?"

"Even with Erick there's no guarantee that you'll be recognized. It would seem you'd be next in line to inherit, if your bloodline could be proven. But that's neither here nor there. William will marry, and he will meet the conditions of the trust.

"Let him settle in and make his plans. There's time aplenty to decide the matter of your parents. I believe he'll be fair with you, Kevin. He was always a lonely child, but one with a good heart. He often shared his tea and biscuits with me because he had no other playmates, except for Darren, when that lad could escape from the clutches of his mother." John sighed. "Now there's a sad case. It's a wonder that boy can even think straight. Warped, he should be. To this day, he follows his mother like a shadow."

"There was Erick," Kevin reminded John.

"No, Erick didn't come to Mayfair until William was sent away to school. 'Tis a pity they never learned to know one another. It would have made all of this easier in the long run, this handing down of the estate."

"It's a cruel method. Mayfair should go to the one best able to work it."

"Even that's not a proven case, Kevin. William's mettle has not been tested."

"Not yet. My claim will come as a shock to the new lord."

"Maybe, maybe not," John said wisely. "Give it a chance. Now stop driving your mother wild with worry and anxiety. You were completely happy and content with your work and the horses until we told you. Look on this as a chance of fortune, a hand of cards."

"Ignorance is bliss." But the irony of his voice was cut with a fine edge of humor.

"Indeed it is, Kevin. Now back to bed with you. I heard Erick say that he's going to bring in the three-year-olds tomorrow. Are there any with promise?"

"Indeed." Enthusiasm had returned to Kevin's voice, and

he sounded like the man Mary had grown to trust as her riding instructor.

Mary picked up the cat and scampered back across the courtyard before she was caught eavesdropping. Her head was reeling with everything she'd learned. Kevin might be William's half-brother! And William didn't have a clue. How would he react? And how would Erick react to such news?

The intricacies of the MacEachern trust were unknown to Mary, but she could see the potential complications. Legal as well as emotional. Although she'd never met William's father, it was strange to think of him having an affair with one of the servants. William's depiction of his father was of a cold man not given to bouts of temptation or emotion. Certainly not an affair with one of the maids.

She went to the kitchen and hurriedly put the kettle on for the tea. Familiar took a seat at the heavy oak table and began to lick his paws.

"You're a mighty sly puss," Mary said, remembering the way he'd grabbed her leg and practically dragged her to the barn.

"Meow." Familiar went back to his grooming.

"What did you find on the third floor?"

"Meow." Familiar stopped licking his foot. He shifted to a sitting position and looked around the kitchen. With a quick hop, he landed on the floor and went to the refrigerator.

"How about something to eat?" Mary asked as she poured the hot water and covered the pot to allow the tea to draw.

"Meow."

She obligingly opened the refrigerator door and motioned for Familiar to indicate his desire.

The cat sniffed the air and put his paw on a small covered dish near the bottom.

Lifting the dish out, Mary uncovered it. "Custard." She realized she was starving. She'd had nothing to eat, nor had William, except for one or two of the pecan biscuits Abby had brought with the tea.

"Good idea." She put a portion on a plate for the cat and then divided the rest into three glass dessert dishes for herself, William, and Dr. Sloan. It had been a long night for all of them.

She left Familiar munching away and returned to the library. Knocking lightly, she entered to find William agreeing to a series of tests at the local hospital. The idea made her blood run cold, but it also gave her a ray of hope. Medical experts could certainly find out what was happening with William. Once he was diagnosed, then surely a cure could be found. Or a priest called to exorcise his demons!

She served the custard and the tea to the thanks of both William and the doctor.

"I'll bid you good-night," Dr. Sloan said soon after, snapping his bag shut. "I'll see you Monday at the hospital." He stood. "If there are any more of these incidents, I'll expect to see you before then."

"You will," Mary assured him. "William is hardheaded, but this time I believe he sees how necessary it is to clear up this matter."

"I do," William said. "Mary and I plan to marry. The sooner all of this is over, the sooner we can begin to make our plans."

"Now that's a smart decision."

Mary walked the doctor to the front door. She was bursting to tell William what she'd heard at the barn, but it really wasn't her place. If Kevin was his half-brother, she did not need to interfere. They would have to work out their own relationship, and much of that would be determined by Kevin when he chose to tell William. She could only keep her fingers crossed that both men would act with compassion toward one another.

Familiar suddenly reappeared at her side as she went back to the library. To her astonishment, William was sound asleep in front of the fire. He'd lain down on the sofa and pulled the blankets over him. His face registered a weariness that made Mary sit beside him a moment and examine his features.

With his clean jaw and high cheekbones, he was a handsome man. She could see the blood of his ancestors in him. Anyone looking at the gallery of MacEachern paintings in the hallways of Mayfair could find more than a dozen likenesses of her fiancé. The MacEachern genes were strong, and they were undeniable between William and Slaytor.

And Kevin? His hair was lighter, his skin more olive and his eyes brown rather than gray. But his hair was thick, his face square and his eyes wide-spaced and kind. He could be a MacEachern.

He also could not.

"Heaven help you," she whispered to William as she stroked his face lightly. "I'll leave you here to sleep." There seemed no reason to wake him. He was exhausted. She looked around, but there was no place where she could comfortably rest. He was home, in Mayfair. He'd be fine if she left him to go to her room and catch a few hours herself.

She stood, tucking her hand into the pocket of her jeans as she did so. She felt the ring, forgotten in the madness of the night. Pulling it out into the light, she was dazzled once again by the brilliance of the emerald and the setting of the ring.

Acting as Slaytor MacEachern, William had left the ring at her door. She'd give it back to him the next day. It was a family heirloom, and one William should keep until they were well and truly wed.

"Come along, Familiar," she said, motioning the cat to follow her. "It's time for bed."

Together they made it up the stairs. On a hunch, Mary decided to check on Sophie. Her friend had slept through the harrowing evening, and it was just as well.

Tapping lightly on the door, she called Sophie's name.

When there was no answer, she tapped harder. Worried,

Mary tried the door. It opened readily, and she stepped into the suite her friend had chosen.

At first she thought the bed was empty, but on second glance, she saw a poorly defined lump beneath the thick covers.

"Sophie?"

Mary advanced. Before she could do anything, Familiar flew to the bed. With a half growl, he caught the covers in his teeth and pulled.

Mary ran forward. Her friend was deathly pale, her eyes closed and her chest barely moving. "Sophie?"

There was no answer.

Mary rushed to the bedside and tried to shake Sophie awake. She was alive, but she did not respond to anything Mary did. "Sophie!" Mary cried urgently. Then she ran from the room, down the stairs, and hurried out the kitchen door, running once again toward the Connery house.

Chapter Nine

"Keep her walking," Abby directed the tiring Kevin and John as they supported Sophie in a slow pacing back and forth across the room. "There'll be no sleep for you this night, but tomorrow you can lie abed and snore yourselves silly."

Mary sat in a chair in front of the fire and watched her friend stumble sleepily between the two men. Sophie's color was good, as was her breathing. But it didn't do to take a chance, not at Mayfair. Mary toyed with the idea of loading William and Sophie into a car and taking them both away. She could do it—and she might. "Do you think Dr. Sloan should take a look at her?"

"Let the poor man sleep," Abby said. "Miss Sophie's taken in a quantity of my herbal tea. She's sleepy, but it isn't a toxic substance. We could let her sleep it off, but it'll make you feel better if we revive her."

"Yes, it will," Mary agreed. Sophie was rolling her head from side to side, resisting all effort to wake her. But Kevin and John struggled on, forcing her to walk.

"Why won't you leave me alone?" Sophie said clearly—and irritably. "I want to sleep."

"See," Abby said. "She's fine."

"I think you're right." Mary was feeling better and better as her friend started to grudgingly wake up.

"How do you suppose she got into the tea?"

Abby motioned for the men to put Sophie back onto the bed. "She came downstairs about nine and said she'd stayed behind so that you and William could have a real date. She'd been reading, but felt nervous. She kept hearing things outside her door and such. I know how Miss Sophie's mind can imagine things, so I gave her a cup of tea."

"One cup wouldn't do this," Mary said.

"Right. She obviously went back and made more. I showed her where the herbs were located."

"She must have drunk several pots," Mary replied. She caught the startled look on John's face, but he quickly averted his eyes.

"I'll go and make us some coffee," Kevin offered. "Caffeine should help bring her around."

"Exactly so." Abby went to the bed and rested her palm on Sophie's forehead. "How are you, Sophie?"

"I was fine until you burst in here, dragged me around the room, and irritated me to pieces."

Mary felt relief wash over her. Sophie had always been grumpy about being awakened. With each passing minute she was sounding more and more like her old self.

"I'll be back," Abby said, excusing herself. John and Kevin followed after her. Their work was done.

"What possessed you to drink all of that tea?" Mary asked as soon as she was alone with her friend.

"Don't make it sound like I've been robbing the cupboards. I went back and made myself a single cup of tea. The one Abby gave me was delicious, and I was beginning to feel very relaxed and sleepy. So I thought one more would bump me over the edge into sleep. I didn't realize I was going to be the sport for every member of the Connery family, not to mention my best friend. Next, William will be here nagging me to wake up."

Mary smiled. "So sorry to disturb your dreams, Sleeping Beauty. I thought you were dead."

"It's this place, this morbid castle."

Instead of denying it, Mary stood and paced the room. "William is going to the hospital Monday for some tests. If we can manage to get through this weekend…"

"Mary." Sophie sat up. "What's wrong?"

"He had another attack." Mary pulled a chair up beside the bed and gave her friend some of the details. Carefully avoiding all references to Lisette, Mary told of William's illness and the ride through the night. "So, things are very tough for William. I'd like to have this dinner party and pretend that everything is fine here. It could be very important to William. In the future."

"Mary, what are you going to do?" Sophie gave Mary's hand a squeeze. "I've been terrible, thinking only of myself. William is really sick. What will you do?"

"He'll go into the hospital, and we should know something in a day or two. I'll remain here." Even as she spoke, Mary knew she sounded unsure of herself. Should she stay at Mayfair? Would that help or hinder William in the future?

"That's good, a show of strength." Sophie sounded more and more assured as she talked. "At least William has consented to finding out what's wrong. I think this is a very positive step."

"Sophie…" Mary looked at her friend. "I've teased you so much lately about this ghost business."

"That's okay. I guess I was being something of a goose. I mean, I saw someone in the hall, but I didn't really see his face. I was being silly."

"Maybe not." Mary felt the flush creep up her face. "William changed." She forced herself to continue. "He changed radically. And he…" She had to stop.

"He what?" Sophie was leaning forward. "What, Mary?"

"He thought I was Lisette." She dropped her gaze down to her lap. She'd intended to keep this part from Sophie, but she needed someone to confide in, and Sophie had been her closest friend for the past five years. From the pocket of her jeans, she extracted the ring. "He left this for me on my door."

Sophie drew in her breath. "It's beautiful, Mary. It must be hundreds of years old. In fact, at least two of the women in the paintings are wearing a ring just like this one."

"It's the MacEachern marriage ring. I think William left it for me because he was Slaytor, and he thought I was Lisette."

"Oh, Mary." Sophie's eyes filled with tears. "That isn't true. If William left it, he meant it for you. He loves you without any reservations."

"Aye, he does. When he's William." Mary turned away before Sophie could see her tears. She was tired and upset, but crying wouldn't do any good.

"Well, I'm wide awake. Let's plan the dinner."

"Now that's a good idea. It's Saturday morning, and though I haven't had a wink of sleep, I'm ready to plan. That will give Abby and the staff a chance to put it all together."

"What, dinner for…seven?"

"Ten, I believe. We'll have the three of us, Mrs. Daugherty, Dr. Sloan, Erick, his lady, Chancey, Clarissa and Darren McLeod and…" Mary stopped. "Who else?"

"William will know. Ten will hardly put a dent in that enormous table." Sophie's hand flew to her forehead. "What a goose I am. I forgot to tell you that Darren McLeod stopped by last night. He was desperate to see William."

"Darren?" Mary was surprised at her reaction of concern. "What did he want?" Maybe it was his mother that set Mary's teeth on edge. She didn't trust Clarissa as far as she could throw her. And Darren was definitely in his mother's thrall.

"He didn't say. I was reading when he knocked on the door. John had gone to bed, so I answered it."

"Did he come in?"

"Only the foyer. He demanded to know where William was. Naturally I couldn't tell him a thing, so he left. His hair was all tousled and he was anxious. But he didn't leave any kind of message.''

''Well, I'm sure William can handle whatever it is.'' Mary forced her mind back to the party. ''Now we have our guest list....''

''Will ten people be enough?''

''More than enough.'' Mary already felt apprehensive. She didn't want to overextend herself on the first entertainment, but she also wanted to put on a show of graciousness and ease. If William didn't get sick. ''It's always in the evening when William has an attack.''

''I know.'' Sophie spoke quietly. ''I was so excited for you last night. I was hoping it was over. The night before had been calm, except for Familiar's episode. And last night looked so promising.''

''I've racked my poor brain. What would trigger such a thing? I've gotten to the point where I'm saying the hall clock chimes eight and William becomes Slaytor. Could it be the clock?'' Mary laughed at herself, but it wasn't a humorous sound. ''I'm getting desperate to find some cause and effect.''

Sophie yawned and stretched. ''Excuse me. Another little twinge of that tea.''

Remembering the coffee, Mary got up and went to the door. ''I'll bring the coffee up. And I want to check those herbs. If you only made a cup, and it nearly turned you into Ichabod Crane, maybe I could keep some on hand for William when he starts to act strange.''

Mary didn't wait for an answer. She was bone weary as she trudged to the kitchen. Abby was nowhere to be found, but the coffeepot and two cups were on a tray. She'd obviously been about to bring them up when her attention had been diverted.

Stepping into the pantry, Mary began to rummage through the different jars and bags that Abby kept. The array was impressive. Some of the goods were store bought, and others

Abby had put up herself. Spices and teas predominated, and Mary made a mental note to come back and check out Abby's pantry at a later date. Herbs fascinated her, and a few cooking lessons wouldn't hurt.

As a member of the symphony, she had found that her life revolved around music rather than food. Now, things were changing. It would be fun to prepare something for the dinner party, some dessert or dish. It would help her to hold on to her dream of life with William at Mayfair.

In the kitchen, she retrieved the tray and a small black shadow that followed her along the halls. At the library, she checked on William. He was sleeping soundly.

"As well he should," she murmured under her breath. "Like a baby, and I'm wide awake." She tucked the blanket under his chin and closed the door behind her.

"Come on, Familiar. We have a menu to plan, and I'm certain you have a few ideas in that direction."

MARY TWISTED HER curls into a loosely gathered cluster and pinned them in place. The effect was perfect with the gown she'd chosen for the evening. It wasn't a formal dinner, but she wanted to look her best. For William.

William was dressing for the dinner, also. He'd awakened long enough to drink tea and eat toast, and then he'd slept through the rest of the day. There had been no opportunity to speak with him about the events of the night before.

The guests would be arriving at any moment. Mary picked up Familiar and stroked him, allowing herself to enjoy the feel of his silky hide. Somehow she'd manage to get through the night. Somehow. She and William would have a long talk on Sunday.

Her nerves as taut as a fiddle string, Mary fought against the worries that seemed to tear at her. She held to the picture of William, sleeping soundly on the library sofa. He was okay. He really was. But the image of him as Slaytor MacEachern superimposed itself on the picture. Rugged, determined, a man who would risk everything to have the woman he loved.

Mary sighed, and Familiar licked her hand with his rough tongue.

"You know, don't you?" she whispered as she placed him on his feet. "I hope Eleanor and Peter are having more luck than I am."

She checked her bedside clock and discovered that she had time for one cup of tea before she could expect the knock of the first guest. Maybe William would join her. She checked her earrings one last time. The opals looked good with her green dress and her eyes. Suddenly remembering the emerald ring, she went to get it. It was amazing how well it fit her finger. And it was beautiful with the dress.

Should she risk triggering an episode with William by wearing it to dinner? She closed her fingers over it and decided to take it to his room. If he didn't remember giving it to her—and he hadn't said a word—it would be better to return it before anything happened to it. There was no safe place in her room, only a dresser drawer or her own jewelry box in a drawer in the bathroom. That wasn't exactly the place for a ring worth a small fortune. Best to return it to William. There was a safe in Mayfair, and it would be much better there. With that in mind, she put it back on the chain and put it around her neck. It nestled just above the curve of her breasts, obscured by the dress.

Passing Sophie's room, Mary had the first truly happy thought of the day. Sophie had gone down to the barn— sneaked, actually—to talk with Kevin. For Sophie, who was extremely shy with men, it was a major step. In all of the years that they had known each other, Sophie had expressed crushes and infatuations with men who were always unattainable. She'd yearned for movie stars and newsmakers, always turning aside the overtures of handsome young men who were actually available. Kevin was a definite step in the right direction. The matter of his parentage might prove to be rocky, but Mary had no doubt William would do everything in his power to be fair. She grinned. Yes, indeed, Sophie might see a lot more of Mayfair than she ever anticipated.

She was smiling still when she made it to the kitchen. Several of Abby's helpers were bustling about, and Mary waved them away as she turned on a kettle for tea. As Marla whirled by with cooking utensils bristling from her arms, Mary stepped into the pantry for the tea. She found the tin marked Abby's Special Blend and shook a portion into a teapot. The excitement in the kitchen was contagious and transmitted itself to her.

As she put the canister back, she saw another, very similar tin. Abby's Sleep Aid was written on the label. Mary held the can, considering. When Sophie had made her tea, she could have mistakenly picked up the wrong canister. Standing on tiptoe, Mary inspected some of the other tins and jars. Pushed way into the back was a small brown vial. Pulling it forward, she discovered it was a prescription ordered for Abby by Dr. Sloan. Nembutal.

Panic clicked in Mary's brain. Nembutal was a powerful sleeping drug. Had some of it gotten mixed in the tea? By accident or deliberately? Were there any other effects of the drug? Her mind raced with a thousand possibilities. She memorized the spelling of the drug and checked the date. It was only two months old. Whatever was troubling Abby's sleep had started about the time that William had made it known he was coming home to Mayfair.

The possibilities rolled and turned, shaping and reshaping. Mary tried to stop them because some were so patently ridiculous. She could not visualize Abby deliberately putting anything in anyone's food. The harsh truth was, though, that William's ''spells'' came during or after the evening meal. During the day, he often ate on the run, stopping at a pub or neighbor's house if he was out on the estate. In the evenings he ate at Mayfair.

She tried to remember each horrible incident. The last two were most vivid. One had been at the dinner table and the other had been with a glass of port. The port! She'd planned on serving it prior to the meal.

Putting the pills back on the shelf, she hurried to the bar and removed the heavy crystal decanter. Several loud glugs came from the decanter as she tipped it into the sink. Better safe than sorry. What would she do with a roomful of Scots who decided to go back in time—especially the McLeods and MacEacherns? They had been at war with each other at one time!

The idea was so ridiculous that Mary had to laugh. Mixed with the terror was a growing measure of relief. If William's episodes were brought on by some substance, then he was perfectly all right. If he stopped getting the substance, then he would never "regress" again.

She started to rinse the port decanter to refill it. Bitter reality hit home; she should have kept some of the port for analysis. She'd poured her proof down the drain.

"Blast me for a fool," she muttered. She tipped the bottle and found a small portion still remained. "Thank goodness." Finding an empty glass, she poured the half ounce of port into it and was holding it when she heard footsteps approaching. Like a guilty child, she pushed the glass into a dark corner of the bar.

"Mary?" William walked into the parlor. "Who are you talking to?"

"Myself, for being an idiot." She looked at him and couldn't help the smile that spread over her face. He was the most handsome man she'd ever seen. And he was fine! She was going to prove it!

"What a lovely smile," he said. "I feel like some charmed character in a fairy tale. After sleeping a hundred years, I awaken to find myself engaged to a lovely princess."

"Oh, William. I have so many things to tell you."

"What happened last night?" His worry showed in the

deep lines etched in his forehead. "I remember bits and pieces. You rode with me in the night."

"I did. And my body has the bruises to prove it." Mary couldn't stop grinning.

"You're awfully jolly about it."

"Indeed I am." She kissed him. "I think I've figured it all out. William, I—"

The doorbell rang, announcing the first guest.

"What?" William had caught hold of her excitement.

"After dinner. Just promise me that you'll switch plates with me."

"Mary?" He was amused.

"No argument. It's important. Promise?"

"I don't understand, but if it pleases you, of course. By the way, Erick called and sent his belated regrets. The woman he's seeing, her child is sick. It must be serious or he would be here."

"I know. It's a shame, though. I was looking forward to meeting this woman. Erick is so private about her."

"We'll meet her soon enough. He promised that."

"If it were up to me, we'd sneak away, to be alone." Mary felt the thrill of her discovery ripple through her. She stood on tiptoe and kissed William again, making sure to remove the traces of her lipstick before she put her arm in his. Together, they went to greet the guests John was showing into the castle.

"HOW QUAINT!" Clarissa McLeod lightly touched Mary's arm. "Is this some Edinburgh custom, to switch food with your intended mate?"

"It's a custom of my family, not my city," Mary said. Her voice was very soft, and she smiled, but she saw Darren's head swivel toward his mother. He gave Clarissa a disapproving look, which she shot back at him, forcing him to return to his conversation with Sophie.

"Since we don't know much about you, dear, forgive my

inquisitiveness. It's just that Lady MacEachern is such an important role to fill. Strange customs will excite gossip.''

"It seems everything excites gossip in this small village." Mary wanted to bite off her own tongue. She was being antagonistic and abrasive, but she'd had as much of Clarissa's indelicate probing as she could take.

"What Mary means is that everyone has a lively interest in what happens at Mayfair." William was about to burst into laughter at the expression on Mary's face. She was furious, and she didn't hide it well.

"There are some very interesting things happening here, William. Very interesting. Night rides. Ghostly appearances. *Undiagnosed illnesses.*" Clarissa's voice cut across the other conversations, bringing the room to a full silence.

"Remember, gossip is always twisted." William's composure did not slip a notch. He poured more wine for Mary. "The sole is delicious, Mary. Why aren't you eating?"

With the entire focus of the table turned on her, Mary lifted a forkful to her mouth. She'd intended not to eat anything. Her suspicions that William was being fed something in the evening meal made her reluctant to eat since she'd insisted on trading her plate for his once they'd been served. She looked around the table. Dr. Sloan was watching her with reserved interest. Darren was openly curious. Chancey was unusually quiet, but her bright eyes were taking in every nuance of the tension-filled meal. Sophie was mortified, and Mrs. Daugherty was so busy with her food that she was paying minimal attention, looking up only when the silence became stretched.

"Mary?" William was watching her more with curiosity than anything else.

She took the food, chewed and swallowed. "Delicious." She looked around the table. "Abby is a wonderful cook. Darren, I understand you were about in the darkness last night, also."

Darren stopped chewing. "Uh, yes. I..." He gave his mother a nervous look. "I stopped by to visit Miss Sophie."

Mary felt a moment of shame. Darren had come courting Sophie and had lost his nerve at the last moment. And now she'd drawn attention to his awkwardness. Judging from Clarissa's glare, Darren would pay for his show of independence, too.

"I think Abby is the best cook in Scotland," Sophie said, fumbling for something to say into the awkward silence that had dropped over the table. "I think I've gained weight since I've been here. All of those scones and breads and puddings."

The conversation stalled awkwardly again.

"Since we've been talking about the strange incidents at Mayfair, I have a surprise for you," Clarissa said, "as I promised." The look she gave Darren was inscrutable.

Instantly Mary knew she would not like the surprise.

"I've arranged for a world-class medium to visit tonight." Clarissa's smile was that of a very satisfied carnivore. "Since the stories we've been hearing about midnight rides, ghosts roaming the hallways, and strange behavior are only gossip, Madame Sianna will simply declare Mayfair free and clear of all spirits. That's assuming Mayfair is free and clear."

Mary couldn't believe her ears. A medium? At Mayfair? A chill ran along the bare skin of her arms.

"Madame who?" William was amused, and his humor bumped the conversation over another dead silence.

"See-anna." Clarissa pronounced the name in a tone that meant she was serious. "She's from Hungary. Very well respected. Members of the royal families all over the continent use her."

"And how were we so lucky to have her in Kelso tonight?" Once again, humor prickled William's tone.

"We're so lucky because I requested her to attend. She was interested in all the stories that have been floating around about Mayfair suddenly being haunted."

"And what stories are those?" The humor was gone from William's voice. "I don't have to ask who's been telling them around."

"Don't be foolish, William. You can't go riding all over the countryside at night and not expect someone to see you. If you've forgotten, you almost gave poor old Rycroft a heart attack the night you jumped the wall in front of his car. Lucky for you Blaze is such an excellent jumper and not easily frightened. And I hear you and your lovely fiancée—" she gave Mary a tight smile "—were out for a little ride last evening. Is this going to be a family tradition?"

"I see Mary has improved her riding skills considerably," Chancey said dryly under her breath but loud enough for all to hear.

William laughed. "Possibly. But it has nothing to do with ghosts."

"Then you shouldn't mind a little entertainment from Madame Sianna. If there's nothing to hide at Mayfair, then there's nothing she can…discover."

Mary sensed William's anger, but he covered it well.

"What's a little harmless party entertainment?" He looked around the table. "Dr. Sloan, if we discover any bodies, you can tell us if they're dead or alive."

"My specialty," the doctor said. He gave Clarissa a disapproving look and returned to his plate. "Dabbling in the occult can be an entertaining pastime, as long as no one takes it seriously. I'd hate to see anyone make a fool of themselves."

"No need to worry on my account," Clarissa said brightly. "Now, Madame Sianna will be here at nine. I think we should gather where we can have a comfortable place to sit and allow our minds to open to the possibilities."

"The library," Mary said instantly.

"How about Lisette's turret room?" Clarissa countered. "If it's ghosts we're hunting, wouldn't it be better to go to

the source of the vile history of Mayfair and Slaytor Mac-
Eachern?''

''That room hasn't been used in years,'' William declared.

''All the better,'' Clarissa said. Her victory was written on
her face. ''So glad I thought of it. I hesitated to suggest it,
since William isn't exactly thrilled with the idea of my little
adventure, but it's all in fun, isn't it, William?''

William shrugged. ''The turret is fine. Just remember,
though, Clarissa, whatever you stir up becomes your problem.'' At the look of sudden panic that crossed her face, he
grinned.

The anticipation of the coming séance dulled everyone's
appetite for the delicious apple pie that Abby had baked.
Instead, they took their coffees and after-dinner drinks to the
turret to set up the room for the arrival of Madame Sianna.

While William, Darren and several of the servants were
putting a table and enough chairs in the room and laying a
fire, Mary saw her opportunity to catch Dr. Sloan alone. Motioning him to follow her out into the hall, she found one of
the hundreds of alcoves that lined the old stone walls and
stepped into it with the doctor for a moment's privacy.

The limited time made her blunt. ''I found a prescription
for Nembutal you'd given Abby.''

''Yes?'' Dr. Sloan raised one eyebrow.

Mary took a breath. ''We've discussed that fact that William has been acting…peculiar.''

''And you're wondering if he could be taking a drug?''

Mary nodded.

''Wouldn't you know if he was taking anything, Mary?''
The question was gently put, but it implied so much.

''I would, if he knew. What if someone's giving it to
him?''

''For what purpose?'' Dr. Sloan was visibly shocked at the
idea.

''I don't know,'' Mary had to admit. ''It's just that I found the drug, and it was hidden in the pantry. It would be so easy…''

"For someone like Abby to drug her employer?"

"I know it sounds ludicrous. But I have some port. It might contain something. Is there any way we could test it?"

Dr. Sloan looked into Mary's eyes. "You're serious, aren't you?"

"If it is something like that, it would mean William is… not sick. It would be a simple matter of finding out who was doing it and why."

"Much preferable to considering that your fiancé suffers from psychotic personality changes." He nodded as he spoke. "I can send the port to a lab that specializes in chemicals and poisons." He tilted his head as he looked at Mary. "So that's why you changed plates with him and were reluctant to eat."

"I'd be willing to eat the stuff if it would prove that William is reacting to a drug."

Dr. Sloan put his hand on Mary's shoulder. "I'll check the port, and I should have William's tests back early Monday morning. I'll check them thoroughly before he's scheduled to show up at the hospital." His fingers tightened on her shoulder. "Don't put too much faith in this idea, Mary. I can't believe anyone would try to hurt William. As far as Nembutal goes, it's never been known to create a psychotic disorder. There's always a first time—some adverse reaction to a drug—but don't pin your heart on it."

"I know." She felt defeat sink into her soul. Dr. Sloan's arguments reinforced her own doubts. Who would hurt William? Abby? Hardly. Kevin? Before he'd even told William about the possibility of his heritage? Not likely. There wasn't anyone who would gain by making William believe he was one of his ancestors. Besides, if there was poisoning to be done, a fatal dose would be more useful. She wasn't a lawyer, but she realized that with William alive but institutionalized, Mayfair would be in a terrible limbo.

"Chin up, Mary," Dr. Sloan said. "We'll get to the bottom of this."

"We have to," she answered softly.

Footsteps coming down the hall made Mary pause. Loud exclamations of surprise and anticipation told her that Madame Sianna had arrived.

Chapter Ten

"What should we do to assist you, Madame Sianna?" Clarissa McLeod asked reverently. She looked across the table that had been placed in the center of the turret room at Madame Sianna's order. Darren looked away from her.

Mary watched the silent exchange of glances, her mind still reeling from the surprise of the tall, dark-haired woman who had taken instant command of the situation. Madame Sianna was striking, from her richly colored dress to her deep black eyes. If she was not a member of a traditional Gypsy family, she absolutely looked the part. Even down to the golden earrings that swung freely from her earlobes among her dark curls.

"It would help if you were quiet," Madame Sianna said matter-of-factly.

Mary sensed rather than heard William's amused reaction to that remark. She, too, grinned. When she caught his eye she could see that he was actually enjoying the entire evening. That made her feel considerably better. Even after her discouraging exchange with Dr. Sloan. She had been so certain she was on the right track. But the doctor was right. Who would want to make William ill? That was foolishness; no one would benefit from an illness.

She noticed that Familiar had slipped into the room. He was perched beside the fireplace, acting for all the world as if he didn't care what was going on. Mary knew better. The cat was watching the entire evening play out with an alertness that was belied by his casual pose. Good for Familiar! She was glad someone was as concerned as she was about what might happen next.

"Before we begin, I would like a moment outside alone." Madame Sianna rose. "Take this time to clear your minds of all distress, all worries. Prepare to welcome the past, those poor souls who have failed to find rest among the dead but who cannot return to the living." She strode across the room and closed the door behind her without a backward glance.

"Mary, why are you doing this?" Sophie's voice was low, her whisper urgent. She sat to Mary's right while William had taken the place to her left.

"Have I a choice?" she asked, careful to keep her frustration out of her voice.

"What if there is a ghost here? What if they really stir it up? They'll go home and we'll be here!"

Sophie's concerns echoed Mary's own. Since Dr. Sloan had burst her bubble about the Nembutal, she was back to the possibility of a real ghost. Even *that* was better than the alternative—William and some form of mental illness.

"This is one of Clarissa's many jokes," Mary said, soothing her friend even if she couldn't soothe her own worries. "This is some bag of tricks Clarissa has engineered. Clarissa and Chancey, judging from the way Our Lady of the Horse is acting." She nodded toward the tall blond woman who was on William's left. Laughing lightly, Chancey was leaning over to William to whisper something in his ear.

"She never gives up, does she?"

"Not until the vows are said."

"Oh, Mary." Sophie's voice was filled with sympathy. "If we can make it through the rest of this night, everything will be fine, you'll see."

"I believe you're right," Mary answered, wondering if she could possibly last for another hour or two.

"Madame Sianna asked us to be quiet and to prepare ourselves," Clarissa said. She was across the table, having taken the seat beside Madame Sianna. Darren was between her and Chancey, and he was staring across the table at Sophie. Mrs. Daugherty was taking in every aspect of the room, her gaze carefully avoiding the place where Madame Sianna would be sitting.

"I think we should be quiet, also," William said. Reaching under the table, he found Mary's fingers and squeezed them. "We want to give Madame every benefit of the doubt."

"Good." Clarissa smiled. "What shall you do if you discover Mayfair is haunted, William? Will you sell the estate? I don't believe Mary is quite up to living in a haunted castle."

"I don't believe I'm going to have to worry about that." William looked up as the door opened and Madame Sianna returned. She took her seat and ordered everyone's hands on the table, little fingers touching the person's on either side to make a circle as palms were placed flat on the surface.

"Maybe we should reconsider this." Mrs. Daugherty glanced around the circle. "I'm not sure this is going to be fun."

"Hush, Emelda," Clarissa ordered. "You have to experience different things before you pass judgment on them. Now, let Sianna continue."

"This is the unbroken circle," Madame Sianna began. "We are the living, the circle of life. Together we can call forth spirits from the other side."

Across the table, someone moved abruptly.

"Do not disturb the circle," Madame Sianna warned. "We can call the spirits back over to us only if we remain united in the endeavor. Should one single one of you betray us by breaking the unity of the circle, for any reason, the results could be grave."

Silence fell around the room. "Before we begin again, I am going to light a candle. Candles purify the air. They burn away the bad thoughts and deeds.'' She got up, went to the enormous bag she'd brought with her and extracted one large candle and several smaller ones.

''I can get someone to bring you more candles,'' Mary offered.

''These are blessed,'' Madame Sianna said. ''You are generous to offer, but it is much better if we light the room with a brilliance that has already received special blessings. Sometimes the dead are difficult to see. They may be only a shadow, a glimmer of light, maybe even the touch of a chill that traverses lightly over the skin.''

Mary felt such a chill as she listened to Madame Sianna. William was sitting beside her, perfectly fine. But the idea of a ghostly possession clung in her mind until she felt actual dread at what Madame Sianna was about to do.

Chancing a look at Sophie, Mary felt her heart drop to her stomach. Her friend was terrified. Totally erect, Sophie was staring into the large candle that Madame Sianna had placed in the center of the table. The skin across Sophie's face was tight with…anticipation? Mary couldn't actually call it fear. Not exactly. But it was almost as if Sophie felt something that no one else in the room felt.

''Now.'' Madame Sianna walked to the light switch and hit it, throwing the room into near darkness. Candles along the mantel and the windows and the single candle in the center of the table gave the only illumination. ''We shall begin.''

She resumed her seat, putting her hands on the table to complete the link of human flesh.

''There is someone here among us. A definite presence. He has been here for a long, long time. Someone filled with anger, yet weary. Someone who looks to the heart of his kinsman to see that all matters are worked out for the best. He has been dead a very long time, but he cannot rest. He cannot rest without finding, first, the woman who holds his heart—and wears his ring.''

Even though Madame Sianna was a perfect hoax, Mary felt her stomach knot. The ring that had been left outside her bedroom was hanging around her neck by the chain that came with it. She'd never had a chance to talk to William about it. The urge to remove her hand from the table and touch the ring was almost overpowering.

"Do not break the circle," Madame Sianna intoned.

Mary gasped, and she felt Sophie stiffen on one side while William started forward in his chair on the other. She slipped her little fingers farther up their hands to indicate that she was fine. Both settled back into their chairs.

"This spirit is very strong." Madame Sianna's voice had changed. There was now a hint of concern in it. "He wants to come back. Even though he knows that it is not allowed, he is determined. There are things he did not finish, goals left unattained. These trouble him. He was a man of great wealth and power, and now he sees what he has built beginning to decay."

"How do you mean, decay?" Clarissa asked. Her voice, spoken into the dark quiet of the room, was as shattering as a slap.

Madame Sianna's voice was terse. "Please do not ask questions. As I learn more and more about this spirit, I will tell you. When you ask questions, you break my communication with the spirit. Often they won't come back."

"I—"

"Be silent. Concentrate. This is a very troubled spirit. He is so desperate, I sense that he would try anything. Possession, reincarnation. Even though he knows it would be stealing a soul and transplanting it with his own. He is a man torn by such battles." There was the sudden intake of her breath. "And he is very desperate. Desperate in his heart!" Her voice grew stronger and she began to speak faster. "This is a dangerous man. Barbaric, uncivilized." She exhaled rapidly. "He is also very determined. He will do whatever it takes to have his way. Whatever."

Mary felt as if the ring were burning into her skin. She knew it was just her imagination, heightened by the powerful suggestions Madame Sianna was making. Glancing at William, she tried to determine what he was thinking. Outwardly he seemed perfectly calm, even amused. Those expressions could be deceiving. She'd seen him change in a matter of a few moments.

"Shall we call this barbarian into our midst?" Madame Sianna asked. "He would make an appearance. He wants to tell us something. And he wants…to return."

Mary wanted no such thing. She didn't want Slaytor MacEachern called into the room. Not for any reason, and not even in jest. She started to break the circle, but she felt William's hand restrain her, signaling her not to interrupt.

"I see him clearly now," Madame Sianna continued, unaware or ignoring the distress Mary clearly signaled. "He is a handsome man. Warlike. Savage, but handsome. Dark of hair and light of eye, he bears a small scar on his right temple. It is the mark of a childhood game with a friend. That scar no longer troubles him. Something much deeper eats away at his soul. Now he is unable to rest because of his heart. His love. They have been separated! The woman he loves… There is danger!"

William's eyes locked with Mary's and, with a look, he urged her to remain still. He—and Clarissa, Darren, and Chancey, at least—knew that the medium was perfectly describing the legends of Slaytor. He could imagine what it sounded like to Mary. Especially with his own unexplainable "attacks." But he wanted to see how far Madame Sianna would take her little charade.

Mary studied William's eyes. He was calm, in control. The pressure of his fingers on hers let her know he did not want her to interfere in the séance. So be it. She wasn't afraid of ghoulies or shades—only of hurting William. If he was content with the proceedings, then she would remain silent.

"A cold wind blows from the past," Madame Sianna was

saying. "Such anguish. Such anger." Her own voice was twisted with emotion. "This man has the force to reach across the centuries to touch us here and now. He does not need my aid to return to this world. He comes and goes at will. He seeks an answer, and his quest gives him strength. He seeks…"

Sophie rose slowly to her feet, but her hands never left the table. "I hear you," she said softly.

Across the room, Familiar sprang up, his back arched and his fur standing on end. Mary watched in horror as her friend turned to the closed door.

"I hear you." Sophie tried to go forward, but Mary held her wrist and Dr. Sloan grabbed the other one.

Before Mary could make a move to halt the séance, the door creaked open. "Lisette, where are you?" the voice was thick with brogue and laced with anger. "Lisette, where is the ring?"

"I'm coming." Sophie struggled to free herself of Mary's grasp.

"Stop it!" Mary's words were directed at Sophie, but they were also appropriate for the séance. "This has gone far enough." She shook free of William and put both hands on Sophie's shoulders. With a quick motion, she shook her friend, and then very calmly slapped her across the face.

"Oh!" Sophie's shock was complete. "Mary, what was that for?"

"Keep her here," William directed as he sprang from the table and ran to the door that was only slightly ajar. "I'm going to find whoever is in this house, and he is going to pay a handsome price for this prank."

Mary wanted to go with William. She couldn't, though; she had her hands full with Sophie, who was sobbing uncontrollably. To her relief, Familiar darted after him.

"What was I doing?" Sophie asked again and again. "What was I thinking? I could hear myself, but it was almost as if I had no control of my own thoughts and certainly not my actions. This place is haunted. You can deny it till the cows come home, Mary Muir. No matter what you say, Mayfair is haunted, and by the very devil himself.''

Mary pushed her friend into a chair. ''Blow out those candles and turn on the lights. We've had enough of this.''

''I quite agree.'' Emelda Daugherty's support was unexpected. She pushed back her chair and went to the light switch. ''This was in poor taste, Clarissa. Very poor taste. I hold you responsible for this foolish night,'' she rattled on as she blew out all the candles.

Mary turned to confront Madame Sianna, who was sitting placidly at the table.

''You may find this amusing, but you've frightened my friend. Whoever you brought along with you to play the ghostly voice of Slaytor, William will find him, and I wouldn't be surprised if he didn't press charges against both of you.''

Madame Sianna's eyes were deep and sharp. ''Mayfair is haunted, Ms. Muir. My advice is to get your friend and your things and get out of here as quickly as possible. Take William with you and don't let him return. The spirit I saw wants your fiancé. He wants his life, his body.'' She leaned forward, her voice almost a hiss. ''His very soul.''

''Get out.'' Mary felt a sudden fury. ''You won't frighten me or William. I don't know what's behind all of this, but it's a hoax.''

''The spirit world is no hoax. Guard yourself if you choose to stay here. But you can't protect William if he stays. You will lose him as he falls more and more under the spell of his ancestor. I've asked for no money here, nor would I take any. My advice is free. Heed it, or suffer.'' She picked up her bag. ''I'd like to leave this place, Clarissa. I'm raw from exposure to this spirit. Raw and bleeding. That seems to be what Slaytor MacEachern constantly leaves behind him, brutalized people.''

"Darren," Clarissa interjected. "Get Sianna's things. We should be going right away."

"I think I'd like to stay. William might need...my help." Darren stared at his mother.

For a split second she hesitated. "If you're ever to get anything you want, Darren, it would be best if you listened to your mother. Perhaps you can come back later and help William." Her smile held no sweetness.

"Whatever you say, Mother." He stepped away from her and began to gather the psychic's bags and candles.

"Mary, see if you can find William." Dr. Sloan's voice was calm but commanding as he put his hands on Sophie's shoulders.

"Yes, dear. He looked distraught," Mrs. Daugherty said as she assisted Dr. Sloan. "Find him."

Mary rushed into the hallway, but there was no trace of William or Familiar. A sense of loss and despair made her want to strike out. If William was out in the night again, she would find him. There had been no sign that he was having an episode, but there was no way to tell what had happened to him since he'd left the turret room.

As she turned the corner and started down the stairs, she almost ran into Abby and John Connery. Kevin was behind them.

"What's wrong?" Abby asked.

"There's no time." Mary tried her best not to sound panicked. "Would you see the guests out, and make sure the psychic goes. And ask Dr. Sloan to stay with Sophie until I can return."

"Certainly," Abby said. As she spoke, John turned back down the steps to attend to his duties at the door. "And you?" Abby asked. "What are you about?"

"William may need my help. I'm going to find him."

"Be careful." Abby's voice was fearful. "There's strange things happening at Mayfair. Strange and terrible."

"I'll be careful." Mary hurried to her room, took off her

dress and found clothes suitable for riding. The one thing she had absolutely no desire to do was crawl up on Shalimar's back for another midnight ride. Her thighs were still sore and aching. For William, though, she'd ride bareback through hell.

Boots clattering on the steps, she hurried downstairs and out into the courtyard. The stables were strangely quiet and she remembered that Kevin was in the castle. If William had already left, no one probably knew which way he went.

"William." She spoke his name loudly as she walked toward the horses. "Are you here?"

Silence answered her.

She continued into the barn, feeling comforted by the sounds of the horses munching hay and shifting in their stalls. She stopped at Blaze's stall. The stallion was still there. William was not out riding. She turned back, caught by the silhouette of someone standing in the barn doorway.

"Hello, Mary," Chancey said as she walked inside. "Lovely dinner party. I'd declare it a smashing success. The gossip won't subside for weeks. Now, there's an asset for William."

"Were you in with Clarissa on that medium?" Mary didn't care that she was hurling accusations. If Chancey was not directly involved, she had every intention of using the incident to her advantage—to play Mary as a fool to the small community of Kelso.

"Clarissa is more than capable of making her own trouble," Chancey said, her voice filled with amusement. "Where's William?"

"I don't know." Mary hated to admit it, but she had no idea where he might turn up, or in what condition.

"Blaze is gone?"

"No," Mary said coldly.

"Then he's around. I checked the cars. He hasn't taken one, and if the horse is here, he hasn't left the grounds. I know him well, you see. Much better than you could ever learn to know him. William and I are alike. We share a common past, a common background. A common desire to see Mayfair prosper and the MacEachern name to continue with strong, healthy heirs."

"You've spoken of your brood mare capabilities before." Mary felt a surge of pure adrenaline. "I don't have time now to continue this discussion."

"Are you pregnant yet, Mary? If not, I'd accomplish that before William is dragged off to hospital."

Stunned at Chancey's knowledge of their personal business, Mary lost her aggressive edge.

"I see I've hit a nerve. William hasn't told you about the terms of his inheritance, has he? I'm assuming he's afraid you'll panic, once you understand that you may be carrying the child of someone who's mentally unstable."

"I don't know what you're talking about. William is fine."

"Save it for someone who might believe you. I don't." Chancey stepped closer. "In order to inherit, William must marry and produce an heir before he is thirty-five. A male heir. That gives you about two years. By my calculations, that's two babies. And if there should be trouble, or they should be girls…" She laughed. "How is your genetic disposition, Mary? Do boys or girls predominate?"

"That's absurd. No one would stipulate such a thing." Mary found that her breathing was shallow. She forced her mind to clear.

"Oh, someone has—and did. Good old Slaytor, whose name keeps popping up all over Mayfair these days. No MacEachern inherits unless there's proof he can continue the line. Slaytor MacEachern was a warrior. Times were very different when he was living, and so he stipulated the heir clause in his will to be passed down generation by generation."

"How do you know so much about the business at Mayfair?" Chancey was a liar, a great liar. This could be one of her tales.

"Everyone knows." Chancey laughed. "Everyone but you. You're the outsider, Mary. You're wrong for William. Did you hear Madame Sianna? Slaytor is stalking the grounds because he's disappointed that William is to marry you." She stepped even closer, until she was only four feet away. "You claim to be so much in love with William. Why don't you think about what you're doing to him? Just think about what it would mean for him to lose Mayfair. No heir, no prospects of one. You're not exactly a robust figure of a woman. In fact, I'd label you nothing more than a terrible liability."

The private moments with William came back to Mary like a slap in the face. William had spoken of his desire for children—soon, and as many of them as she wanted. Was that merely to meet the demands of his inheritance? She felt her trust begin to crumble. No! She had to give him a chance to answer the accusation. Before she believed anything, she had to ask him. And she would.

"Go home, Chancey. The evening is done." She wanted Chancey out of her way so she could find William. Find him and ask a few questions.

"If you want to stay at Mayfair, get pregnant before William goes in hospital. After that, it may be too late. But if you're with child, a boy child, perhaps you can save Mayfair for William. If you're not willing to do that, then get out of my way. Because I am."

"Does this look like I'm leaving?" Mary, goaded beyond clear thinking, drew the ring from beneath her sweater by the chain.

Chancey's indrawn breath let her know it had been an effective tool. "That's the MacEachern marriage ring," Chancey said.

"I know. William gave it to me. We're to be married November first. I hope you can attend, Chancey." Mary's speech was cool and formal. She'd regained her composure and the upper hand.

"Where did you get that ring?" Chancey's voice was half command and half frightened question.

"I told you, William gave it to me."

"That's impossible." Chancey's voice held no challenge, only fact.

"Impossible to you, but it happened to me."

"That's the marriage ring, the one every MacEachern from Slaytor down for more than four centuries has given his wife. On their wedding day!"

"I know that," Mary answered impatiently. There was something she wasn't getting. Besides, the enormity of the half lie she'd told Chancey was beginning to weigh on her. "I'm giving the ring back until we're wed."

"That should impress William."

Chancey was too smug. Mary felt the trap close before she heard Chancey's next words.

"That ring is never shown before the ceremony. It's tradition, Mary. The ring is placed on the bride's finger at the wedding. William would never give it to you beforehand. Never. In fact, he couldn't give it to you, even if he wanted."

"Why not?" Chancey's expression was so smug, so knowing, Mary couldn't help but ask.

"The ring has been missing for at least a hundred years. I'd like to be around when you explain to William exactly where you got it."

Chapter Eleven

Very clever. Very clever, indeed. Madame See-anna needs to see the inside of a good old-fashioned jail. That was a very interesting locket she was wearing. Very interesting the way it caught the candle flame and reflected just perfectly. The question with the madame is, who is she with and what does she hope to gain?

There's something rotten in Kelso, and it isn't the haggis, either.

Here's my opportunity. She's bending over to get something off the floor. One flying kitty leap! A terrible yank! Dodge a few glancing blows and make my getaway out the door.

"THAT DAMN CAT! He attacked me!" Madame Sianna turned to Clarissa. "You're responsible for this. I've never been attacked by an animal in my life."

"Really, Madame Sianna. How can you accuse me because that cat jumped at you? Besides, you aren't hurt. There isn't a mark on you." Clarissa motioned to her son. "Let's get out of here as quickly as possible. There's no telling what else might jump out at us." Her eyes were sparkling. "I've proven exactly what I hoped to prove—Mayfair is haunted. Something strange and dark has been happening behind these old walls. Did you see the way William jumped up and ran out of the room?''

"Mother," Darren started, his voice tired and disapproving. "If you continue to harass William—"

"I will continue." Clarissa's eyes snapped. "Until he's ready to sell Mayfair."

"I've told you, William will never sell." Darren's voice held the tiniest spark of anger. "He won't give up Mayfair voluntarily. You can't railroad him like you do me."

"Railroad! I only make you do what's good for you."

"Well, I've had just about enough of 'what's good for me.' Mark that down and remember it." Darren picked up Madame Sianna's bag. "I'll be downstairs, waiting for you. Make it fast, or you might discover that my patience isn't as endless as you like to think. I'm about fed up with your treacheries and manipulations. It might surprise you to learn that I have plans of my own."

"Darren!" Clarissa called after her son, but he walked out of the room, ignoring her.

"The night hasn't gone exactly as you wanted," Madame Sianna said. Her hand went to her throat and her face went white. "My necklace. Where is it?"

Clarissa looked from the medium's bare neck to the floor. "It has to be around here somewhere. You had it on not two minutes ago."

"The cat!" The medium looked around the room quickly. "That cat took my necklace."

Clarissa laughed. "That's rich. Mayfair has a warlord ghost and a thieving cat. A nice little fillip to my stories."

Madame Sianna's eyes were burning coals of fury. "This may amuse you, but that necklace is invaluable. It's a family heirloom, and I rely on it in my work."

"A necklace?" Clarissa was only mildly interested. "You use it in your work?"

"Yes. I must have it back."

"Then I suggest you take the matter up with William, *if*

you can find him. Heaven knows where he might have gone to hunt down a ghost.'' She laughed softly at her own wit.

"This is not a matter for laughter.'' Madame Sianna's eyes grew even hotter. "I must have my necklace.''

"Darren is waiting for us. We don't have time to hunt for it now.'' Her eyes widened. "But it would be a perfect excuse to come back here tomorrow. Maybe do some exploring on our own.''

"I will not leave here without my necklace.'' Madame Sianna plopped down at the table.

"Is there some problem?'' Abby moved up to the two women, her mouth set in a firm line.

Madame Sianna nodded. "That black devil of a cat stole my necklace.''

"Familiar doesn't wear jewelry,'' Abby replied, never even giving the hint of a smile.

Sophie, who'd stopped her crying, and Dr. Sloan both laughed. Even Mrs. Daugherty, who was standing uncertainly at the door, joined in.

"That necklace is valuable.'' Madame Sianna smoldered. Her large golden earrings swung free of her dark hair as she looked around the room, checking the floor and under the table and chairs. "It has to be here somewhere.''

"I'm sorry you've lost your necklace,'' Abby said. "I'll search the room thoroughly. Tomorrow. When, and if, I find it, I'll make sure and return it to you. No one at Mayfair, not even a cat, has ever been accused of being a thief.''

Madame Sianna stood tall. "Thank you.'' Without waiting for Clarissa or Mrs. Daugherty, she swept out of the room and down the stairs.

"Come along, Emelda,'' Clarissa said sharply. "Darren is waiting, and he gets to be such a boor about it.''

"Certainly, Clarissa.'' Mrs. Daugherty turned to Sophie. "It was a very…interesting evening. Please give William and Mary my regards. I hope everything is…fine here at Mayfair.''

Sophie, still shaken by the séance, nodded. "I'll tell them. I hope everything works out, too." Her voice was only a little wobbly as she spoke.

NECKLACE, NECKLACE, who's got the necklace? I dare say it's some handsome bewhiskered fellow. Impeccably dressed in formal black. I can't imagine why that woman sets such store in this old piece of costume jewelry. Could it be because she uses it for something other than adornment for her dress? Yes, I do believe that's the case. Nice little hinge and tiny compartment for a small amount of almost any substance, à la Borgias. They used to make these ornate necklaces and rings so substances could be hidden in them and used discreetly. Snuff was often put in them, but arsenic was carried in others. Many a wealthy lord or lady was sent to his or her grave with a dose from a locket or ring. And this locket works exactly the same way. If I only had a thumb, I could snap it right open! I learned about these things from one of those wonderful British mystery writers. It's amazing what tidbits of fascinating knowledge a well-traveled cat picks up along the way. Simply amazing.

Now, with a little shake and rattle, I can tell this compartment is empty. At the moment. But that's not what caught my eye. It was the way the opal-like surface reflected the candle flame—directly into Sophie's eyes. That Madame See Nothing was pulling the wool over somebody's eyes, and not with poison. It was the motion of the locket that she was employing.

I never would have noticed the good madame's game except for Sophie's glass of wine. From my vantage point behind the good Madame, I saw the reflection of the necklace in the wineglass. Then, bingo, I knew exactly what was happening. And no one else at the table suspected a thing. They all thought Sophie was communicating with some otherworldly personality. Not.

In my mind, Sophie is explained, but I don't understand

the voice. All along I've been thinking maybe William was involved. You know, the old "I'm Slaytor reborn" scenario where he undergoes some kind of psychotic split. But William was sitting right at the table. He didn't open his mouth. I watched his lips carefully. And there have been no claims to ventriloquism. This will take some work, unless William has trapped the intruder, which I doubt. Whoever is making the rounds of this castle knows it pretty darn well.

I'll zip down to the barn and see what's going on there. I haven't heard the thunder of hooves, so I'm thinking everyone is still on the grounds. Mary should be there. Fingers crossed—or toes as the case may be.

"KITTY, KITTY!" Chancey caught the glint of gold in Familiar's mouth, and her natural curiosity drove her to try to grab the cat.

Spry as a young kitten, Familiar leapt sideways and darted into the barn where he found Mary. One look at her face told him plenty was wrong.

He garbled a meow around the necklace and deposited the jewelry at her feet.

"Familiar!" Mary recognized the necklace immediately as belonging to Madame Sianna. "Where did you get this?"

She examined the opal-like, almost liquid surface. "It's not expensive, but it's pretty. I'm sure Madame Sianna will be looking for it."

"Me-ow." It sounded exactly like "No doubt."

Mary couldn't resist holding up the necklace to catch the dim barn lights. Even without a direct source of illumination, a multitude of icy fires swirled in the stone.

"This is beautiful. Now we'd better go take it back." Mary looked down at the cat. He'd never shown any interest in jewelry before, but the necklace reminded her that she'd still not returned the MacEachern marriage ring to William. She hated to admit it, but Chancey's gleeful thrusts had twice nicked her heart—and unlocked a series of demons. Why hadn't William told her about the urgent need for an heir? Point one. Point two—if the ring had been lost for over a hundred years, how had William suddenly found it? Was he possessed by Slaytor? Had Slaytor hidden the ring?

Worry for William drove almost every other thought out of her mind. That voice! It had been positively terrifying. And Sophie had acted as if she were responding to it.

"I don't believe in ghosts," she muttered to Familiar, but even to her own ears the statement lacked conviction. "But I do believe in hobgoblins. There's one outside the barn right this minute." She nodded toward the courtyard where Chancey had set up a guardpost to wait for William. "So let's take the back way and avoid her."

Familiar needed no urging as he took the lead toward the side exit at the barn. Mary and the cat made it inside just in time to watch Clarissa, Darren, and Mrs. Daugherty drive away. Dr. Sloan, after making sure that Sophie was okay, was also preparing to leave. His tall forehead was wrinkled in concern as he motioned Mary aside.

"Our conversation is troubling me," he said, looking around to make sure that no one could overhear them. "Your friend should be sent back to Edinburgh, and it might not be a bad idea for you to accompany her. This has been a trying trip for her, and she's worried sick for you, Mary. Is there something you're not telling me?"

"I won't leave William."

"That's what she said you'd say." He sighed.

"What did you make of tonight?" Mary asked.

"Scientifically, I have no real clues. I heard the voice, but I don't believe in ghosts. I'd say someone is out to play a prank on William, but it's gone beyond the measure of a jokester."

"I agree." Mary was relieved to hear the calm tone of her voice. Somewhere along the way she'd become much stronger. She clenched her fingers around the necklace, then realized what she was holding. She opened her palm. "Familiar took this."

The doctor showed surprise. "That crazy medium said the cat stole her necklace. I thought it might be another ruse to try to get back inside Mayfair." He lifted the necklace, caught by the sparkle and swirl of the surface of the medallion. "It looks like opal, but it isn't. Highly reflective."

"Meow!" Familiar sat at his feet. As both Mary and the doctor watched, he started moving his head back and forth.

"Familiar." Mary bent to him but the doctor restrained her.

"Wait! It isn't possible…? Sophie was sitting across from the medium." He swung the medallion, allowing it to pick up the light. "Yes, it's more than possible. I'd say your friend suffered from a subliminal command given to her while she was lightly hypnotized."

He swung the medallion into the air, catching it deftly in his hand. "Yes, I'd say that was exactly what happened. Your friend is perfectly okay."

"Madame Sianna was…"

"Hypnotizing Sophie and urging her to speak aloud." Dr. Sloan picked up Mary's hand and deposited the necklace into it. "I feel much, much better about her. And possibly about you. With William in the hospital, we'll be able to get to the bottom of what's happening here."

"And the voice?" Mary didn't want to bring it up, but it had to be resolved. Somehow.

"That's beyond my experience, Mary," Dr. Sloan said carefully. "My best advice is not to let Clarissa McLeod or Madame Sianna back in this house. Whatever mischief they're up to, you don't need it."

"Good advice," Mary said. "I only hope William heeds it."

"He will, Mary. In time, he will." He took her hand that held the necklace. "Now I'd better be off. Early hours tomorrow. A fascinating evening, on all counts."

"Thank you." Mary closed the door after him. She looked down at the black cat. "You're a fine detective, Familiar. Let's go find William."

I HATE IT when I'm forced to play the role of some slobbering, drooling, red-eyed bloodhound, but I can hardly refuse the request of such a beautiful lady. To be truthful, I'm a little concerned about William myself. He's been gone far too long. The stairs go up five floors, but the top floor is unused and the fourth floor is mostly storage. I know. I've checked. William couldn't find anyone in that mess. I believe everyone who ever lived in this old pile of rocks has stacked some furniture into the storage area. Jeez! There's enough stuff up there to fill several stores.

Nope, it's going to be up to my superior nose to find William. I've tried tracking down "the voice," but it disappears, virtually into thin air. Not a nice sensation, chill bumps, especially not for a black cat. In thumbing through the library, I've discovered that black cats have not been well thought of in Scotland, all in all. Folks used to believe we consorted with the devil. Of course, that foolishness has been all over the western world. Humans just don't like it when cats are smarter. And believe me, we don't have to go far in some cases!

I must say, though, that Dr. Sloan and Pixie lady caught on quickly to the hypnosis. So they're smarter than the average Homo sapien.

Now, up the stairs to the third floor where William disappeared. Jeez, this place is creepy at night. I see Mary stopped long enough to grab a flashlight. Good for her. She's getting smarter and smarter in my estimation. Of course, if she had superior cat eyes…oh, well, enough bragging.

I can pick up William's scent clearly here.

Trouble is, his smell disappears right into the wall. Maybe I bragged too soon. This isn't possible. William couldn't have walked into the wall.

Unless…

"WHERE IS HE?" Mary watched as Familiar dug at the solid stone of the castle wall. "He didn't go in there, did he?" She couldn't believe it. Familiar was acting as if William had been absorbed into the stone.

"Let's see, Familiar." Kneeling beside the cat, Mary began to run her fingers over the stones. She held the flashlight under one arm, directing the beam as best she could while she used her sensitive fingers to feel the stones. "I don't know."

Beside her, Familiar dug, also.

The triggering device was cleverly hidden in the space between two large stones, and as soon as Mary touched it, she felt the wall shift inward, away from her. A crack barely large enough for a man to squeeze through opened.

The air that rushed out was dank and nasty-smelling, and Mary had a sudden wave of real fear. Looking up and down the hall, she saw there was no one to witness her actions. She thought of getting Sophie, but Dr. Sloan had given her a mild sedative and put her to bed. Abby and John were already at home in their cottage, probably with Kevin. There was no one in the castle to offer her help.

Even as she hesitated, she imagined William in some trouble. He'd obviously gone in here. And he hadn't come out! What if he were hurt? Bleeding? That image was enough to prompt her to step through the opening in the wall with Familiar right beside her.

The passage was extremely narrow. Mary traveled it almost sideways, moving step-by-step. Familiar had taken the lead. Though several feet ahead of her, he was matching his pace to hers. The terrible thought that if William were injured in the passage, she might not be able to get him out made Mary stumble. She righted herself and focused on moving along the rough, uneven floor.

She was no student of history, but she could tell by the way the stones had been roughly cut that the passage was extremely old. In the inhabited areas of Mayfair, there had been many attempts made at modernization. On the first, second and third floors, some of the passages had been enlarged throughout the centuries. It was possible that this passage was a leftover from some renovation project.

Or it could have been part of the original castle.

She couldn't be certain, but she felt a slight decline in the angle of the floor. Were they going down? If there was a descent, it was so gradual that she couldn't tell. There was a definite curve, and then another, both to the left. Several step-downs made her certain they were descending to the second floor.

As she became more familiar with the passageway, she increased her speed. She was moving rapidly when her flash-light beam fell on Familiar. His hair was prickled into angry spikes. Without uttering a sound, he dashed forward.

"Familiar," she called after him, moving as fast as she could. Familiar was a great comfort, and she didn't intend to lose him. She didn't want to be left in the tunnel alone.

As she made one final curve, she stopped. She saw a pair of long legs scrunched against the wall. In the beam of the light she recognized William's slacks. He was crumpled against the wall, motionless.

Stepping past Familiar, Mary hurried forward and dropped to her knees. Instead of the raging fever she expected to feel when she touched him, William was cool. Very gently, she moved his head so that she could look into his face. As she touched his right temple, she felt something sticky. Without even looking, she knew it was blood.

In the narrow confines of the tunnel, there was no way to tell how badly William was injured. His breathing was regular and his color seemed fair—as much as she could judge with the flashlight. But he needed to be out of the stale air of the passage. It was enough to make a healthy person hold her breath.

It would take fifteen minutes to go back the way she'd come, but then she didn't know how she could manage alone to get William out if he remained unconscious. As she was about to head back, Familiar started forward.

"Meow!" He seemed to be commanding Mary's attention.

Trusting the cat, she stepped over William and followed Familiar. In a matter of a few yards, they hit a solid stone wall. It was the end of the passage; it looked as if it went nowhere.

Familiar dropped to his side and began clawing at the wall with all four feet. In a second, Mary heard the shift of stone against stone, then a narrow exit appeared.

"Where are we?" she asked, poking her head through. An enormous tapestry blocked her view. With as much care as the situation allowed, she pushed it aside. "William's room!" Her surprise was complete.

The heavy old tapestry came down in Mary's hands as she tugged at it. "I've probably destroyed a part of history, but I don't care," she said to the cat. "We've got to get William out of there."

Stuffing the tapestry into the opening, Mary nodded with satisfaction. Even if the stone wall should suddenly begin to close, the heavy tapestry would block the opening. It was a precaution that made her feel much better about going back to try to move William herself. The distance was short, and she was determined to get him into his bed without telling anyone else about the passage. Once she'd learned that it led to William's room, a million doubts began to form in her mind. And one way or another, those doubts included everyone in Mayfair. Now she understood the swordsman's pelt she'd found on William's floor—how it had come to be there and how it disappeared.

Edging back to William, she was relieved to see that the burst of fresh air that had entered the passage when she'd opened the wall had improved his color.

"William." She knelt beside him on the cold stone and touched his cheek.

His eyes opened and he reached up to her, stroking her face. "Mary?"

"Yes." She realized he couldn't see and turned the light so that it illuminated her face. After a few seconds she adjusted the light so that it fell between them. Although William's skin was still cool, his eyes were feverish.

"I was after him! I saw him, Mary!"

"The man who was speaking during the séance?" Her pulse raced. If William could identify the man, then they'd be well on their way to solving what was happening at Mayfair!

"Yes. I saw him. True and certain." William looked beyond her, down the passage. "I don't know how he came to be here, but he was here."

"Who was it, William?" Clarissa had brought some confederate with her—some hired hand she'd paid to imitate Slaytor. Darren had been in the house the evening before. He might have slipped past Sophie, at least long enough to scout out the area to set up the séance. She felt her hopes leap. They'd work out this mystery, and then William would be able to explain why he hadn't told her the complete truth. "Who was it?" she asked again, eager to know.

He looked back at her, his expression perplexed. "Why, it was Slaytor. Who did you think it would be?"

Chapter Twelve

The narrow passage seemed to shift closer around Mary. William's words were completely insane.

"He nearly knocked me senseless when I caught up with him in the passage." Excitement intensified William's voice, and he spoke in a breathless rush. "I'd forgotten the stories about these hidden links from floor to floor. They've been a part of the lore of Mayfair for centuries, little passages created during one or another of the renovations. I never believed they were real. Imagine my shock when I saw him dodge into one." He looked at her and grinned. "I managed to follow. I knew I had him then. I knew I had Slaytor!"

Mary couldn't believe the torrent of words that came from William. She'd hoped for a human solution to their problem, not an encounter with an ancient ghost. She'd hoped for something they could combat together, not a delusion. She'd hoped for the truth—the truth only William could tell her. Chancey's revelations had badly shaken her. But she had to be strong. At the moment, there was no alternative.

"William, it's awfully dark in here," she said gently. "You had no light."

"I didn't need a light, Mary. I didn't need a light at all."

She swallowed. "Why not?"

"He spoke my name, just as he knocked me to my knees."

"Just because he knew your name doesn't mean it was

Slaytor.'' It was a sign of his complete disorientation that he wasn't thinking logically. Mary reached out and smoothed his forehead. A sheen of sweat had broken over him. ''We should get out of this passage and go to your room. It's only a little farther.''

''You don't believe me, do you?'' He reached out and caught her hand.

''I don't know, William. I was hoping we'd find someone to blame for all of this. It's hard to blame a ghost. And rather pointless.'' The hopelessness of the situation struck Mary hard. She fought to keep defeat from her voice.

''Not at all, Mary.'' William tightened his grip on her hand. ''At least now I know what Slaytor wants.''

''And what might that be?'' Her interest was piqued, despite herself.

''He wants me to leave Mayfair.''

''Why?'' The information was so unexpected that Mary felt herself being pulled in, if just for the moment.

''He wants it for himself.''

''But he's dead.''

''Aye, Slaytor is dead.'' William pulled her down closer to him so that he could whisper. ''He's dead and moldering in his grave.''

''But...''

''The man who clotted my noggin was very much alive, though he wanted me to believe he was Slaytor.''

Mary sank beside William to the rough stone. ''Then you know he wasn't a ghost!''

''Hush, now. These passages carry noise very effectively. Just help me out of here and we'll talk.''

The relief that touched Mary made her feel superhuman. Jumping to her feet in the cramped quarters, she gave William her hand. She didn't know how much she helped, but he did stagger to his feet, and in a few moments they were in his room. He cleared the tapestry from the entrance to the passage and allowed the panel to close. "We'll rehang that in a little while. We need to keep that passage a secret."

"How many more do you suppose there are?" Mary hesitated about broaching the subject of Slaytor. Even Familiar, who'd followed them out of the passage, gave William a questioning look.

William signaled her to keep her voice low. "There could be at least two or three more. I don't really know. I'm going to ask Erick if there are any old drawings of Mayfair. We might be able to figure it out."

"I doubt anyone would include a secret passage on a floor plan," Mary noted.

"You're right. And Erick didn't grow up in Mayfair. He's always lived in the village with his family. I doubt he'd know as much about the castle's past as I do." William sat down on the edge of his bed. "My head is pounding."

"Let's take a closer look," Mary said, stepping forward and turning on the bedside lamp. The gash was hidden in William's thick hair. After cleaning it, Mary decided it wasn't worthy of stitches, but the knot that was forming indicated that William had been struck with a great deal of force.

"Who do you think hit you?" she finally asked, dropping the antiseptic-soaked cotton into the trash.

"I don't know. He was bigger than me."

"There's no one at Mayfair bigger than you. Both Erick and Kevin are shorter, though Kevin is sturdy and Erick is strong."

"This man was big. Maybe two inches taller."

"Six-four?"

"At least." William looked directly at her. "Exactly as big as Slaytor was said to be. He was a giant for those days."

"Then it was no one from Mayfair. Could Madame Sianna have brought a sidekick?" Mary quickly filled William in on what she'd discovered about the medium's necklace and her penchant for hypnotizing her clients.

"It could be. But you've heard that voice before tonight."

"Yes." Mary had thought about that.

"And what would Madame Sianna have to gain by trying to drive me out of Mayfair?"

"That I don't know. Unless she's working for Clarissa. She'd love to get her hands on Mayfair. Is that a pipe dream, or could she afford it?"

William considered that question. "Possibly. She came into considerable money when her husband died. And her parents also left her an inheritance, and Darren, as well. Mayfair would be a feather in her cap, sort of a vindication of history, returning the original property and all."

"Would Darren go along with her?"

"Possibly. Not because he wanted to, but because he hasn't the backbone to deny Clarissa anything she demands from him. As a boy she dominated him, and now that he's an adult, she'll ruin the rest of his life for him."

"It's a pity."

"It is. And a man can take only so much twisting and mauling before he snaps."

Mary looked up, catching the pain on William's face. "You think it's Darren, don't you? You think he's behind this."

"It would please his mother to get Mayfair back. Perhaps it would please her enough to leave him alone. You know, Darren will never marry unless his mother dies. She can't find anyone good enough for him. But if he could divert her attention, he might be able to grab a little bit of life for himself. Or it's possible he'd want Mayfair for himself. To thwart her."

"How horrible to have to live like that."

"He isn't the same boy I knew growing up. I've met him several times, when I was out checking the estate. There's no spark, Mary. He had no interest in the things we once found so important. I believe Clarissa has stomped it out of him with her demands and nagging and ridicule." He paused, thinking. "He's taller than me, a little. But he was in the room, seated at the table. It couldn't have been him in the hallway."

"Yes, he was in the room." She thought for several seconds. "He could have left his mother, you know."

"Aye, he could have made that choice. I did. But Darren was never like me. He tried to please her, where I was determined never to please my father." William laughed. "I could have lived abroad and been happy. Darren could not."

Mary patted the side of the bed for Familiar to jump up. The black cat was sitting not three feet away, taking in everything that was being said.

"By the way, Familiar found you."

"That cat must be part dog."

"Meow." There was an indignant tone in Familiar's voice.

"I don't think Familiar appreciates that comparison," Mary said. She cleared her throat. Now that she knew William was neither injured nor deluded, she had to broach the subject of the heir—and she had to tell him about the ring.

"What is it, Mary?" William sensed her difficulty. He watched as she bent her head and stroked Familiar's back.

Mary looked up at him. In her book, the omission of such a crucial bit of information was a lie. And she didn't want to bind herself to a liar. How was she to tell him that?

"William, I—"

Familiar sprang from the bed with such suddenness that Mary jumped. The black feline pulled open the door to the hall, which had been left slightly ajar. The sound of running footsteps came back into the room.

"It may be him," William said as he dashed after the cat.

It took Mary a few seconds longer to get to her feet, but she was right on William's heels as they tore into the hallway where the footsteps echoed louder.

"Hold!" William called after a fleeing figure. The man was running down the hallway toward the stairs. "Hold!" William didn't break his stride as he yelled.

"You there! Stop!" The fleeing man yelled, also, and he kept running.

"You! Stop!" William was gaining on the man as he made it to the stairs and ran down them, boots clattering. As the running figure passed a light mounted on the staircase, William caught a glimpse of a familiar profile. "Erick!" He called his cousin's name. "Erick."

Turning to confront William, Erick finally stopped halfway down the stairs. "William, he's getting away! We have to catch him." He looked down the stairs, the desire to pursue obvious on his features. "Damn!" He struck the stone wall with his fist. "He had too big a lead."

"Who?" William asked, slowing to a jog as he caught up with the manager of the estate.

"I didn't get a look at him, but he was standing outside your doorway. I'd come up to bring Miss Sophie her gloves. She'd left them down in the barn while talking with Kevin." He held out the gloves to Mary as she caught up with them. "When I knocked on her door, she didn't answer, so I was going up to the office. But when I turned the corner, there he was, listening at your door."

"What did he look like?" William's voice was eager.

"Tall. Very tall. A big man." Erick stared down the empty stairway as if he could make the intruder materialize. "For a split second, I thought he was going to stand his ground and fight, but when he ran, he had the speed of a stag. I've never seen a big man move so swiftly."

"I didn't hear any other footsteps," Mary said. She held Sophie's gloves just as Erick had given them to her.

"He was wearing those athletic shoes," Erick said. "He was quiet. Sneaking around outside your door, eavesdropping."

"Erick, why didn't Kevin return Sophie's gloves?" Mary stared at the black gloves as if they held some strange fascination.

Erick shrugged. "The truth is, Abby called me in town

and told me about the troubles this evening. I was using the gloves as an excuse to look around the castle.'' Erick looked at his cousin. ''There's strange business brewing here at Mayfair. I was worried about you, William. Abby said you'd taken off and that Mary was looking for you.''

''As you can see, I'm fine. How's your friend's daughter?''

''Anna is fine. Asthma. It gave us quite a scare.'' Erick's smile was half apologetic. ''We were sorry to miss the dinner, but there was little else we could do. She's a clever child, and she's dying to visit Mayfair. If you don't mind, I might ask Kevin to give her a riding lesson or two.''

''That's a fine thing for a young child.'' William smiled. ''I'm glad she's okay.''

''And I'm glad you are,'' Erick said, clapping his cousin on the shoulder. ''I'm going to talk to the staff. I want them to be on the alert for any strangers who might be on the estate.'' He frowned. ''We'll catch this fellow. He has no right to be snooping about. For the moment, I'm going to check the garage and the barn. He might be hiding on the premises.''

''I'll help you,'' William said.

''Take care, the two of you,'' Mary said as she watched them start down the stairs.

She'd lost her chance to speak with William, but she would find the time. Later. When she'd prepared what she was going to say. When she was certain she could face the consequences.

MARY SAT on the side of the bed and watched William as he slept. It was early morning, not yet six o'clock. He'd come in from the search, tired and distressed that they'd found no clue. She'd waited for him, wanting the comfort of his arms as much as she wanted to comfort him. After making love, they'd gone to sleep, tangled together. But something had awakened her, and she felt a compulsion to return to her own room. Familiar had left hours before, to forage in the kitchen, no doubt. That cat could eat twenty-four hours a day. It seemed all he did was eat and sleep, yet whenever there was a crisis, he always showed up to help. He was some kind of cat.

And William was some kind of man. She watched the way his fingers curled softly in his sleep, a gentle motion. He looked younger at rest, the tension gone from his face. Somehow vulnerable. At that thought she felt a fierce desire to protect him, as she knew he would protect her. "You're not the only Scot with a heritage of loyal blood," she whispered. Leaning over to kiss him, she was careful not to awaken him. Deep sleeps had been few and far between for him, and she wanted him to rest as much as possible. There was much to be done.

Now that she knew Slaytor MacEachern was an intruder, she intended to come up with some foolproof plan to capture him, and that would require all of her resources.

Too restless to stay still, Mary rose and picked up her jeans from the floor. There was the tinkle of something on the stone. Groping in the darkness next to the bed, she found the necklace and the ring. Damn! Didn't she have her own secrets to tell? And she would, as soon as William awakened. But the ring brought up another train of thought.

Who would know enough to find and leave the MacEachern wedding ring, if it wasn't William? Where had they found it? Goose bumps soldiered over her arms. William had not mentioned the ring, was completely unaware that she had it. She slipped the chain around her neck.

Mary padded down to her room. The stone floor was freezing, and she couldn't suppress a shudder as she hurried into her room and to the thick pile carpet beside the bed. The old castle had modern heating, but nothing could really remove the chill in the enormous corridors or in the rooms once the fires had burned out.

The idea of a fire appealed to Mary, but it occurred to her

that now would be a perfect time to snoop around the pantry. Abby was certainly asleep and could take no offense at Mary's nosiness. She might not have another chance.

Another thought followed closely on the heels of her plan—in the confusion following the séance, she'd forgotten to give Dr. Sloan the portion of port she'd wanted tested. For the safety of everyone, she needed to remove the glass from the bar. Even though it was tucked out of the way, it could be poured out or inadvertently drunk.

After pulling on thick socks, she laced her shoes, added a turtleneck under her sweater and tiptoed downstairs.

Mayfair slumbered around her, all except for a black cat. Familiar was perched on the kitchen table, a testimony to the fact that cats can open doors.

Mary patted his head. She thought of a cup of tea, but coffee was what she wanted. A pot of it while she went through the extensive pantry. She set up the coffeemaker, turned it on and decided that it wouldn't hurt matters to turn the oven on and open the door for a little heat. The kitchen was always warm and toasty whenever Abby was around, but the predawn hours were chilly.

Although tea was easily found, the coffee was another matter. It wasn't often consumed at Mayfair. Feeling slightly uncomfortable, Mary opened cabinets and began pushing cans, tins, jars and bags, all filled with the wonderful ingredients Abby used to cook, out of her way.

The pestle and mortar caught her by surprise. It was such an ancient-looking piece of crockery that she pulled it out of the back corner of the third shelf and bent to examine it. It reeked of antiquity—another of Mayfair's priceless heirlooms that was used or displayed with little thought by the people who knew them so well. Never before had Mary lived where history was so revered, yet so much a part of day-to-day life.

A tiny residue of yellowish powder remained in the container. She sniffed it curiously, interested in the lack of odor. Or maybe there wasn't enough of the substance left to smell.

"It isn't curry. What could it be?" she asked the black cat who'd come up on the counter to investigate what she was doing.

Familiar bristled. A tiny bit of foamy saliva collected at his lips as he glared at the container and then at Mary. A loud hiss, like a nest of thoroughly angry snakes, erupted from his throat.

"Familiar!" Mary backed away from him. The transformation had been so complete, so total, and without any warning. He was acting exactly as he had the night he'd attacked William.

Familiar circled the pestle, the hair on his back rising to stand straight on end. Ignoring Mary, he hissed at the container.

The implication of what the cat was doing struck Mary with a force that made her sit down abruptly in the kitchen chair. She looked at the cat, who now sat on the counter staring amiably back at her.

"It's poison, isn't it?" she asked.

"Meow."

"You got the same thing in your food that someone has been grinding up and putting in William's food."

"Meow." Familiar waited.

"I'm going to take this up to William," Mary said. She approached the counter and gingerly stuck out her hand to pick up the pestle. Familiar, purring, brushed against her hand and allowed her to take it.

"Let's go, cat. We've finally unraveled what's going on. Or at least, a portion of it."

IT'S ABOUT TIME I got some assistance from the tall, vertical people around here. There was no way I could get into that shelf, even if I could have somehow sensed that bitter stuff was up there. Truth be told, I hadn't a clue it was there. Once Mary brought down that old container, I recognized it. It was that little tang I remembered when I woke up at the vet's office. Bitter, but not really. Undetectable, except as an aftertaste, and then it's too late. That's why it blended so perfectly into the egg custard. Same color. No taste, no smell—except to my highly developed feline olfactory system. It was almost a perfect crime. Bold even, with the implements of destruction left hidden in the kitchen cabinets. Maybe too bold, or at least that's what my feline intuition tells me. We'll see what William makes of it. And, oh, yes, Pixie lady, while you're hauling poison up to the love nest, don't forget that glass of port in the parlor. Methinks that will be the final coup.

"OKAY, OKAY," Mary said as she allowed Familiar to edge her into the parlor. "I'll get it." As she started across the room, she noticed the first pink light of dawn. Mayfair would be awakening within the next half hour. It was a place where daylight ruled the comings and goings of all, even William, to a great extent. Since the economy centered around farming and the land, the sun was the best of friends or the worst of foes. No matter what part it was playing at the time, it was always the starring role. As winter drew nigh and the days shortened, the moments of daylight were even more precious.

The glass of port was just where she'd left it, and she breathed a sigh of relief as she lifted it in her right hand. Her left held the pestle with the yellowish residue.

"If this isn't what I think it is, we're going to feel awfully stupid," she said to the cat. "You'll take your fair share of the blame, believe me, Familiar. Though folks will think I'm a half-wit if I try to convince them I was led down this path of logic by a cat."

Her rubber-soled hiking boots made little noise as she ascended the stairs. Her heart was racing with the thrill of her discovery when she heard something that made her stop. She was outside Sophie's door, which was open a tiny crack. It was the sound of voices raised in anger that had caught her ear.

"I will not have it, Kevin." Sophie's normally timid voice was full of emotion.

"I thought I could rely on you." Kevin's voice was flat. "I should have known you'd stick with her. I thought...I thought there was something between us."

"I thought you were the kind of man who stood up for his beliefs." Anger sharpened Sophie's tone.

Mary clutched the glass of port. She'd never heard such passion in Sophie's voice.

"I have my beliefs, but I have no rights. I'm just a horse trainer."

"Feeling sorry for yourself won't solve anything, Kevin. If you don't tell William the truth, you have no right to complain." Sophie's voice was completely unsympathetic.

"Exactly my point. I have no rights." The anger had dissipated from Kevin's voice. "Except what I take."

"Why don't you just come out with it and state your demands, Kevin? Why lurk in the shadows? You've no reason to be ashamed of your birthright. You had nothing to do with it. But if you are William's half-brother, you should tell him. You both have a right to that information."

Mary thought her heart would burst.

"Aye, William's rights. That's my concern now. And thanks for your support. I'll be getting back to my *job* at the barn." Kevin's voice was filled with pain. "I can see I'm going to have to take care of this situation on my own."

Mary bolted away from the door and into her own room. She'd barely had time to close her door when she heard Kevin's footsteps. His stride was long and angry as he disappeared down the stairs.

"Sophie." Mary spoke the name to herself. She held the pestle to her chest with one arm and she could feel her heart beating against the hard, marblelike substance. The one question that popped into her head was when had Kevin and Sophie become close enough to be confidants? They'd only really begun to speak to one another with any kind of interest in the last day or so. In twenty-four hours or less, Kevin had revealed to Sophie that he was possibly William's half-brother? That was preposterous. Kevin wasn't loose with his lips. So how had they become so close so fast? Or had they been hiding it?

Mary put her burdens on the bedside table and sank down onto the bed. What should she do? The implications that could be drawn from the conversation between Kevin and Sophie were very clear. Kevin might stand to gain a lot if William didn't marry her. *And* produce an heir, as she'd learned from Chancey the night before. That was something she was going to have to take up with William. She still could not understand why he hadn't told her about that himself.

Unable to sit up any longer, Mary flopped back onto the bed. It was more than she could bear. Someone—and this she no longer doubted—had been tampering with William's food. But everyone around her was a suspect, even those who lived down the road. If this was the benefit of wealth, power and prestige, she wasn't certain it was worth the price. Maybe it would be better if William didn't inherit. Then they could go back to Edinburgh and resume the old life they'd built together.

Music, pubs with good food and entertainment, the casual ease of her friends around her. William had enjoyed that life. Was it too much to ask to live someplace where people weren't trying to poison, frighten or maim one or both of them? She didn't think so. Coming to Mayfair had been a terrible mistake. It had nearly cost her William and, very possibly, Sophie.

She closed her eyes for a moment to ease the pounding in her head. She would clear her mind of everything and relax for five minutes, and then she'd get up and go talk with William.

Mary's chest rose in a shallow rhythm as she drifted into a light sleep. She did not awaken when a portion of the stone wall beside the fireplace eased open. Lips slightly parted, she slept as the tall, strongly built man moved beside her bed and stopped.

He held a sword in his hand, the hilt splotched by a small patch of dried blood. Dark hair curled around his face.

Very carefully, he picked up the pestle and the glass of port. ''The past is never dead at Mayfair, lassie,'' he said in a voice rippling with brogue. ''You'll learn you're never done with it. 'Tis a pity, the lesson may be costly. Especially for you.''

Chapter Thirteen

"Mary! Mary, wake up. It's Eleanor on the phone!"

Mary felt as if a steel rod had been welded to her spine. She tried to sit, but her back was stiff and unyielding. To her horror, she discovered sunlight was streaming into her bedroom window. Bright sunlight—as in noon. She'd fallen sound asleep, legs dangling off the side of the bed.

William was standing over her, his face flushed with excitement. "Eleanor has some news. She said we'd want to hear it together. Take the phone in the library, and I'll pick up an extension in the hall."

"Okay." Mary struggled to sit up.

"Here." William gave her a hand and then rubbed the small of her back, loosening the muscles that had tightened from her unnatural sleeping position.

Moving as fast as she could, she stood and hurried down the hall, down the stairs and into the library.

As soon as she picked up the receiver, she could sense the tension on the line. "What is it, Eleanor?"

"Good, we're here," William said. "What news, Eleanor?"

"It's taken me forever to find the right musty old stack of records to dig into, but I've found something that may well throw an entirely differently light on your situation."

"What?" Mary hummed with the sense of excitement, too.

"Well, it would seem that the legends about old Slaytor aren't exactly on the up-and-up."

"What legends?" William asked.

"The ones about him and his wife, Lisette."

"You can't mean that they weren't married?" Mary heard the distress in her voice. Another complication of parentage would only add to the mess, especially with Kevin's claim hanging in the wind.

"Oh, no, quite the contrary." Eleanor's voice bubbled. "You see, Lisette was never really kidnapped. The entire kidnapping was staged by Lisette and Slaytor because Lisette's father would never have consented to his fair, English daughter marrying a savage Scotsman."

"If she wasn't kidnapped, what about the turret room and all of the moaning and hand wringing?" William asked. "That's the major portion of Mayfair's legendary past."

"It was all staged, for the benefit of the servants. So the tales of mistreatment would get back to Lisette's father. Then when she became pregnant, and Slaytor made her his wife, it was a much better fate than any her father could envision for her if she were simply a captive. Lisette's father didn't want the marriage, but it was better than a pregnant daughter held as little more than a slave. He accepted the marriage, with apparently some degree of grace. Voilà, a happy-ever-after ending MacEachern style."

"She was never a prisoner in the turret room?" Mary asked, but she knew the answer.

"Never. In fact, the records I've discovered, some ancient, crumpling letters, indicate that the entire kidnapping scheme was Lisette's plan. She even rode over to Scotland by herself so that Slaytor could more easily kidnap her."

The night of the wild ride she'd taken with William came back to Mary. He'd gone to meet someone. A woman who'd crossed the border alone. A woman willing to risk everything for her man.

Mary clutched the telephone to her ear. "You're sure of this, Eleanor?"

"Positive. The legends about Slaytor—the savage kidnapper of women who kept them locked in a turret until they yielded to his carnal desires—it's all pure fabrication. Just another example of how a story can supercede historical fact. Slaytor and Lisette were so effective in creating the tale, and spreading it, that it is now regarded as the true history of Mayfair."

"Amazing," William said. "But how does that relate to my problems here?"

"Don't you see? You're being possessed by this brutal, angry, savage ghost of Slaytor. But he was never that man. Whoever is setting you up, however they're doing it, they don't know the real history of Mayfair at all. If you were really being possessed by Slaytor MacEachern, he would be a firm but gentle man."

"Who loves Lisette." Mary had whispered the words.

"What?" Eleanor asked. Her voice crackled again. "This line isn't the best. You'll have to speak up."

"How's Peter faring?" Mary asked instead. She had to think about this wrinkle. About the kiss that "Slaytor" had given "Lisette" in the cold moonlight. Possessed. They had been, indeed, by a powerful passion.

"So far, the MacEachern family medical history is boring stuff. There's no heritage of lunacy, delusions of grandeur or of any other kind. No brain tumors, religious fanatics, or even heart disease. Other than a fondness for the bottle and a tendency to work too hard, a very uninteresting bunch."

"That's good," Mary said automatically.

"Mary, are you okay?" Eleanor, even at such a distance, was quick to pick up on Mary's tone.

"Fine. Just a lot to think about. Eleanor, will you and Peter be coming back here soon? I have something I need tested. Dr. Sloan said he could do it, but he'd have to send it away to a lab. He doesn't have the equipment at his office."

"Peter would face the same problem," Eleanor reminded her. "What is it?"

"Two things. I think both of them contain some kind of poison. Something that has made William, and Familiar, act out of character. It could explain a lot of things that have been happening here."

"Yes, it certainly could. If we can identify the substance. Why don't you express them to us here? We have the lab facilities, and we could test them right away."

"Excellent idea." Mary felt a great relief.

"What did you find?" William asked.

"I'll show you when we're finished. In my room," Mary said. "Thanks, Eleanor. I may send them up with Sophie." She felt her voice thicken at the mention of her friend. One thing she'd decided was to get Sophie out of Mayfair. The sooner the better. Her "friend" could hardly refuse to run this errand. It would be the perfect excuse to put her on a train.

"Send her on. Just call and let us know when to expect her."

"First thing in the morning," Mary said. "I'll see she gets on the seven o'clock train out."

"Well, goodbye for now. Give my cat a hug for me."

"Familiar is fine," William reassured her. "In fact, we don't know if we can do without him."

"None of that talk," Eleanor warned. "He's going back to the States with me, as soon as we get to the bottom of the haunting of Mayfair Castle, and my cousin."

"Goodbye," they said in unison as they replaced the receivers.

Mary met William at the head of the stairs. Neither spoke at first as they tried to gauge the other's reaction to the news they'd just learned.

"Who?" William finally asked.

"It could be anyone, William. I have to tell you something about Kevin. And Sophie. And about a MacEachern baby."

William took her arm. "Let's go for a ride, Mary. At least that way we'll know no one can overhear us."

"Let me get the port and pestle from my room. I want to seal the liquor in something and get this package ready to go before I let it out of my sight."

As they walked to her room, she told him of her findings and her suspicions. "Odorless, as far as I could tell. Yellow in color. Remember the night Familiar went wild? You fed me fresh berries in the bath."

"I well remember that night." He couldn't stop himself from touching her arm. The feel of her warm, smooth skin was easy to remember.

Mary ignored the flush of heat that sprang from his touch. "You put your custard down on the floor and didn't eat it."

"I had other things on my mind."

She couldn't help but smile at the memories he evoked. "Yes, well, Familiar ate your custard. That's when he had his fit, or whatever you want to call it."

"You're right!" He twisted the knob of her bedroom door and pushed it open. "You're absolutely right. And my attacks have come after eating, as you said a while back."

"Or after drinking. The night we were going to hear your friend play, you drank port while I went to change. In an instant, you reverted. I know there's nothing wrong with you, William. It's just a matter of figuring out who's trying to do this to you."

"I hate to admit it, but I believe you're right about Clarissa and Chancey. If I had to pin the guilt on anyone right now, I'd say them."

"The only trouble with that theory is that there are other people who have access to your food. Chancey and Clarissa weren't around every time you've had trouble." Mary didn't want to look at him.

"Who are you thinking of?"

"Abby. John." She sighed. "Kevin, and Sophie. Kevin has reason to believe he's your half-brother. That's more of a claim to Mayfair even than Erick. And Sophie may be reluctantly helping him.''

''My half-brother? This must be some kind of joke. I've known Kevin since he was born.''

''He isn't Abby and John's son. His mother, who claimed that he was your father's child, abandoned him. Apparently she worked in the house in some capacity. Abby and John took him in. All this time he's believed he was their natural son, but they told him recently, so that he could stake his claim to a portion of Mayfair after your father died.''

William looked up and down the corridor. ''This is incredible, Mary. Don't tell me any more until we get out of here. This place has ears, you know.''

''I have to talk with you about something Chancey told me.'' Mary was determined to clear the air once and for all. ''This is important, to us.''

William put his finger to his lips. ''Later. Now grab your riding boots, and I'll get the port and pestle.''

''Beside the bed,'' Mary directed as she entered her room and went to the bureau to get her riding gear. She'd wait until they were mounted, but they *were* going to talk.

''Mary?''

The question in William's voice made her look up from the search for her right boot. ''What?''

''There's nothing on the bedside table. Except a book.''

''But I...'' She dropped everything and walked to the bed. The small bedside table was still bathed in the glow of the lamp, but its polished surface was bare of everything except her book.

''I put it right there.''

''Did you lock your door?''

She shook her head. ''I didn't think. I didn't expect to go to sleep.'' William had been standing at the end of the hallway while they'd been on the phone. No one could have slipped past him.

William's face was white. "I think it might be best if you went with Sophie back to Edinburgh," he said slowly.

She could see the tension in him and understood the fear. "No, William. I won't be run off."

"If this person is creeping into your room, standing over you while you sleep, I can't protect you. There's nothing here at Mayfair I value more than you. I won't let anyone harm you."

"And no one can hurt me as much as you can." She grabbed his hand. "Chancey told me about the terms of your inheritance. That you must have a male heir within two years. Why didn't you tell me that?"

"Could we talk about this outside?"

"Just tell me when you were planning to tell me."

"I had hoped never to tell you. Now let's get outside." He took her arm in his left hand and her boots in his right.

They'd made it as far as the stable yard when Erick flagged them down. "William, Darren was looking for you. He said it was urgent. He was headed around the west side, and he seemed terribly agitated. You'd better go find him. He might have finally had enough and killed his wicked mother."

MARY SWUNG INTO the saddle with more confidence than she'd expected to feel. As she'd saddled and bridled Shalimar, she'd listened to every nuance of Kevin's voice. He was as kind and gentle as he'd always been. William had gone with Erick to find Darren, so Mary was going to have it out with Chancey—horsewoman to horsewoman.

"I think I'm going for a ride. Alone." She forced a confident smile.

"Is that a good idea?" Kevin's worry was instant. "I'll come with you if William is too busy."

"I'm going to ride to Chancey's. I'm sure she'll be glad to show me more of the area." She watched for a reaction, but the only thing she saw was concern.

"Chancey isn't the most trustworthy companion," he said.

"It would be better if you let me, or one of the grooms, take you around. You won't be calling on the gentry—" he lifted an eyebrow "—but you could see the country."

"I want to prove to Chancey that she can't frighten me." It was the truth, but Mary also wanted to test another theory.

"I think you've proven that, Mary. It would be a shame to snap your neck to make a point with the likes of Chancey."

No matter how she tried, Mary couldn't believe Kevin was a man who would stoop to any underhanded activities. Not even for an inheritance worth a fortune. But she'd heard him! He and Sophie.

"Perhaps to you, Kevin, but not to Chancey, or Clarissa, for that matter. Well, I'm going to serve notice to her and anyone else who endangers me, William or Mayfair. There will be a terrible price paid. I don't intend to give up William, or his heritage, without a bloody struggle."

"Spoken like a true MacEachern," Kevin said. He slapped Shalimar's rump. "Off with you, then. Sow your warnings on the women of Kelso." He grinned. "I fear it's barren ground you plough, but you must try it for yourself. Chancey and Clarissa will both make a hard end. Clarissa has been walking that road since Darren was born, and it looks as if Chancey will follow. But warn them if it makes you feel better." He turned and walked back into the barn, his back straight and his posture untroubled.

"Blasted inscrutable Scot," Mary said under her breath as she turned Shalimar toward Chancey's and the challenge that hung in the wind between the two women.

William had reluctantly given her directions. He'd been unhappy with her decision to go, and her insistence that she was going alone. What had to be said, though, was between only the two women. She'd heard another side of Sophie, and it had shocked her to learn that someone she'd known for so many years could have a hidden facet to her personality. Mary was discovering that she, herself, had a strength and aggressiveness that she would never have guessed at. It came into play only when William or their future together had been assaulted. Chancey, deliberately and with malice aforethought, had done just that.

Sensing the renewed determination in Mary's seat, Shalimar lengthened her trot, stretching into a gait that smoothly covered the distance.

The day was bright, even though it was chill, and Mary found herself enjoying the ride. The borderland of Scotland was incredibly beautiful, a long, rolling land that lent itself to crops and pasture. Vistas of green dotted with sheep were broken by bands of hardwoods and cut with the fast flow of small streams. Large estates were set back in ancient trees, a reminder of a way of life when the very rich owned most of the entire country.

Chancey's house was old stone covered in a thick ivy on one side that gave it a look of sensual disorder. It was a modest size, but wonderfully built and decorated. Behind the house was a barn with four stalls and plenty of room to store the hay that would hold the horses through the winter.

Shalimar's hooves rang on the stone drive, and Mary kept a tight rein on the mare as she tried to look through the barn. There was a quiet, a stillness, to the place that made Mary suddenly ill at ease. She had the distinct sensation that someone was hiding, watching her.

"Chancey!" She called the woman's name and waited. There was no answer. In the barn, the horses shifted, and one neighed a greeting to Shalimar.

"Shall we?" Mary asked the mare. She rode up to the open door of the barn, noticing how thick the stone walls were. Chancey's place was old, historic, and it was kept in beautiful order. Funny, Mary had never thought to ask if it was an inherited home or one that Chancey had purchased on her own. In fact, Mary knew little about the woman. Did she work? It was an interesting thought. Mary considered the types of work Chancey would be suited for—in her opinion. Nothing she came up with was very flattering.

She had already dismounted when she noticed that the horse calling to Shalimar was saddled and tied outside the barn beside a large tree. Inside the barn, four horses shifted back and forth over the stall doors. Chancey's horses, or at least a full barn of them, were already in. Who did the fifth horse belong to?

The fact that Chancey had company struck Mary, and she felt a twinge of regret and a big spurt of relief. If Chancey had a guest, then she couldn't possibly take Mary up on her offer to go for another ride. That was the relief. But it would also interfere with Mary's plans to try to question Chancey. A third party would be a definite handicap.

But it would be interesting to see who had ridden over to pay a visit to Chancey. Another horsewoman, no doubt, Mary thought grimly as she found a halter, slipped it over Shalimar's bridle and tied the mare.

Kevin had been adamant about never tying a horse with the bridle reins. He'd explained at great length how even the best trained horses could become frightened or excited and pull back. When that occurred, the bit could damage the horse's mouth, or the leather reins could snap and the horse would be free, possibly running into even greater dangers in unfamiliar territory.

The halter Mary found hanging beside the door on a wooden peg was forest green, a color theme that was repeated, she saw, in the blankets and leg wraps of the horses. A brass plate had been engraved with Chancey's name and address. "Nice touch," Mary said as she made sure her knot was secure. "Be good, Shalimar. I'll be back."

She didn't hear the step behind her, but she caught sight of the moving shadow just as she was turning to walk to the house. She tried to step aside, but she saw the blow coming at her before she could really shift out of the way.

"Stop!" she managed to yell just as a fist crashed into the

side of her head. The blow was a glancing one, but it made her ear ring and knocked her to the ground. For a moment she felt as if the world swayed dangerously around her. Then her vision cleared, and she forced herself to her hands and knees and started crawling toward the door.

The sound of running footsteps led into the bright sunlight. In a matter of seconds there was the sound of hooves striking the stone exit.

At the sound of frantic hooves on the cobbled drive, Chancey came out the side door of the house, her expression plainly amazed. When she saw Mary crawling out of the barn on her hands and knees, she ran over.

"Mary, did you take a spill? Was that your horse running down the drive?"

"No, to both questions." Mary sat down and looked down the drive, hoping to catch a final glimpse of the man who'd struck her. "Who was here?"

"Here?" Chancey looked around. "I don't know. I mean, no one, to my knowledge. Did you see someone?"

"This isn't a game." Mary started to stand, but the dizziness washed over her again. "Someone was here. His horse was tied at your barn. He hit me."

Chancey stooped down and put a palm on Mary's forehead. "No one was here, but you must have taken a nasty spill."

"Chancey, his horse was tied at the barn."

"A horse might have been tied here, but no one was visiting me. I've been in the house all day waiting on a call from a breeder over near Melrose. I've not left the house and I haven't had a single visitor."

Head throbbing, Mary forced her eyes to stare directly into Chancey's. The other woman never flinched.

"Help me to my feet, please," Mary said.

"Maybe you should consider giving up horses," Chancey said as she braced herself to pull Mary to her feet. "Every time I see you, you're on the ground, smashed and broken.

I suppose I can safely assume you and William haven't started a family yet.''

''I didn't fall,'' Mary said as she got her balance and shook free of Chancey. ''My horse is *tied*. Do you understand? And my state of pregnancy is none of your business. That's exactly what I came to tell you.''

''You'd better hope possession by ghostly spirits isn't hereditary.'' Chancey grinned. ''What will you do if William locks you in the turret until you conceive? Actually, I'm shocked that he's going to marry you until he knows you're pregnant. If I were him, I wouldn't take the chance that you might not conceive.''

''My mother was one of fifteen children, and I have eight brothers and sisters. We're a prolific family. I'm certain William looked it all up before he popped the question.''

''Well, you aren't much for staying on your feet, but you have a bit of wit about you,'' Chancey said, completely unabashed. ''Come in and I'll make you a cup of tea. I suspect you came to ask me to go riding, but I can't leave the phone and I don't think you're up to it now. That's a bad knot over your ear.''

Mary put up her hand and felt the bump swelling beneath her fingers. It was terribly sore. If she and William didn't get to the bottom of what was happening at Mayfair, they'd both need skull reinforcements.

''I will take some tea.'' Her head didn't bother her nearly as much as Chancey's attitude—the woman was practically bubbly, as if she had something to hide and was working very hard not to show it. Mary wanted to get inside Chancey's house. No way did she believe the blonde was innocent.

''What kind of horse was your mystery man riding?'' Chancey asked. ''Did you see him?'' She motioned Mary up the steps in front of her.

''I didn't get a look at the man. The horse was a bay. Very nice. Well behaved.''

''No distinguishing marks?''

Mary looked back at Chancey. Was that relief in her eyes? "I didn't see clearly," Mary confessed. "I'd recognize it if I saw it again."

"Lots of bay horses around these parts."

"Yes," Mary agreed as she took a seat on the sofa where Chancey waved her.

"I'll get some tea. It won't take but a minute. Make yourself at home, and maybe you should call William. I don't want him coming over here and blaming me for this incident. I thought he was going to lynch me over the fall you took."

"William is very protective of me," Mary agreed. She craned her neck around to make sure Chancey had gone to the kitchen and could not see her. "I'd like to borrow your bathroom, please."

"Down the hall, second door to the left."

"Thanks." Mary got up and tiptoed to the stairs. Chancey's bedroom would be on the second floor, as would her bath. Moving as silently as possible, Mary forced her protesting body up the stairs. She found the bath and quickly went through the medicine cabinet. To her disappointment, there were no prescription drugs anywhere in the bathroom.

"There was a bath downstairs." Holding a plate of cookies, Chancey was standing at the foot of the steps as Mary came down. Her expression was wary. "Were you looking for something?"

"Some aspirin," Mary said, knowing she wasn't a good liar.

"I don't like people wandering around my house." Chancey's voice was edged with anger.

"Sorry, Chancey. I didn't want to worry you by asking for aspirin. I thought I could find them myself."

"Next time, ask." Chancey put the plate down. "I'll be right back. With some aspirin."

Mary took a seat on the sofa, eager now to get back to Mayfair. She'd learned nothing concrete and had gotten herself knocked in the head. It wasn't much of a record for an investigator.

Chancey returned with the tea tray and a vial of aspirin. She shook out two and gave them to Mary.

"Thanks." Mary took them with a swallow of tea.

"Glad to see you're able to drink. One day you're going to break your neck in a fall."

"You'd better keep an eye on your horses. Someone was out there." Mary felt her temper begin to flare.

"I don't believe that for an instant. What I believe is that you were pretending to be injured as a perfect scheme to get in my house."

"So what horse did you hear running down your drive?" Mary felt she'd hit the winning question. Her smile was victorious.

But Chancey wasn't about to yield so easily. "Maybe it was Slaytor, tired of haunting Mayfair. Maybe he has better taste in women than his heir."

"Maybe." Mary stood. "I'd better start home."

"Why did you come here, Mary?" Chancey stood, too.

"For tea, what else?" Mary sensed the anger of the other woman, and she knew that backing down was the worst thing she could do.

"You came to spy on me." Chancey was furious. Two high spots of color marked her cheeks. "Admit it, you were spying."

"Do you have something to hide?" Mary saw the dart strike home. Chancey tried to cover her reaction, but she wasn't quick enough.

"How far are you willing to go to try and get William? Or is it Mayfair, Chancey? How far?"

Chancey stepped forward. "You'd better watch yourself, Mary Muir. You aren't a MacEachern yet, and there are plenty of people around Kelso who would just as soon see you go back to your symphony seat in Edinburgh. You aren't the right woman for William. I'm not the first to say it, nor the last.''

"I doubt William will be greatly influenced by your choice in picking his wife." Mary's own temper was stretching the limits of her control.

"William is a fool. His entire heritage is at stake, and he doesn't even realize it."

"Don't underestimate him, Chancey."

Chancey walked to the door, opened it and pointed out. "Leave now, Mary, while you still can."

Brushing past her and going down the steps, Mary felt a tingle of panic. Chancey's warning had more than one meaning. And she was the type of woman who acted on her threats.

Chapter Fourteen

Mary rubbed the towel over Shalimar's body. The horse had actually worked up a good sweat on the ride home. "You're a lovely lady," she whispered as she worked. In a very short time, Mary had learned to love riding. Each time she was around Shalimar she learned more and more of her horse's unique personality. They were well matched.

The hard-bristled brush was missing from the grooming kit, so Mary walked into the tack room to look for it. Kevin kept everything neat, tidy, and in its place. The brush had probably fallen out of the kit and was lying on the floor of the tack room.

Moving around the saddles and other equipment, Mary went to the back of the room and bent down to search the floor. Beneath several old saddles she caught a glimpse of a tangle of nylon and pulled it forward.

The forest green halter was almost new. Her fingers beginning to tremble, Mary turned it over. There were two holes where an oval brass plate had been attached.

"What are you studying, Mary?" Kevin's voice was soft.

"Nothing." She dropped the halter to her side.

"A mighty fascinating nothing."

"It's a halter. I found it while I was looking for a brush."

Kevin closed the distance between them. "Whose halter do you suppose it is?"

His voice was so soft, so gentle, that Mary had to imagine it contained a note of threat. She felt her heart begin to accelerate. "I think it belongs to Chancey. Our halters here at Mayfair are blue. Hers are green."

"As are other farms in the area." Kevin's eyes caught the afternoon light. Little lines drawn tight around them made him seem tired, upset.

Mary wanted to back away from him, but she knew better. If he was the one who had been poisoning William, she could not show him she was afraid of him—or that she suspected him. "Shalimar was excellent today. She gets better and better. You're doing a wonderful job with her."

Kevin held out his hand for the halter. He took it, flipping it over and over again in his hands as he examined it.

"She's a wonderful mare. It was generous of William to give her to you. I expect he paid a lot of money for her. And I'm sure Chancey got her cut of it by one hook or crook."

"Chancey?"

"She's got a finger in every horse deal that goes down around here. She knows buyers and sellers. I'm certain she must have helped find the horse."

"But she was here when Erick brought Shalimar up." Mary remembered the day as if it were only hours before. What she couldn't remember was what color halter the mare had been wearing.

"She was here, so what? It doesn't mean she didn't tell Erick about the mare. Chancey comes from nothing, and she's done well by herself, finding horses and trading horses. She's an accomplished business lady, and I have no doubt she was handy in finding that mare for you." He held up the halter. "I'd say this proves it. Forest green is Chancey's color, as you say. I'll see this gets returned to her."

"Thanks." Mary turned away from him and busied herself looking for a brush. "Kevin, has anyone else been out riding today but me?"

"I've been up at the ring with a young horse I'm training over the fences. I couldn't say. Why do you ask?"

"Just wondering. It was a lovely day for a ride. Have you seen William?"

"Here he comes now." Kevin nodded toward a tall figure walking rapidly toward the barn.

"Mary." William's face showed barely concealed excitement. "Come up to the house, quickly."

"Is it Darren? What happened?"

For a moment the excitement left William's face. "I never found him. He wasn't about the grounds or in the house. I checked thoroughly. I suppose whatever he wanted, he figured out himself."

Not likely, Mary thought to herself, but said nothing. William did not want to believe his childhood friend could be involved in the happenings at Mayfair, but she was not as generous. She would ask a few questions herself. "What is it that has you so excited?" There were things she had to tell him, too.

"Remember Dr. Faulkner, the veterinarian we rushed Familiar to? He has some news on Familiar's condition."

Mary suddenly went still in his arms. She'd completely forgotten the possibility that something in Familiar's lab work might show up. "Oh?"

"Come inside and I'll tell you." He kissed her cheek. "I've ordered a special dinner for tomorrow evening." He turned to Kevin. "I hope you'll join us, Kevin. Erick is staying, and I've invited some of our neighbors. This is a celebration."

Mary felt her misgivings double. The last time they'd had a dinner party, Clarissa McLeod had turned up with a medium and a bag of tricks. "Are you sure this is wise?" she asked in a soft whisper.

"We're celebrating, love. It's time we set the date for the wedding."

"What about tomorrow?" She whispered the question,

knowing William had not forgotten his appointment at the hospital.

"It's all taken care of. All of it!" He kissed her cheek, then turned to Kevin. "I want you and your parents there, Kevin. This will be a special day for Mayfair."

"We'll be there," the younger man said before he moved away to check on a horse that was stomping impatiently in a stall.

"This is crazy," Mary whispered urgently in William's ear. "Whoever is trying to hurt you will love this opportunity."

"Perhaps, but we'll be ready for them."

He took her elbow and started toward the house. "In the meantime, let's have a cup of tea, a few fresh scones, and a chance to plan our evening."

"William!" She pulled away and turned to face him.

"What?" he asked, startled by the expression on her face.

She started to speak but stopped, glancing over her shoulder to find Kevin staring after them. She remembered exactly what tack was on Shalimar the day she came to Mayfair—a saddle and a bridle. She'd arrived already tacked up! She hadn't been wearing a halter at all.

"KEVIN LOOKS suspicious, but I can't imagine him working with Chancey. They've been competitors for so long." William was still mulling over Mary's recital of the turn of events at Chancey's barn.

"And if Kevin is in this, so is Sophie," Mary said bleakly. "I wish Dr. Faulkner would call back." She glared at the black telephone on the desk in the library.

"He will," William assured her. "He had an emergency. I know the medical doctors here work hard, but the veterinarians have it even tougher. I don't believe they ever sleep."

Mary picked up the telephone. "Maybe I can track him down."

"He'll call as soon as he gets back in the office." William

looked up to find Familiar walking into the library. The cat leapt onto the sofa and brushed against William's arm.

"I was just curious where he had to go." Mary knew the sudden anxiety she felt was foolish, but she couldn't help herself. "I think I'll call, just to ask. Maybe we could meet him somewhere." She didn't wait for William to object. In a moment she had the vet's nurse on the phone.

"We're expecting important news from Dr. Faulkner. If we knew where he was, we might be able to meet him on his way back," she explained. As she spoke, she felt her dread grow. It wasn't unreasonable for a vet to go out on an emergency call. She had no reason to worry—still, she did.

"I see," she said. "Thank you." She replaced the receiver.

"Mary?"

"He's gone to Chancey's."

William's jaw tensed. "Well, she could have a sick horse. Maybe this is just a coincidence."

"I was there not two hours ago. None of her horses were sick. They were fine. She's called him there because somehow, some way, she learned what he was going to tell us. He could be in great danger!"

"How could Chancey learn such a thing?"

Mary's green eyes were blazing. "I don't know. But I think we should go there. Now! If Dr. Faulkner is in danger, it's because of us."

William didn't waste time agreeing. He grabbed his jacket and the car keys. Mary was right beside him, and not two steps behind was a sleek black cat.

AT LAST, they're beginning to put two and two together. It took me a while. That little spell of snarling, biting, clawing and foaming must have addled my brain. But now all of my gray matter is clicking, and things are beginning to come into focus.

For one thing, I was out in the barn earlier today when

the Queen of the Pixies returned from her visit. Kevin was also at the barn when Mary left. He's a much better rider than she is, and I'm sure he knows the shortcuts, but why would he go to Chancey's when he knew Mary was heading that way? It just doesn't make sense. Unless he and Chancey had to hide something or get rid of something. Now, that's a possibility. But he could have telephoned Chancey. She could have pretended not to be home when Mary arrived, if there was something to hide. Gads, I don't think my brain has cleared sufficiently yet! The more I think this through, the more loopholes I find.

At least by going to Chancey's I'll get a chance to scope out the lay of the land for myself. I know the bipeds are going to be looking for clues, but their vision is inferior, and they work at a disadvantage, being so high up there above all the really interesting stuff.

I only wish I'd stayed in Mary's room this morning. I'm curious about that glass of port and the pestle. Mary had the evidence right in her hand. To think someone broke into her room and stole it!

I was lurking up and down the hallways, so I know he or she didn't come through the door. They might have come through the walls. Now, maybe this is a clue we can use. If I can find the entrance to the passage in Mary's room, maybe we can trace it back to the room where the intruder came from. That would be very revealing. It might give a bit of coloring to the shade that lurks in the walls of Mayfair. I like that idea, shadowing the shade.

Oops, the motor is cranked, and William is spinning gravel as he takes off. My, my, is that Abby looking out the front window? And Kevin, there, in the parlor. And, my stars, John near the hallway from the kitchen. Last but not least, Erick, from the third floor, peering out the window like some creature hidden away in the attic. All of them, just waiting to poke their noses in everyone else's business. And there she is, face as pale as a ghost, peeping out of the window in the *second floor hall, little Sophie. Looks like a panel of Hollywood Squares. One of them has the correct answer, or at least is linked to it somehow. I still haven't ruled out the battle-ax Clarissa and that Valkyrie, Chancey. And they'll be here tomorrow night. I can't wait. I have a little kitty performance lined up for them. I'm going to be the first cat to win an Oscar in a dramatic series.*

THE VET'S combination truck/clinic on wheels was parked at Chancey's house when William roared into the drive. They got out and stood beside the car, halted for a moment by the eerie silence of the place.

"Chancey! Dr. Faulkner!" William called.

One of the horses in the barn whinnied a greeting.

"Let's take a look." William nodded toward the barn.

"William." Mary put a hand on his arm. She had a bad feeling about what they were getting ready to find.

"Maybe you should wait here," he suggested.

"Not on your life," she answered, falling into step beside him. Familiar was already two paces ahead.

The black cat scurried into the barn, made a beeline for the tack room and then clawed on the door.

There was a thumping sound, as if something large was jostling against the heavy wood.

"Hold on," William called. He put his shoulder to the door, but it was latched or blocked from inside.

"Push!" Mary urged him, putting her own weight with his against the door.

A low moan came from behind the door, giving William the extra incentive he needed to push the door open several inches. Familiar shot into the opening. He gave several rapid meows as William and Mary pushed harder, gradually forcing the door open wider.

"I can make it," Mary said, slipping in before William could stop her.

"It's Dr. Faulkner," she called out. "He's tied, gagged, and leaning on the door. Just a minute."

There was the sound of something heavy being dragged on the floor, and William was able to push the door open the rest of the way. He burst into the room to find Mary bending over the prone figure of the veterinarian.

"I'm okay," the vet gasped as soon as Mary was able to remove the gag that had been tied around his mouth.

William cut the ropes that bound his hands and feet, and the vet sat up on the floor and began to rub the circulation back into his limbs.

"He caught me from behind," he said ruefully. "I didn't even get a chance to see what he looked like. He must have used the handle on one of the tools." He rubbed the back of his head.

Mary felt a sympathy pang where she'd also been struck. She glanced up at William. They were both thinking the same thing. A lot of people were being injured at Chancey's barn.

"Where's Chancey?" William asked.

"I don't know." Dr. Faulkner stood, working the kinks out of his arms and legs as he paced. "I got the call, and I should have thought it was strange."

"Why is that?" Mary asked.

"It wasn't Chancey who called. It was a man. He didn't give his name, he just said he was calling for her and that she was in the barn with a sick horse. Emergency."

"And you never saw her."

"The place looked deserted. I came in here, in a hurry, as you can imagine. From what the caller said, I was afraid I was going to find Sprint down in the stall with a twisted gut. I rushed right in. Whoever it was, was hiding behind the door. I'd barely gotten inside before he thunked me on the head. When I woke up, I was in here, tied like a steer."

"You keep saying 'he,'" Mary commented.

The vet paused, thinking. "I suppose that's because I don't think of a woman as being able to knock me out." He shook his head. "Old-fashioned, I suppose. It could have been a strong woman."

"We'd better check on Chancey," Mary suggested.

Familiar darted out of the shadows of the barn and ran toward the house. The back door was standing ajar, and he darted into the house before Mary could stop him. Dr. Faulkner was almost fully recovered, and he and William rushed past Mary to go inside.

"Chancey!" William called.

There was a thumping noise from the second floor. William started up the steps, but Mary's voice stopped him.

"Be careful," she said. "It could be a trick."

"What—" But the vet didn't pursue it. "Someone poisoned your cat," he said. "I gather there's more going on at Mayfair than I thought."

"A bit," William said, his gaze straining up the steps to look for any movement. "Familiar wasn't the only one poisoned."

"Well, poison is a rather harsh word—"

A loud thump-thump from upstairs stopped the vet. "It seems I'm not going to be able to tell you the test results. At least, not for a while longer." He nodded at William. "Shall we?"

"Stay here, Mary. You'll have to get help if anything happens."

Mary knew William was simply trying to protect her, but someone had to stay below, and she'd be of less use than Dr. Faulkner, who was a strong and fit man.

"Be careful," she said.

Gripping the rail, she watched as the two men eased up the stairs. If only they'd brought a weapon of some kind. Even a sledgehammer or an ax from the barn!

They disappeared from sight, and she felt her breathing grow shallow and tight as the seconds ticked by. She was about to call out to them when she heard her own name.

"Mary!" William's voice was concerned.

"Yes? Is everything okay?"

"Come on up."

She dashed headlong up the stairs and stopped abruptly. The sight that greeted her was so unexpected that she almost didn't believe it. Chancey was seated in a straight-backed chair. A gag bound her mouth, and her arms and ankles were tied to the chair.

"I think we should leave her." Mary spoke the words before she thought, but she saw the red color rush to Chancey's cheeks.

"She's only teasing," William said as he approached the chair and quickly untied the knots. "Are you okay, Chancey? Who did this?"

"I'd like an answer to that myself. It's a fine day when a woman isn't safe in her own house." She rubbed her right wrist. "I've been tied here for over an hour. And when I find out who sneaked up behind me and put that foul-smelling cloth over my nose, I'm going to…do something terrible to him."

She looked at Dr. Faulkner. "What are you doing here?"

"I thought you called me. An emergency," Dr. Faulkner said. He was calm, thoughtful. "They said Sprint was down with the colic."

"I didn't call you. There's nothing wrong with Sprint," Chancey said. A strange look passed over her face. "Did you go to the barn? He isn't sick, is he?"

"He's fine, but I spent the better part of an hour down in your barn, tied and gagged, also."

Chancey shook her head. "What's going on here? I don't understand any of this."

Familiar, who'd been standing in the doorway of the room, trotted up to Chancey and brushed against her legs.

"Meow." He appeared to be oozing sympathy.

She reached down to pick him up, revealing both wrists as she did so.

Mary saw the slight chafing on her right wrist, the place

where the rope had bound her to the chair. Both of Dr. Faulkner's wrists were slightly irritated. Chancey's left wrist was unblemished. As if she'd tied herself in the chair. Familiar jumped to the floor, moving over to stand at Mary's feet.

"You didn't see the person who attacked you?" Mary asked.

Chancey noticed the change in Mary's voice. "I said I didn't. Did you, earlier today? Maybe it was the same man. Maybe he was intending to rob me."

"Maybe," Mary agreed. She felt both men looking at her. She could make an accusation against Chancey now, but she couldn't prove it. It would be better to wait and discuss her suspicions with William.

"Dr. Faulkner, do you have any idea why someone would want to call you out to Chancey's so they could knock you out, tie you and gag you?" Mary turned her attention to the vet.

"No." He walked to the window of Chancey's bedroom and looked down on the barn below. "Nothing was taken from me, and it doesn't seem that anything has been disturbed here at Chancey's."

"Nothing except the fact that I've been tied and gagged, too." Chancey's anger was rising. "You act as if I'm somehow to blame."

"Are you?" Mary asked.

"You'd do and say anything to make me look bad to William." Chancey stood. "You're terrified you're going to lose him, aren't you?"

"Chancey!" William's voice was angry.

"She came over here and pretended to be hurt so she could go home and gain your sympathy. Now she's trying to set me up to make me look like I'm involved in some sinister plot to abduct Dr. Faulkner." Chancey's normally lovely complexion was red. "What could I gain by this? What?"

"I think we should go," William said, taking Mary's arm. "Dr. Faulkner, could we have a word?"

With Mary in the lead, the three of them took the stairs and exited through the back door. Mary looked up to find Chancey staring out the window at them as they gathered by the vet's truck.

"What did you find?" William asked.

"It's very strange. Poison is a strong word, but it could be appropriate, although the chemical substance I discovered, in the amounts that I found, would not be deadly."

"What was it?" Mary wanted to shake the answers out of the veterinarian. He was being so careful.

"It's a chemical called Drixilocaine. A mind-altering substance. When I got the lab reports back on the initial tests, I sent some samples to the University of Edinburgh medical school for more tests. I lucked up and found someone interested in the case, and he put it all together. The drug is not toxic in the amounts I found in Familiar's saliva."

"In his saliva?" Mary asked.

"Yes, that's what took me so long. The chemical is activated by saliva. That's where I found the strongest indications of it. Once I detected it, I was able to find traces of it in his blood and elsewhere."

"What is it?" William asked.

"A hallucinatory. The U.S. military was experimenting with it for a while, but they gave it up as too unstable. Or at least, it is assumed they gave it up."

"How do you get it?" William asked.

Dr. Faulkner shrugged. "That's a good question. Now I have one for you, William. What's going on at Mayfair? I hear tales of ghosts and hauntings, and you riding around the countryside late at night like some wild man."

William put his hand on the vet's shoulder. "Is it possible that if I took this drug I might begin to believe I was some warlord?"

Dr. Faulkner didn't smile. He considered the question. "I don't really know enough to say, but my first guess is that it's likely. My understanding is that the drug was being tested to release the aggressive tendencies in fighting men. Sort of a drug-induced fighting machine. Horrible. Trouble was, the results weren't predictable. There's little material available on the drug. As you can imagine, no government would want such test results spread around, but it seems some of the soldiers who volunteered to try the drug became obsessed and tried to injure their own comrades.''

"I see." William turned away from the vet and from Mary.

Mary went to him, touching his arm. "But you didn't become violent," she said. "Not with me, or with anyone else."

"Familiar did, though."

"It could be if the cat took a dose intended for you, he reacted more aggressively. He's a much smaller creature," Dr. Faulkner continued.

"Indeed," Mary said. Hearing Familiar's name reminded her to look around the area for him. He'd been the first one out of Chancey's house.

"William, why would someone want to do this?" Dr. Faulkner asked.

"I think someone is trying to drive me out of Mayfair," William said.

"By making you belive you're crazy."

"By making me believe I'm possessed by the ghost of Slaytor MacEachern."

Instead of laughing, Dr. Faulkner nodded. "This drug could work in that fashion. The power of suggestion on someone taking it is very strong. But who would know of this, and who would have a chance to do this to you?"

"I already have a list of suspects," William said. He looked up at the window to see Chancey still staring down at them. "What's become obvious is that whoever it is doesn't want to kill me, they simply want me to leave Mayfair."

"Or else they want to frighten me badly enough to make me leave you," Mary said. She, too, was watching Chancey.

"Without a bride, you won't inherit," Dr. Faulkner said. "That's common enough knowledge in these parts. The MacEachern trust has been a topic of speculation through the generations."

"And continued speculation now," Mary added. Her glance at William let him know that there was unfinished business between them.

"There are those who aren't glad to see me back," William said.

"That's a mild way of putting it. Whoever would use that drug is either completely ignorant or very dangerous. The long-term effects aren't known. Watch yourself."

"I'll be careful," William promised.

"Be careful, and be smart," Dr. Faulkner said. He looked over at Mary. "And watch out for her. If it's your heritage at stake, Mary is in as much danger as you are, now."

Chapter Fifteen

"What are we going to do?" Mary paced her bedroom, her voice a constrained whisper. "Someone's trying to poison you and drive me away, and all you want to do is plan a dinner party."

William's smile was amused. He made a grab for Mary when she passed and pulled her with him on top of the bed. "I want you to relax," he whispered in her ear at the same time he stroked her waist.

"You're not even worried." Mary was indignant.

"I am, but I'm not frantic." He slid her down beside him on the bed and pulled her into the comfort of his arms. "The truth is, since I don't believe I'm going crazy or possessed by a ghost, I feel much better."

"An external foe instead of an internal one." Mary couldn't help but agree, even though it gave her small comfort.

"Excellently put. An external foe." William kissed her temple. "Now all we have to do is figure out who it is."

"Who stands to gain from your 'insanity'?" Mary asked.

"Obviously Erick and Kevin, if he is indeed my half-brother." He looked at Mary. "Does Erick know about Kevin?"

"I don't know." The thought was intriguing. "If he did, Kevin's claim would supersede his, wouldn't it?"

William nodded. ''If his father is my father, then his claim by blood is greater. Sorry to say that the bloodline of the mother has never counted for much. Since men have always been in charge of setting the rules, we like to think we're the most important element in establishing the line of descent.''

''And there's been many a man who greeted another's son as his own.'' Mary enjoyed the verbal sparring with William.

''That would never happen in the MacEachern line.'' William whispered the words against her throat.

''And how do you know that?'' Mary was finding it difficult to keep up the bantering. William's lips brushed lightly across her skin, and she forgot whatever she intended to say next.

''It's always been a fact that the MacEachern men have been able to cast a spell of loyalty, fidelity and…complete surrender over their women.''

''Surrender?'' Mary tried to gather her wits, but her body seemed to have other ideas.

''Yes, my love, complete surrender.'' He kissed the pulse point at her neck and slowly began to move down.

''And once these women were in the throes of complete surrender, they were seduced and were soon heavy with child?''

''Not exactly.'' William's voice indicated that he knew the topic that was at hand.

''And what if we marry and I don't produce a male heir?'' Mary's heart pounded. She'd dreaded asking this question, but this was the perfect time. William was physically and mentally fine. The future was not completely ironed out, but it would never be between them until this matter was settled.

''Then Erick will inherit.''

''That simple?''

''That simple. I didn't tell you about the issue of an heir because I didn't want you to feel pressured. I know that you love children and want them, as do I. If we start our family in time to meet the deadline, that will be fine. If not… You see, I could have married years ago if meeting the stipulations of inheritance was all that mattered to me. Had I not met you, I would never have married.''

"Surely…"

"I would not tie myself to a woman to inherit a pile of old stone. Never." He kissed her cheek. "And remember, my sweet—" his grin was infectious "—Erick has no male heir. Nor Kevin."

"That we know of." Mary made her point yet she couldn't help but smile. William was everything to her. She'd never known that love could be so full and rich.

"Even Slaytor would not settle for less than the woman he loved. I believe he was right fond of Lisette. And it was marriage he wanted, not just a romp on the furs."

"William…" She reached for him.

He kissed her lips. "It's part of the MacEachern male heritage. We want to marry the women we love."

Mary returned his kiss with all of the passion that had grown between them. For a little while they put their troubles behind them and enjoyed the luxury of intense emotions and desire. The sun dipped below the horizon again, and the lonely sounds of someone in the barn playing bagpipes marked the end of the day.

"Who is that?" Mary asked, leaning up on an elbow to listen.

They were twined together beneath a sheet, and William stroked her hip. "It's one of the grooms. At Mayfair we used to always have an employee who could play, but it's not easy to find someone with that degree of skill. I like it."

"I do, too. There are many traditions that I'm growing to like more and more." She kissed his chest. "I think we should establish a few of our own. Such as retiring to our chamber each afternoon to watch the day disappear."

"Merely to watch the changes of the light?"

"And whatever else comes to mind." Mary kissed him again, then rested her head on his shoulder. The silence between them was comfortable, and together they listened to the last notes of the bagpiper's dirge.

William broke the silence. "I've been giving it some thought. Inheritance follows the first male heir. If I'm proven ineligible, for any reason, Kevin would stand next in line if he could support his claim."

"Then Erick?"

"Yes, and possibly then Eleanor. Her relationship is distant, but the great MacEachern clan has dwindled throughout the years. There may well be more relatives in America and Australia, but I have no idea of how to get in touch with them. And I don't even know if I should try."

"There's no reason now, William. You're fine. We'll uncover who's behind this, correct it, and then you and I can be married, just as we'd planned."

"And begin to repopulate the world with MacEacherns?"

"At least three or four of them." Mary laughed.

"That's a fair start."

"When we do have children, I want to see about a different kind of inheritance." Mary spoke slowly. "You were an only child. But if you'd been the second son, you would have gotten nothing. I don't want that for our children."

"We'll get a solicitor, just as soon as we're married. For now, we'd better make our plans."

"We need to be able to trick whoever is doing this out into the open."

"Exactly, but I'm not sure how to do that." William stretched, drawing her closer against him. "Given a choice, I'd rather stay here and figure out what exactly makes you make those interesting little noises."

Mary snuggled closer. "Given my preferences, I'd like exactly the same thing." She kissed his ear lightly. "What time are our guests coming?"

"For cocktails at seven, tomorrow." William sat up. "And we're going to have to think hard and fast before they get here. I've invited everyone who was here before, along with

Erick, and Kevin's parents." William swung his legs off the side of the bed and stood. "I'm beginning to doubt everyone. Except you."

"Me, too," Mary answered ruefully. "Even my best friend."

"I want to go down to the kitchen and talk with Abby about the menu. I'm going to have her help me plan it, but then get it catered in. I don't want anyone on the staff except those who will be attending the dinner to be here. Everyone else will be hired from the outside."

Mary nodded. It was a good start.

"And how do you think we can flush out the culprit?"

William's eyes brightened. "Why don't we announce at the dinner that we're getting married right away? That we'll be leaving for our wedding trip in the morning."

"Yes!" Mary swung her legs out of bed and got up, grabbing for her clothes. "That's it. We have to take the initiative, and if our calculations are correct, this person doesn't want to hurt you. I mean, not really, or they could have poisoned you with arsenic or something."

William buttoned his shirt. "Right. They could have killed me instead of making me believe I was crazy."

"So if that's their goal, our marriage would be the worst thing that could happen. Even if you were institutionalized, if we were married and I produced an heir, Mayfair would be passed on to your child."

"Exactly my thinking."

The light of excitement and happiness dimmed slightly in Mary's face. "I wish I could ask Sophie to help me." She rolled her eyes at William and gave him a crooked smile. "It's just difficult. Sophie has been so much a part of my life...."

"By all means, involve her. If she's innocent, she'll have great fun helping you. If she's involved with Kevin somehow, then she'll pass our plans on to him."

Mary took a breath. "It's sort of deceitful to do this to her."

"If she's innocent, she'll never know. If she's guilty..."

"You're right." Mary tucked her shirt into her pants and slid into her boots. "Shall I help you talk to Abby about the meal?"

William's smile also dimmed. "No, I'll do this. Abby has been with the family since she was a young girl. This is hard on me, too. I'd never imagined how difficult it might be to suspect someone you loved and trusted."

Mary went to him and hugged him close. "We can only hope that it's Clarissa or Chancey. That way we won't feel too badly when we see them carted off to jail."

"Are you sure you wouldn't rather see them flogged in the square at Edinburgh?"

Mary knew he was teasing, but he'd struck a cord in her. She looked up at him, her green eyes suddenly brimming with tears. "I thought I was losing you, William. I thought something terrible was happening to you and there was no way I could help you, or even get close enough to give you comfort. If I can find who did this to you, to us, I'd be delighted to see them flogged. Publicly, privately, or any way I could manage it."

William kissed her nose. "You are a bloodthirsty little wench," he said. "Perhaps it's that fire in you that has brought Slaytor out in me."

"Perhaps," she said, thinking back to the savage and tender moments they'd shared. "We're both capable of great passion. And great tenderness."

"And great love," he said. "We're going to have a glorious future together, Mary."

"Why don't we really marry?" Mary's brain spun with the possibilities. "It isn't a bad idea at all."

William kissed her forehead, her nose and her chin. "Because I want a proper marriage here at Mayfair. I want you to be introduced as who you are—Lady MacEachern. I don't want to run away and marry in haste. I want to do it with all the pomp and dignity and splendor that you deserve.''

''And that the people of Mayfair expect?'' She was teasing him, but she didn't really mind. It was so like William to want to meet the expectations of those he cared for. And in doing so, to firmly establish her role in his life.

''They do expect it, and I want them to know you are my bride, my love, my wife. With nothing to hide or hurry.''

''Ah,'' she said. ''I'd forgotten that. A hasty wedding might signal a match made of necessity.''

''To those with hard spirits, it would, and I don't want that for us. But no matter, the illusion of a speedy wedding will serve our purposes for the moment.''

''Go and make your plans,'' she said, ''and I'll involve Sophie. It won't be long before it will be all over Mayfair what we're planning to do.''

''That's exactly what I'm counting on,'' William said as he kissed her one last time before heading to the kitchen to seek out Abby.

A PLAN! At last, they have a plan. After Mary has been knocked on the head at least once, and William has gone into fits a number of times. Just let me point out that if a cat had suffered such abuse, a plan would have been conceived a long time ago. But then, humans have never been as nimble-witted as a cat. I shouldn't be so critical. After all, they're just rather large, lovable animals who have to be trained to meet a cat's needs.

Case in point. I've sniffed around this room and discovered where I'm certain there's a hidden passage. Both Mary and William, in the throes of passion, have forgotten to look for the way someone sneaked into her room and stole her evidence.

I, the ever vigilant detective cat, have continued my sleuthing, immune to lust or weariness or... Well, I did take a little break for some broiled chicken livers Abby made just for me.

But it was only for a few brief moments, and now I'm back on the trail.

Look at Mary. She's sitting on the bed all starry-eyed and dreamy, thinking about her wedding and her future. She is a beautiful sight. It does even my jaded old cat heart good to see such love.

Too bad I have to interrupt her daydreams for a little business, but I need someone to trigger this door, and then I need to figure out where this passage goes. It's a blow to my ego to admit that I need a human's help, but…

Here goes, a little meow and a dig with the claws!

"FAMILIAR." Mary jumped up. The cat had planted all of his claws in the top of her foot. She looked down. He hadn't drawn blood, but his tail was twitching as if he intended another attack. "You'd better not."

The words were hardly out of her mouth before Familiar sprang forward, swatted his sheathed claws across her toes, and darted back.

"Why, you little devil, you're wanting to play." Familiar darted behind a sofa. Mary followed. She found him digging frantically at the wall.

"What is it?"

"Meow."

She knelt beside him and began to press where he was digging. In a moment there was a soft grinding sound and the wall in front of her began to slide in, revealing another passage.

"So that's how he stole my port and the pestle," she said aloud.

"Meow." This time Familiar answered with a definite note of impatience in his voice.

"Let me get a light and we'll find out where this goes." Mary's voice was filled with excitement. She hurried to her bedside table and found the flashlight. The beam was good and strong, and she darted back into the passage before she thought to prop the door open. The soft grinding noise sounded much more ominous as the door closed behind her.

In the total darkness of the passage, Mary felt faint with sudden fear. The light picked out the narrow stone walls and floor, and the two golden eyes that let her know Familiar was with her.

"Boy, am I glad you're here," she whispered as she slowly worked her way along the narrow tunnel, following the black cat.

"No, NO. I insist that you and John and Kevin join us." William gently pushed Abby into a chair at the kitchen table. His heart twisted at the expression on her face, one of doubt and apprehension. When his mother had been too busy with social engagements, it had always been Abby who'd sat with him while he ate his cookies and told stories. Often Kevin would be sitting right beside him, just a baby, but so much a part of the warmth of the kitchen and the woman who now sat in front of him.

"At least let me cook," Abby said. "This must be an important occasion. It wouldn't do to have strangers prepare the meal."

Her choice of words startled William. That was exactly what he was after—strangers preparing his food. The idea was wounding. To both of them.

"You've worked too hard. This is a party, Abby. Mary and I have an announcement to make. I want you and John to be my guests. And Kevin, of course. Mayfair wouldn't be Mayfair without Kevin."

Abby looked up at him, her light eyes clear and questioning. "What are you saying?"

"Only that Kevin is part of Mayfair. A large part."

Abby's indrawn breath gave her away. William saw she knew that he was alluding to Kevin's parentage.

"It wouldn't be proper." She tried to rise, but William was standing so close that she couldn't do so without creating even more awkwardness. She resumed her seat, but looked away from William.

"It's proper if I say so, Abby. You and John and Kevin will be my guests, just like the other members of the community. Erick will be there. And Chancey."

Abby's smile was tremulous. "I suppose someone should be in the room to keep that snake cornered."

William chuckled. "There's no love lost on Chancey, is there?"

"None." Abby's smile was stronger. "If she can't have you as a husband, she'll be after Erick. Or my Kevin. She's determined to get as close to you and Mayfair as she can."

Abby's observation was interesting, and William was also growing more and more certain of one thing—if Abby was involved, it was through ignorance. If she was somehow putting something in his food, and she did have the easiest access, then it was done without knowledge of what she was doing.

"What shall we cook for the occasion?" Abby was already concentrating on the menu.

"I know. For the dinner, do you think you might be able to provide the caterers with that wonderful egg custard you made last week?"

"Egg custard?" Abby was taken aback. "I would think you'd want something a little…fancier."

"It was wonderful, Abby. Even Familiar thought so."

"Where is that rascal?" Abby asked. "He hasn't been in the kitchen but once. Devoured an entire pan of chicken livers I broiled for him." She shook her head. "I swear, it does a body good to watch that cat enjoy his food."

"He's up in Mary's room, I believe. Don't worry. In about another hour, when his stomach alerts him, he'll be back down here to con you out of some other delicacy."

"He will at that. He's a charmer, that one. Now, about that custard." She frowned. "Are you sure?"

"Positive."

"Then I could make it ahead of time and leave it for the caterers."

"No, you'll have the whole day tomorrow to relax so you can be fresh for the party. Just tell me what's in it."

When Abby started to rise this time, William stepped back, giving her room. She went to the shelves and drew down a large cookbook stuffed with recipes old and new.

"I've collected these things for years, and my mother before me. She cooked here, though I know you don't remember her. She was retired by the time you were born."

"I remember stories about her." William watched the cook riffle through the pages of the book, looking up the recipe he'd requested. Her eyes traveled over the battered cookbook with genuine love. He wanted to tell her that he would look into Kevin's birth claim, but he couldn't. If Abby was someone's foil, he needed her to remain that. If it was Kevin, then better to learn it now than later.

"Here it is." She took the book to the table and began to copy the recipe on a card for him.

"Do you have any exotic recipes?"

"You should know the answer to that." Her handwriting was slow and proper.

"I mean, something that requires unusual spices."

"Sure, Scotland isn't the tropics. Any of the Caribbean dishes call for spices some might consider exotic. There's that lime and cayenne fish you like so much."

"Wonderful. How do you go about getting the correct herbs?"

"I can buy them now. There was a time when I had to special order and then grind my own. Everything is so much easier to come by."

"It seems I remember you standing at the counter, mixing up something like a powder. Crushing it, I suppose."

"Plenty was the time when I did that, but almost everything comes crushed or chopped. I still grate a few of my own spices, but not like I used to." She snapped her fingers.

"Everything is instant now. Truth is, I miss some of the old ways. But that's progress for you. I have little enough time for my work as it is. I can't see me crushing peppers or grinding ginger into powder. Those days are gone."

"I suppose they are," William answered, but his tone was absent as his eyes roved the shelves. "You haven't noticed anything amiss in your kitchen, have you?"

"Why do you ask?" Abby was suddenly very still. She put her pen down and pushed the recipe toward him.

"Mary thought someone was prowling around the kitchen one night when she came down for some tea. She was badly frightened, so she didn't investigate. I was just wondering if anything has gone amiss."

"Strange, but I am missing one thing, an old pestle and mortar that I used to grind spices. I don't have much call for it, but it is very old. Probably very valuable. I was hoping maybe you'd removed it."

William held her gaze. "No, I didn't. It's a strange item for someone to take, isn't it?"

"Very strange," Abby said.

"It would take a thief who knew the value of antiques. Or one who had a use for such a device."

Abby closed the cookbook. "I hadn't thought of it before, but Kevin has used it in the past to grind up some medicines for the horses. Those big tablets, for their aches. He puts it in their feed, all crushed. Maybe he's borrowed it and taken it to the barn. If that's the case, I'm sure it's safe and sound and will be returned."

William turned away from the sudden concern in the cook's face.

Chapter Sixteen

Mary's knees were throbbing from her position on the cold stone floor. She pressed again and again at the stones that Familiar indicated, but the exit to the passage would not open. She'd found the end—to no avail. She'd been unable to open the door. Now she was back at the point where she'd begun, and she could not manage to force that door open, either.

Familiar circled her feet, his anxiety showing in his restless pacing.

"We'll get it open," Mary assured him. They had to. No one knew where she'd gone—or even where to begin looking. William had no inkling that there was a passage in her room.

Panic bloomed like a deadly flower, and Mary forced her thoughts back to the moment. The air in the passage was dank, musty and unpleasant, but she did not feel as if she would suffocate.

"Let's try the other opening again," she said to the cat. Her fingers were sore and bleeding from pulling, tugging and clawing at the stones near the base of the opening to her room.

Step-by-step, they traveled the passage again. At times Mary felt as if they were definitely going up an incline, bu there was no way to really tell. In the dark and twisting passage, she'd lost all sense of direction.

Finally reaching the end, she felt her heart pound. It was a solid stone wall. As far as she could tell by shining the light up and down the length of it, there might never have been another opening.

Familiar flopped on his side and began frantically digging near the base. It was the same area that triggered the door in her room, Mary knew. But no matter how she pressed and pushed, it seemed to have no effect. Not on either end of the tunnel. Why hadn't she been smart enough to block the opening with something? Or even left William a note saying where she'd gone? Why hadn't she taken a few simple precautions? Now it was too late. She and Familiar could figure a way out of the tunnel, or they could die in there of dehydration.

A terrible thought winged through her brain. What if someone had deliberately rigged the door? What if it had all been a trick to lure her into a dead-end passage with no escape? That would resolve the problem of William's marriage.

"Easy now," she said, bending to stroke the cat. But the words were for herself.

The flashlight beam bounced back at her from the dead end, flickered once and died.

"Great," she said, the darkness complete. "Now we can't even see."

Creeping forward on her hands and knees, she found Familiar. The cat's rough tongue licked comfort along her forearm, and Mary snuggled him against her. He was the one thing she could count on at this time.

Despair chased all rational thoughts from her brain, and Mary curled against the stone wall and held the cat to her chest. She felt very small, and very alone. The thought of crying came to her, but she knew it would do no good. She could only rest her fingers for a little while and then try again to trigger the mechanism that opened the doors. And wait for William to start hunting for her.

Without the flashlight, she couldn't even tell how long she'd been in the passage. It seemed like hours, but she knew it hadn't been that long. Maybe an hour. So William would miss her soon. Maybe she'd hear them searching.

She stretched out on the stone floor with Familiar against her. With her ear to the wall, she hoped to hear something, some sign that someone was searching for her.

The darkness was so total that she shut her eyes against it. Trying to see only made it seem that much worse. She felt Familiar's paw on her cheek, and she heard his kitty motor kick into overdrive as his purr echoed off the stone walls.

"I've gotten us into a mess, Familiar, and you aren't even mad at me, are you?"

He lightly nipped her nose, still purring.

"What?" she asked. She knew the cat wanted something. She could tell by the way he was patting her face with his paw. Slapping it would be a more accurate term. He was actually slapping her firmly in the face with his paw, claws carefully sheathed.

"Okay," she said, sitting up and reaching into the darkness for him.

The supporting wall behind her swung back and light flooded the tunnel.

Mary gave an exclamation of surprise and threw her hands up to ward off the light. It was so bright after the blackness of the tunnel that she couldn't see at all.

"Hey!" There was a startled exclamation from a large man who towered over her. He stood at the entrance, ready to dart inside.

"William?" She couldn't see at all.

"You're a meddling lass, and one who deserves the consequences of her actions." His big hand clasped on her hair, and he began dragging her back into the tunnel. She braced her feet and fought.

The man wasn't William. It wasn't anyone she knew. Though her eyes were still blinded by the sudden light, she was able to tell that the man was enormous and clad in kilt and furs. A sword broad enough to cleave an oxen's—or a man's—neck in two hung at his side.

She focused her gaze up to his face, and a cry escaped her. His face was painted red and black, a curious and extremely pagan pattern of war. He was completely terrifying.

"Damn ye for an interfering wench!" he cried as he shifted his grip to her arms and drew her into the black maw of the tunnel.

Her glimpse was brief, and Mary still didn't believe what her own eyes had seen. Flattened against the wall where he'd flung her, she dropped to her hands and knees and began to crawl toward the opening. The door slid shut when she was still a good six feet away.

"Familiar! Get William!" Mary cried through the wall to the cat. "Get him! Quick!"

Mary sank back against the wall. The darkness in the tunnel enveloped her, and her heart was pounding so loudly she couldn't tell if anyone was near her or not. It was evident she'd seen Slaytor MacEachern, or the man masquerading as him. And he was no one she could identify. He bore no resemblance to anyone at Mayfair. He was far too tall for Kevin, or even Erick. He was, as William had said, a good two inches taller even than he, with dark hair wild and tangled around his shoulders.

Who was he? Where was he?

At first she didn't hear the rasp of angry breathing. It wasn't until she heard the clank of the broadsword on the stones that she knew the terrible figure of Slaytor Mac-Eachern was standing over her.

"You've done enough damage here, Mary Muir. I tried my best to frighten you away, but you wouldn't heed me. It's in the wind that you're to marry William very soon. I can't let that happen."

One hand closed in her hair as his second hand covered her mouth. With almost no effort, he pulled her against his chest and disappeared down the passage.

WILLIAM WAS PANTING as he topped the third floor landing and ran behind the black cat. Familiar was in a wide-open run. He skidded around a corner, then stopped in the open doorway of the turret room.

Even in the natural light, William could see the room was empty.

Familiar's hair rose in a line down his back, and a low growl escaped his throat.

"Where is she?" William asked.

Familiar's answer was a deeper growl. Very slowly, he entered the room. In a moment he was digging at the wall.

"A passage." William knew what the cat was trying to show him. "She's in the passage."

He felt along the wall, his fingers encountering the loose mortar that indicated that stones had been shifting. "It's here. I can almost feel it." Just as he spoke, the panel began to slide open.

William started into the darkness, but Familiar hooked a claw into the cuff of his pants. With a great tug, the cat held him.

Pausing for a moment, William heard the sound of muffled sobbing in the distance.

"Mary!" he cried, shaking loose of the cat and running into the darkness without a light or a weapon. "Mary! I'm coming!"

I WONDER if playwright Sam Shepard had these two in mind when he penned Fool for Love. *Now it's up to me to find something to block this door. I tried to warn the big galoot, but would he listen? No. And he almost tore my left claw out by its roots. All because Miss Pixie is whimpering.*

Truth to tell, she did sound pretty unhappy. Oh, well,

here's a cushion from a chair. I'll drop it in the opening before the door can close, and then we'll have an exit. I'm not about to get trapped in this place with these two. I don't think I could take the heat.

"I'M OKAY," Mary whispered again as she held on to William. "I'm really okay."

William crushed her against him, terrified to let her go. He could feel the pounding of her heart, and it reassured him. He never wanted to let her out of his arms again.

"I saw him," Mary said, trying hard to remember the details. With the paint on his face, it completely distorted his appearance. The only thing she could say for certain was that he was big, and that he had long, black hair. Because his features had been obscured by the weird pattern of paint, she couldn't describe him, but he did bear a passing resemblance to the rows and rows of MacEacherns hanging on the walls of the castle.

"We'll talk later. Let's just get out of here."

"The door!" Mary struggled to her feet. "It jammed when I was in here before."

"Meow!"

Familiar's mew echoed against the stones. It was a demanding tone.

"Is it possible he wants us to follow him?" William asked.

"Highly possible, but we're closer to the end that comes out in my room."

"Meow!"

"He's a demanding cat," Mary said as she yielded to Familiar's direct order. "He's also almost always right. Let's go."

William led the way in the darkness, and was tremendously relieved to see a three-inch slot of light. At the base of the door, a green velveteen pillow was almost crushed. Beyond was the turret room.

"Familiar did that. He knew the door would close and we wouldn't be able to get out."

"Just exactly what your relative had in mind," Mary said. "I don't know who he was, but his entire game is to prevent our marriage. He told me…" She faltered. It was one thing to hear the threats, it was another to repeat them to William.

Putting his shoulder against the door, William heaved it open enough for them to make an escape, Familiar at their heels. William picked up the pillow, and the panel slid back into place. There was no trace that it was even there.

"What did this man tell you?" William tossed the cushion onto a chair and pulled Mary into his arms. "More importantly, what did he do to you?"

"Nothing that won't mend," Mary said, rubbing her scalp. "He had a fondness for dragging me about by my hair. I felt as if he were my flipping brother."

William kissed her, touched by her attempts at humor when he'd been so afraid for her. That was like Mary, to make light of the damages she'd suffered so that he wouldn't worry.

"What did he do?" he repeated. The cold knife of real anger forged as he waited for her reply. It was one thing to drug him, but it was another to touch his Mary.

"He picked me up by my hair, more than once. Sort of hauled me around, in and out of the passage. He threw me up against a wall, and then scared ten years off my life by dragging me into the passage with him." She took a breath and refused to looked at William. "In the darkness in there, I remember his sword clanking against the wall. I thought he was going to cut my head off. That would have pleased Chancey, that I would have died like my namesake."

Even though her words were spoken in jest, William felt his blood chill. The idea that Mary had thought she might die was intolerable. Whoever had done this would pay.

"I think we owe Familiar a great deal of thanks," he said, veering away from the cold fury that was growing inside him.

He didn't want to frighten Mary with his own dark emotion. The MacEachern clan was descended from bloody warriors, and not even generations of peace had completely destroyed the hum of his blood.

"William?" Mary was looking at him with concern.

"What, my love?"

"I'm fine now. He only wanted to scare me, I believe. He told me if I didn't leave Mayfair tonight, you'd be in terrible danger. So, he did mean to let me out."

"Possibly." William wasn't ready to give up his anger.

"No, I'm sure he was. He could have hurt me. To be honest, he could have easily killed me. No one would have been the wiser…" She turned to the black cat, who was perched on the chair and cushion, watching them. "If it hadn't been for Familiar."

"Let's get out of this room." William looked around at the faded draperies, the daybed that was against a wall with a large window. "Slaytor and Lisette obviously had some enjoyable times here, but I'd just as soon redo this room when you have time to think about it."

Mary smiled. "That would be fun. Maybe I could use it for my music room."

William's smile was genuine. "That's delightful. I can hear your cello against these stone walls. It will be like my own private symphony. Now, everything is set for the dinner tomorrow, and I've spoken to Abby."

"News travels fast in Mayfair. That man knew we were planning on marrying soon."

William paused. "Then he had to overhear me telling Abby about the announcement."

"But those walls are solid. Abby told me they were more than three feet thick, reinforced with all kinds of things because the kitchen was part of the original castle."

"That's true, but there's no telling what hidden passages are behind those pantry walls. I did ask Erick, and he said that the castle had been through so many additions and renovations that it would be impossible to determine where they might be. But he said we could measure the rooms and try to make an educated guess.''

''Well, we know one leads from here to my room.''

''And one from my room to the hallway up here. There could be a dozen more. Why not one into the kitchen? Or at least, an opening where a person might eavesdrop.'' William was more certain of it as he spoke. There had always been stories at Mayfair about maids who knew exactly what William's parents wanted even before they could call for it. Maybe the staff knew something about the old castle that the MacEacherns had forgotten.

''Well, at least we know how he got the glass of port and the pestle.'' Mary felt at least one loose end had been tied. Her satisfied expression gave way to one of real concern.

''What is it? Did he hurt you?'' William's worst fears resurfaced.

''No, it's just that it dawned on me, whoever he is, he could be living in those walls. He could have been there for some time now, William. And the fact that you've come home might have driven him out—and made him danger-ous.''

Mary's conclusions were like drops of water hitting a crys-tal surface, shattering into a million little droplets and spread-ing out in every direction. Too clearly, William saw the dan-gers. With his father old and infirm, someone could have lived within the vast stretches of the castle with no difficulty. There was always abundant food in the kitchen, and rooms where no one ever entered—just the maids on an irregular basis. Mayfair was simply too big for one small family to inhabit all of it.

''You're thinking exactly what I'm thinking,'' Mary said, her voice dropping to a frightened whisper as she looked around the room. ''He could be some local crazy who's been here all along, pretending to be Lord MacEachern and wait-ing for his chance to rule. Now that you're back, you threaten him. And if he's been in Mayfair, he knows the terms of the will."

"And he would view *you* as the ultimate threat," William said, finishing for her. "Without you, I can't inherit."

"Yes, and I would be the easiest target, the weakest. There's also clan loyalty to consider. If he's playing at being a member of your family clan, he wouldn't really want to injure you. An outsider would be far more acceptable."

"He doesn't object to making me think I'm crazy, but he might shrink from putting a dagger in my heart."

Mary felt the blood squeeze through her own heart at that image. "What are we going to do?"

"I don't know." William hadn't considered this possibility. "I'll tell you, though. I almost prefer this to the idea that someone I've known all my life might be trying to send me to a mental ward."

"I'm not so certain I feel the same way. You didn't see this man. The black-and-red paint is not merely bizarre, it's terrifying."

"There were times when members of a clan used paint as a symbol of war," he said.

"I thought that was the province of Native Americans," Mary noted.

"The clans of Scotland were much like the American tribes in some ways. Not nomadic, though. But the painting of the face has been a part of ritual and tradition in many different parts of the world."

"What would you say red-and-black paint might mean?" Mary asked, almost afraid to hear his answer.

"I'd say it was serious business, whatever else it might signify."

"What are we going to do?" Mary asked again. Now the plan to stage a fake wedding seemed dangerous. "Maybe we should cancel our announcement. This man lurking about in the walls might go over the edge. He could try to injure us, or anyone else who happens to be here."

"We have to flush him out, whoever he is," William insisted. "We can't continue to live here, never knowing when he's going to appear."

"You're right," Mary said, though she wanted to insist that they pack their belongings and leave. Surely there was some professional they could call in to find the passageways and hiding places, to drag out the man who'd been tormenting them.

"Mary, we have to right this ourselves. The old legends of Slaytor aren't that important. It's a part of history here, and it adds to the aura of Mayfair. But if I allow anyone— anyone at all—to drive me from my home, I'd never have the respect of the people here. The symbol that Mayfair is would crumble. I'm not bragging when I say that it would be economically devastating to the community. Even if I didn't want to stay and fight this out for me, I'd have to do it for the people who depend on me. Do you understand that?"

"I do," Mary answered, slightly ashamed of her desire to flee. "I do, and I stand beside you."

Familiar wedged himself between their legs and looked up at them. "Meow." It was as if he were declaring his intention to also stand with them.

OF ALL THE GUESTS at the dinner party, Abby and John were the most uncomfortable. They stood in one corner, drinks melting in their hands as they looked around the room and forced smiles.

"Maybe this wasn't a good idea," Mary whispered to William. She felt sorry for them, so obviously ill at ease.

William excused himself and walked over to the couple. "Abby, everything is fine. The caterers followed your instructions to the letter. I only wish you could relax."

"She'd rather be working," John said, almost snapping to attention when the doorbell rang to announce the arrival of

Clarissa and Darren McLeod. He plainly wanted to go and perform his duties, but Abby's gentle hand restrained him.

"Where's Kevin?" William asked.

"One of the fillies took a bad turn. He's down there with her now, but he promised he'd be here in time for dinner—and in a suit," Abby said. Her pride peeked through her discomfort. "He loves those horses, he does."

No matter what Kevin might or might not have done, William's heart went out to Abby. "I want you to know that when I inherit the estate, Kevin will be treated fairly."

Abby and John exchanged quick glances, then both looked down.

"We have no doubt of that," Abby said. "How long have you known?"

"Not long." William took her hand and squeezed it. "Abby, you and John did a wonderful thing, taking Kevin in. If he is my half-brother, he'll be treated fairly."

Worry furrowed Abby's brow. "I told him to be straight with this, to talk with you. But he wouldn't. He said he wanted to do things his way." She glanced at John, and a look of pain passed between them. "He's a good boy, but he can be stubborn, and it's been hard for him, what with Miss Sophie and all."

"What about Miss Sophie?" The conversation had taken a turn William hadn't anticipated.

"His feelings for her are strong. All of these years, he's never given a girl the time of day. It's been hard for him, wanting to make Miss Sophie an offer."

"He wants to marry her?" William was surprised.

"He does, but what can he offer her? A life here as the wife of a servant? Especially with her friend marrying the Lord of Mayfair." She shook her head, but not before tears were evident. "Pride is not a bad thing, but it can make a man foolish."

"Kevin's feelings for Sophie aren't foolish."

"No, but his actions have been." Abby saw the look of

warning on John's face. "I'd better check to see if everything is going smoothly in the kitchen." She turned away abruptly and left.

"She's upset," John said, following after his wife without another word.

William motioned Mary to his side. "This is going to be an interesting night, my love. Whatever happens, don't leave the dining room without me."

"What is it?" Mary felt her heartbeat accelerate.

"Promise, Mary. Stay in the dining room. Your life and mine might depend on it."

Chapter Seventeen

Kevin strode into the dining room just as everyone had started taking their places. Although he didn't go to Sophie, his look lingered on her, and she, in turn, couldn't take her eyes off him. But whenever they felt someone looking at them, they dropped their gazes and pretended they were not interested in each other.

Mary watched the exchange with a feeling of sorrow. Not Sophie. Not her friend. She could take anything except betrayal by her friend. What was going on between the two of them, and how deeply was Sophie involved in Kevin's personal business? She and Sophie had been so close for so long, and now they hadn't really spoken to each other in several days. Why hadn't Sophie confided in her? The sense of betrayal made tears well in her eyes. She blinked them back. How did William feel, thinking his own relatives might be plotting against him? She felt Sophie's gaze on her, and she forced a smile.

"You look beautiful," Sophie said to her. Her dark gaze met Mary's green one and then slid away.

"And you." Mary wasn't exaggerating. Sophie's dark hair glistened against her pale skin, and the red dress she'd chosen was perfect for her complexion. But it was more than clothes or makeup. Mary could see the flush that heightened Sophie's coloring and put an extra sparkle in her eyes. She was in love with Kevin. What once would have given such joy was now an occasion for worry.

Mary looked around the table. Dr. Sloan had not been able to attend, but Clarissa, Darren, and Mrs. Daugherty were there. A pang of concern for Darren made Mary turn away. He was caught in a web of anger spun by his unhappy mother. Soon he would be completely cocooned in her harping, nagging ways. Unless he made good his escape soon, she would suck all vital elements from him and leave only a shell. But was he willing to sacrifice William to make his escape? Did he want Mayfair for his own?

"Mary, are you okay?"

She looked up to find Erick staring at her. His blue eyes, so much like William's, were narrowed with concern. His short, dark hair glistened.

"I'm fine." She smiled. "Just serious thinking." She looked behind him. "Where's this wonderful woman we've heard so much about?"

"Edna couldn't make it tonight."

"Is her little girl sick again?"

Erick's smile was careworn. "No, it's her mother, I'm afraid. Edna carries a lot of family responsibility. But on to more pleasant things. I hear William's going to make an announcement."

"Now, that's for William to do." She tried to read something in Erick's face, but there was nothing there but a smile.

"Excuse me," he said, "but I think John and Abby are having difficulty finding their seats."

Mary watched as Erick helped maneuver the couple to their seats. Everyone else had begun to settle around the table, and she found her seat at William's left. She glanced at him only to find that he was alertly scanning the crowd. He was looking for the snake in the garden, or at least some sign of one.

Before the party they'd spent half an hour tapping at the walls to see if they could detect a hollowness anywhere that might lead to another passageway. They'd found nothing—and had almost been caught by Erick, who'd shown up earlier than expected.

They'd also managed to open the passage in Mary's room and thoroughly search it from end to end, without finding a single clue to the man who'd frightened Mary.

"Maybe no one here is involved," Mary whispered to William. His gray gaze swept the room for the hundredth time.

"I wish I could believe that. There's someone in Mayfair. Someone who doesn't belong here. I have to be certain, though, that he's working alone." He looked at Mary, a piercing look. "You see, the problem I have is, why would a stranger try to destroy my marriage, and my future?"

"He might not be normal," Mary said, hesitating to state it any more forcefully.

"If that's the case, he could be extremely dangerous."

Mary sighed. "I know that." She took her seat as William held her chair. The other women sat, followed by the men. Abby looked as if she wanted to jump up and take charge of serving the meal, but she sat between John and Kevin, her glance falling occasionally on William as she waited to see what he would do.

While Mary barely picked at her food, William ate with gusto. The sound of laughter, cutlery and crystal filled the room, giving the enormous hall a sense of real warmth.

Even Clarissa seemed determined to enjoy the evening and to contain any negative remarks she might want to make. For his part, Darren drained his wineglass more than once, but his slightly flushed face gave way more often than usual to a smile.

"I can't believe it's anyone in this room," Mary said, bending close to William's ear while the table was distracted with the serving of the dessert.

"We'll soon find out." He took a spoonful of the custard. "This isn't as good as Abby's."

"No, it isn't," Mary agreed.

William took another bite before he folded his napkin. He stood at the head of the table and cleared his throat. "I've asked you here on such short notice for a special announcement. You've all gotten to know Mary." He ignored the angry stare Chancey threw his way. "We've decided to marry as soon as we can possibly arrange it. We'll be leaving in the morning."

The exclamations around the table ranged from consternation to surprise. Clarissa McLeod looked as if she'd been slapped.

"What about the ceremony? There's never been a Lady MacEachern without a huge ceremony to mark the wedding. The community has to meet her. If you fail to introduce her properly, she'll never be accepted." Clarissa leaned forward impolitely on her elbows in her eagerness to make her point.

"It's a lost cause," Chancey said. "William can hire an orchestra and rent a circus to perform. None of it will make that woman acceptable as Lady MacEachern. She hasn't the backbone for the job."

"Chancey, that's enough." William's voice was harsh. "We will have a ceremony," he said, directing his comment to Clarissa. "But it will be after we're wed." He picked up Mary's hand and kissed it. "We simply can't wait any longer. If I had the proper ring, I'd marry her this moment."

"She has—" Chancey's remark was interrupted as William assisted Mary to her feet.

"At this time, I'm going to formally pledge my vow of love and marriage to Mary Muir." He turned Mary to face him. "At one time, this was considered the formal vows of marriage. The head of the clan would announce his choice of wife, the MacEachern marriage ring would be produced, and hopefully accepted. And the marriage would be legal." He frowned. "The ring has been…"

Mary's hand went to her chest, where the ring nestled beneath her dress. In her concern over straightening out the heir business and the plans for the evening, she'd never gotten around to telling William about the emerald. Slowly she withdrew the ring from beneath the folds of her dress, slipped the chain from around her neck and placed it in his hand. "I accept your proposal, and your ring," Mary said, her voice shaky with emotion. Out of the corner of her eye, she saw Chancey's furious look.

"Mary!" William looked shocked.

"The ring!" Erick stood, surprise clear on his features. He strode to William's side and examined the emerald. "By God, it's the ring! This calls for a real celebration. We need champagne."

"Champagne," Sophie agreed, also rising. "I'll help Erick."

In less than five minutes they returned with filled glasses of champagne. "Mayfair's finest," Erick declared as he and Sophie made sure everyone had a glass. "Now for the ceremony. It's been many years since Mayfair has seen this ritual."

"Mary—" William took her hand "—where did you...?"

"Later," she whispered. "I don't know that I can explain."

Lifting her left hand to his lips, William kissed it. "In the tradition of the Clan MacEachern, I take Mary Muir as my wife." He slid the ring on her finger. "I will love and protect her for all of her life."

Darren clapped. "Bravo, William. A long and fruitful marriage." He lifted his glass and everyone followed suit.

"Darren!" Chancey's face was white. "I don't believe ancient tradition will be accepted as law. This isn't a legal marriage. It's a farce."

"This will never hold up in a court." Clarissa's lips were pinched tight.

"Think about it, Mother. William has married. He will inherit Mayfair. There's nothing you can do about it." Darren's smile was bitter. "Nothing I can do." He turned to

William. "My congratulations, William. Now, if you'll excuse me…" He placed his napkin carefully on the table and left the room.

"Well, Darren certainly knows how to make an exit." Clarissa fought for composure.

"My warmest congratulations," Mrs. Daugherty said. She rose to her feet and held up her glass of champagne. "A toast to the bride and groom. To many years together, and a long, happy and fruitful life." She swallowed her wine.

Mary turned to William to seal the marriage with a kiss. To her horror, she saw his face flush with color. Tiny drops of perspiration were gathering on his forehead. "William!"

"I think some strange and awful evil is among us." He glared around the table. "Tricks and pranks and gossip-wagging tongues. 'Tis time to right the wrongs that have been done in my castle."

Mary couldn't believe it. Before her very eyes, William was changing. A terrible silence fell over the table.

"Now, William—" Mrs. Daugherty began.

"Still that tongue if ye wish to keep it," he snapped at her, and she clamped her mouth shut. "Now I want the guilty parties to step forward." His hand went to his side as if he searched for a weapon that was not there.

"William." Mary touched his arm. "We need to talk." She looked at Erick for some assistance. "Help me get him out of here."

"Let me have a word with you, my lord," Erick said, stepping around the table to take William's arm. "I need a favor of the highest order. Only you can grant it."

"I'm not done with these…invaders." He looked at Kevin. "These impostors."

"Just one word," Erick said. "It won't take long, and then we'll come back here to finish your business."

William nodded and allowed Erick to lead him from the room.

"So this is the man you're going to pledge your life to,"

Chancey said. There was a waspish sting to her words, but she was obviously shaken by what she'd seen. "I've had enough of this boorish treatment. I'm going home." She gathered her coat and stalked out of the room.

"Chancey!" Kevin stood swiftly and followed her. "Don't be a total fool. Come back here."

"Excuse me." Mary rose, her own legs shaking.

"Mary, I'll help you." Sophie jumped up and went to stand beside her friend.

"I'll find the villain who's been wandering about my castle. I'll chop his fingers off one by one!" William's voice echoed off the stones of the castle.

Mary looked around the room. "Excuse me." She turned and fled, running blindly down the hallway. What had come over William? How had this happened when they'd taken such care about the food? She caught a glimpse of Chancey disappearing into the kitchen, but she hurried on to the library. With a great shove, she swung the big door open—to find an empty room. There was no sign of William or Erick.

She whirled, the long dress floating out behind her as she ran toward the kitchen. Members of the catering crew were busy cleaning up.

"Has anyone been through here?"

One young woman scrubbing the stove looked up. "A tall woman prissed through about three minutes ago. Had a very high opinion of herself, she did. Near knocked me down."

"Did anyone come into the kitchen this afternoon? Anyone at all?"

"Mrs. Connery stopped by and looked around." The girl smiled. "She was very nice. I think she wanted to help us."

"No one else?"

The girl frowned. "No one. I've been right here. Just you and his lordship, when you were looking at the walls. No one else."

"Thanks." Mary dashed through the room and out the back door. Chancey was going to the barn. She must have followed Erick and William. Mary could only pray that Erick would not allow William to ride. He'd been lucky so far, but there was always a good chance he'd break his neck taking walls and fences in the dark.

The barn was disturbingly quiet as she entered. Except for the movement of the horses in their stalls, it seemed empty. With a quick check, Mary made sure that Blaze was still in his stall. The striking stallion nuzzled her hand and went back to his hay.

A sudden movement at Mary's feet made her draw in her breath. It took a second for her to realize it was Familiar, wending in and out of her legs. She was about to speak to him when his sharp claws penetrated the skirt of her gown and struck her calf.

"Ouch!" she cried, trying to jump back, but Familiar followed, one paw still attached to her dress.

"Meow." He retracted his claws and started down the long, dark barn. "Meow."

Mary followed, trusting the cat. When he scratched at the door to Kevin's office, Mary hesitated. No matter what she suspected, it was still difficult to force herself to enter another person's quarters without their permission. Only William's safety and his future motivated her to turn the knob and enter.

Familiar circled the room, quickly surveying the entire area. In a moment he was pawing a brown paper bag on the floor beside the desk. "Meow!" His tone was demanding.

Mary reluctantly opened the sack, and a long, low sigh escaped her. "Damn." The pestle and port glass were in the sack. They'd been broken into many pieces, but she still recognized them. "Kevin!" She spoke his name in sorrow. "This will break Abby's heart."

"Meow!" Familiar was sitting on the floor looking up at her.

"What?" The cat definitely wanted something. She could tell that much, but she didn't know what.

"Meow." He patted the sack with his paw.

Mary narrowed her eyes as she looked at what Familiar was doing. Something was wrong. What? She couldn't understand what the feline was trying to tell her.

"We have to find William, and now," she said. She'd worry about Familiar's antics later.

Kevin had left the room shortly after William and Erick. He could be bird-dogging them. And Chancey? Was she working with Kevin? It would seem so. She was somewhere in the night running around, also.

Mary scooped up the cat and left the office. She made sure the door closed behind her, and then she hesitated. Mayfair was aglow with lights in the distance, but the barn was still very dark.

After hiring caterers and trying to make sure that nothing went amiss, someone had still been able to put something in William's food. Who? No one had been in the kitchen. Or at least, not anyone that the caterers had seen.

Mary started to go back to the kitchen. Maybe one of the other caterers had seen something. She should have asked them all. She was halfway across the yard when she heard Kevin call her.

"Mary."

She felt a chill run through her body. She stopped, but she didn't answer.

"Mary! It's William. He needs your help!"

"Kevin?" She didn't want to answer him—or go to him. "I have to go back inside."

"No, Mary. You have to help me. William's life depends on it."

She turned around to find him, but the barn door was a large black opening. There was no sign of human life at all. She felt the cat brush against her lower legs, and she felt a measure of comfort. "What is it, Kevin?"

"Come here. Hurry. We have to help William."

Mary took three steps toward the barn. She had to force her feet forward. "Kevin, don't hurt William."

"Get over here."

"I'm coming." She tried to find something to pick up, some weapon. If she walked into the barn defenseless, then she'd be dooming William and herself. With each slow step, she tried to figure out a way to prevent what was happening.

"Get in here now, before it's too late."

The urgency in Kevin's voice shut out everything else. She had to obey, or he would injure William. Step-by-step, she approached the barn. Familiar was beside her—and unusually quiet, for him.

"Where's William?" She spoke to the darkness, unable to see Kevin or anything else.

Before she could utter another sound, strong hands clasped over her mouth and around her waist. She felt herself being lifted, much as she'd felt in the tunnel. She managed one muffled cry before she was whirled into the barn and thrown against stacks of baled hay.

"Hush!" Kevin's voice cracked with anxiety. "Running about all over the barn. You nearly spoiled everything. I've been waiting, watching, hoping for this chance. Sophie and I have discussed it."

Mary's heart was pounding. She fumbled in the hay beside her, trying to find some object she could wield as a club. Her fingers clutched only straw at first. In a moment she felt something soft and silky. She tugged at the material, finding more. Her fingers worked along it until she felt something smooth and warm. Long and smooth and warm.

A leg!

"My God!" She spoke the words before she even thought.

"Don't worry, it's only Chancey. But if you don't shut up, I'll have to hit you, too."

Chapter Eighteen

I don't know whether to jump on Kevin or Mary. He's acting like a complete dunce and she's about to scream bloody murder. If we're to find William, then Mary is going to have to cooperate. That was what I was trying to tell her in Kevin's office. Would a person who stole evidence leave it lying about on the floor in a paper sack? That's a plant if ever I've seen one—set up perfectly for Mary to find. With my help, I might add. I was played like a cheap fiddle! I used my detective skills to lead Mary directly to the wrong assumption. Now I'm going to have to think quick. Not difficult, for me, but the problem is trying to second-guess these humans. They are totally irrational! At least Kevin has given that sassy Chancey exactly what she deserved—a knock on the noggin. Now she sleeps the sleep of the innocent. Maybe somebody should record this event for historical purposes.

MARY'S GROPING fingers moved from Chancey's leg along the hay until her fingers found the large knife the stable boys used to slash the twine that held the bales together. The blade was so dull she could almost pass it over her palm without concern for a cut. But it was heavy, and if she struck at Kevin in the dark, she might be able to surprise him.

"Don't even think about the knife," Kevin said matter-of-factly. His voice was a harsh whisper. "Just sit still and listen. If you want William alive, listen."

For all of the fact that he had just knocked a woman cold, Kevin's voice was still calm. He spoke to Mary as if he were reasoning with a child.

"What have you done with William?" Mary demanded.

"Nothing yet, but if you don't lower your voice and hush, you're going to cost him his life."

The totally reasonable tone was infuriating. Mary tightened her fingers around the knife handle. She was dealing with a maniac. She'd just have to take her chances.

Just as she was about to lunge across the short distance and try to stab Kevin, she felt Familiar's weight on her arm. His claws dug into her tender skin and he effectively pinned her entire hand and arm.

"Listen!" Kevin's whiplash command and the sudden sound of another voice made her complaint die in her throat.

"Ye must ride after Lisette, Slaytor. She's escaped from the turret room and headed home. If you don't stop her, she'll go back to England and you'll never see her again."

"The lass will never escape me. She's mine. I am her husband and her master." William's voice swelled.

"Aye, you're the master, but not for much longer." Instead of anger, Erick's voice was filled with sadness. "I didn't want it to end like this, William. I did everything I could to frighten you or Mary away. But once you wed, Mayfair is yours. There'll be a child, just as planned. I thought if I could stop the wedding, I might have a chance."

"We are wed! Well and truly!" There was the sound of a fist banging into a wall. "I want Lisette back within the keep of my castle before the moon is full up."

"And you shall have her." There was no satisfaction in Erick's voice. "Before this night is over, the two of you will be together. Forever."

"And you?" William's voice was suddenly cunning.

"I don't know." There was the sound of something being

dragged about. "Now, sit here while I saddle Blaze for you. Mary almost caught me the last time. You're eager enough for the ride, but you lack a little on getting there."

"I can saddle my own horse." William was belligerent.

"Sure you can. But I'll help." Erick shifted along the barn until he'd brought Blaze out of the stall and hooked him in the cross ties. "I think she went toward Dundee. That's the road I'd take."

"What about the creek? Are the waters not over the bridge?"

"If she made it, so can you."

"He's going to try to drown William." Mary had given up all idea of trying to stab Kevin. At the first sentence of the dialogue between Erick and William, she'd known who was behind it all. She knew who and why.

"Yes, he is." Kevin's agreement was quietly put.

"What are we going to do?"

"Distract him." Kevin touched Mary's arm. "If you can draw him away from William, for just a few moments, I can take him."

"Why are you doing this?" Mary asked.

Kevin squeezed her arm. "William may well be my half-brother. But he is without a doubt the Lord of Mayfair. Abby said you knew about my birth claim. You should also know that no part of Mayfair is worth the price of William's life. At least, not to me."

"And Erick?"

"I believe he's a sick man. Abby told me that she's been getting prescriptions for him from Dr. Sloan. Medicine to help him sleep because he couldn't rest. He wouldn't go to the doctor, so Mother faked his symptoms. Ever since William decided to come back to Mayfair, it's been downhill for him. And there's more. I found some boots of his. There were lifts in them, to make him taller."

"He wants Mayfair for himself."

"I believe he thinks he deserves it, Mary. I've been doing

some checking around. All of those stories about a woman he loves, his life so busy away from here. They're all lies. Mayfair is the only thing he has. And there's no telling what other kinds of medications he's been taking. Some of the medicines I use on the horses have been tampered with.''

"My God," Mary whispered. "He could be completely irrational."

"I think that's the assumption we're going to have to take."

"Irrational and very cunning. He must have put something in William's champagne. The same thing he's been putting in his food. It had to be the champagne."

"He's almost got Blaze saddled up. Now we have to intervene before William leaves the barn. Once he starts riding, I don't think there's another horse that can match Blaze."

Mary nodded, drawing a lungful of air before she stepped away from the safety of the hay and into the aisle of the barn.

"Let him go, Erick, and we'll leave Mayfair. You have my word. Leave William alone, and I'll see to it that you inherit."

"Too late, too late," Erick said. He turned to Mary, and she almost let a cry escape. His face was painted in the red-and-black mask that had terrified her in the passageway.

"It isn't too late. We'll leave. No one will be the wiser."

"It's too late!" Anger choked him. "This is your fault. You should have left when you could. But you wouldn't. You stayed and stayed and stayed. William would have followed you back to Edinburgh. He loves you more than he loves Mayfair. But I love Mayfair. I could have married. Chancey would have finally had me for her husband—if I had inherited. We could have taken care of Mayfair and lived here forever."

The singsong quality of his voice let Mary know that he was high, or completely unbalanced.

"Just talk to me," Mary begged. "Come into the house

and let's talk. Nothing bad has happened. We can work this out.''

''No. This is the only way. William will ride into the creek, and then you'll have to leave. I'll be here. Mayfair will be mine.''

Mary had a sudden thought. ''Did Chancey tell you this?''

''No, not Chancey. Not at all. I told her, but she said it would never work. She said I could never do it. But she'll see, and then she'll marry me.''

''You tied up Dr. Faulkner at Chancey's barn, didn't you?''

''He found the drugs in the cat. That blasted cat. I should have killed him first.''

''And you tied up Chancey?''

''She tied up herself. I wouldn't do it, even when she said I should. I couldn't hurt her.''

Mary sighed. So it was Erick who'd brought Chancey's halter back to Mayfair. She could see William slumped against the wall. Blaze stomped the hay-covered ground as he blew and fidgeted in the cross ties. He'd never been a horse with a lot of patience. He was ready to ride.

''Let's go to the house and talk about this.'' Mary stepped forward. She could see the confusion in Erick's eyes. ''Everyone is locked in the dining room. No one will bother us.''

''No. It's a trick.''

''There's no need to hurt anyone, Erick. William and I will leave. You can have Mayfair. You've worked hard here. Let us go. You can have the estate.''

Erick shook his head slowly. ''It's not up to William to give it to me. It's the inheritance clause. He gets it whether he wants it or not. Unless he dies.'' He looked at William. ''He has to die.''

''No! Leave him alone!'' Darren sprang out of the loft, landing between Erick and William. Holding the wooden handle of a pick, he assumed the stance of a swordsman. "Get back, Erick. Leave William alone."

"Darren." Mary breathed his name but couldn't believe what she was seeing.

"Stay back," Darren warned the stouter man. He stepped forward menacingly, but his foot struck something and he stumbled.

"Get back!" Erick drew a dirk from beneath his coat and held it aloft. "Don't attack or I'll have to kill you."

"Erick!" Mary could plainly see that Darren had stumbled. He had no intention of attacking. "Erick!"

She saw the blade of the knife begin its descent. Everything was happening too quickly, and there was nothing she could do to stop it. Out of the corner of her eye, she saw Familiar take a leap toward Erick. Her own foot moved forward in a long sweep, but she knew she wasn't fast enough.

She didn't believe at first that William was arcing, head first, through the air toward Darren. Even as she took another step herself, she saw Familiar stretch out, long and lean, a black blur that balanced for a moment on Blaze's withers before bouncing onto Erick's head. The cat struck just as William's shoulder caught Darren.

The blade of Erick's knife slashed downward, missing Darren by mere inches as he rolled backward under William's weight.

Mary stopped, unable to decide where she was needed next. Kevin dodged past her, running to Erick and pinning him to the ground.

"William?" Mary watched her fiancé stand and offer his hand to Darren. In a moment, both men were brushing dirt from their clothes while Kevin held the subdued Erick.

William caught sight of Mary, poised but unmoving. He opened his arms to her, and she ran into them. "You're fine. You weren't poisoned."

"I was faking. When I saw his face the minute you showed the ring, I knew it was him. When he got the champagne, I knew not to drink mine. But I pretended because I wanted to get him out of the room, and I felt he'd make his move. I was afraid someone innocent would be injured if we remained.''

Kevin looked up at the two of them. His face showed sadness and relief. ''William, you know that Erick is ill.''

''I know,'' William reassured him. ''You have my word that I'll see to it that he gets the best medical care. He could have injured me or Mary at any time. He didn't. Whatever delusions he suffered from, he really did not want to hurt us. And, Kevin, I want to assure you that if your claim to Mayfair is legitimate, you'll share the estate with me.''

Tears stung Mary's eyes, but she blinked them back. Now wasn't the time to get sentimental.

''I can't wait to tell Sophie,'' Kevin said. ''She assured me that you and Mary would be fair. She begged me to talk with you. She even tried to browbeat me into it. If you can imagine that. But I was afraid you wouldn't take me seriously.''

Mary felt a flood of relief. That had to be the scene she'd overheard. And that went a long way to explaining how her friend had ''changed'' so radically. She'd misjudged the conversation—and Sophie.

''Familiar.'' She called the black cat over and knelt down to stroke his hide. ''I don't know how we'll ever thank this rascal. All along he's been here at Mayfair, discovering secret passageways, eating William's poisoned food. If it wasn't for Familiar, William might well be locked in some mental ward.''

''Meow.'' Familiar rubbed under her hand, stopping so that she could scratch under his chin.

''How can we thank him?'' William stroked the cat's sleek hide. ''Maybe Eleanor will give him to us. I think we're going to see about updating the crest of the MacEachern clan. A horse—and a black cat.''

''An excellent idea,'' Mary agreed.

"Let's get Erick inside and call Dr. Sloan. We can keep this among us and not press charges," William said, "if we all agree."

"I don't think that will be a problem." Kevin grinned. "Except for Chancey. I'm not going to admit that I crunched her on the head."

"Nor I," William said.

"I will." Darren grinned, too. "It's about time someone other than my mother accused me of doing something wrong."

"Who knows?" Kevin remarked slyly. "Chancey may decide she likes a man who exerts a little authority over her."

"She'd be a match for Mother," Darren agreed.

"That's out of the frying pan into the fire," Mary warned.

"I think I'm ready for a different kind of roasting," Darren said as he helped Kevin lift Erick to his feet. "Watching you and William tonight made me decide that I'm going to move to the city. I'm going to start my own life, before it's too late. But we'll discuss all of this later. We'd better take care of Erick."

With a nod from Kevin, they started toward the house.

William's hand restrained Mary. "Wait a minute. The ring! Where did you find the MacEachern wedding ring? It's been missing for decades."

Mary watched Kevin and Darren lead Erick toward the bright lights of Mayfair. The mystery was solved, or almost. "I didn't find the ring. Someone left it for me on the door of my room. On the chain. At first I thought it was you. But it wasn't, was it?"

"No." William caressed her cheek with his fingertips.

"Do you think it was Erick?"

He shook his head. "No, love, I don't. I think that once, a long time ago, a MacEachern fell in love with a woman with all of his heart. Slaytor was willing to risk everything to have Lisette. I think our love, as strong as the bond between my kinsman and his wife, made Slaytor return the ring.''

''You think Slaytor left the ring for me?'' Mary snuggled into William's arms. She couldn't be certain if he was teasing her or not. She didn't care. All that mattered was that they were together, and the future stretched before them.

''That's one thing we'll never know,'' William answered. He turned her to face him. ''But now that we have the ring, we should return to our guests and set out the plans for a real Mayfair wedding. Then I have other matters to…discuss with you.''

''Meow.'' Familiar closed the subject, twining about their legs.

So ELEANOR *and Peter are late. I'm all packed, got my best black suit on, and I'm ready to travel. I've avoided Mary all day. William was bad enough, but if Mary lets those crystal tears leak out of those big green eyes, I'm undone. I'd rather just walk into the sunset like John Wayne. You know, cast a big shadow and get out of town.*

Damn! Here she comes, and her eyes are already red. They want to adopt me, but I'm a traveling kind of cat. Besides, I can't keep my mind off my Clotilde. It's been a long time since I've seen her, and I have this nagging kind of feeling that she needs me at home.

Ah, here comes the car. And Eleanor is as beautiful as ever. I've known some classy broads in my day, but none will ever compare to the Dame. Even Dr. Doolittle looks good to me. I must be suffering from some Scottish fever to think that.

Too bad we can't stay for the wedding. Mary's going to make a beautiful bride. And reports of Erick are that he's improving with some new type of mineral therapy. He was more than a little unbalanced, but they think they may be able to put him back on line. And Kevin and Sophie can't keep their hands off each other. It may be a double wedding here at Mayfair.

Okay, Mary, don't rumple the fur, and God knows, salt water might spot my coat, so don't drip on me. Just put me down and answer the door. That's a good girl.

"FAMILIAR!" Eleanor dropped her purse and knelt on the cold stone floor as the black cat darted across the room and jumped into her arms. "Let's go home."

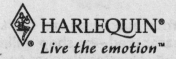

Silhouette®

Silhouette SPECIAL EDITION™

Emotional, compelling stories that capture the intensity of
living, loving and creating a family in today's world.

Silhouette Desire®

Modern, passionate reads that are powerful and provocative.

Silhouette INTIMATE MOMENTS™

Romances that are sparked by danger and fueled by passion.

SILHOUETTE Romance®

From today to forever, these love stories offer
today's woman fairytale romance.

Silhouette BOMBSHELL

Action-filled romances with strong, sexy, savvy women who save the day.

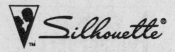

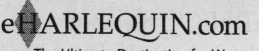

HARLEQUIN®
Live the emotion™

HARLEQUIN® AMERICAN *Romance*®
Upbeat, All-American Romances

HARLEQUIN® flipside
Romantic Comedy

Harlequin Historicals®
Historical Romantic Adventure!

HARLEQUIN® INTRIGUE
Romantic Suspense

HARLEQUIN® HARLEQUIN ROMANCE®
The essence of modern romance

HARLEQUIN® *Presents*
Seduction and Passion Guaranteed!

HARLEQUIN® *Super* ROMANCE®
Emotional, Exciting, Unexpected

Temptation
Sassy, Sexy, Seductive!

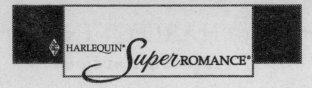

HARLEQUIN *Super* ROMANCE®

...there's more to the story!

Superromance.
A *big* satisfying read about unforgettable
characters. Each month we offer *six* very different
stories that range from family drama to adventure
and mystery, from highly emotional stories to
romantic comedies—and much more! Stories
about people you'll believe in and care about.
Stories too compelling to put down....

Our authors are among today's *best* romance
writers. You'll find familiar names and talented
newcomers. Many of them are award winners—
and you'll see why!

If you want the biggest and best
in romance fiction, you'll get it
from Superromance!

Emotional, Exciting, Unexpected...

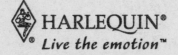

HARLEQUIN®
Live the emotion™